LUSH

ANNE-MARIE YERKS

ODYSSEY
BOOKS

Published by Odyssey Books in 2020
www.odysseybooks.com.au

ISBN: 978-1922311207 (paperback)
ISBN: 978-1922311214 (ebook)

A catalogue record for this
book is available from the
National Library of Australia

Look how the leaves drift in the darkness.
We have burned away
all that was written on them.

— Louise Glück, *The Letters*

For my students

PART I
OUR FARM

CHAPTER 1

NAUDIZ, 2151

*M*uch of history was missing, the man had said.

Yes, it was. But its remains were in our custody.

Behind the back field was a stretch of land surrounded by pines. The tall trees, planted decades before, obscured a vacant village of crumbling houses and trailers. The structures had been eroding for nearly a century, each one pulled from its foundation and carried in on my grandfather's truck. The Polity never paid for Grandpa Effort's work, but instead offered a deal: Our family would perform the year 1856 for tour groups, joining with our neighbors to form *Cherish the Past*, a tribute to the Mennonite ways.

Maybe because I grew up in a time not my own, I often wondered who'd lived in those houses and what exactly had happened to send them running for their lives.

"Isla, stay away," Papa warned. "That old lot is no place for a young girl." I listened at first, but eventually joined my older brother Perrin to rummage for clothes and trinkets. I once found an interesting relic inside a battered plastic box hanging on the oldest and most eroded of the houses—a card with a photograph on one side and a handwritten message on the other.

But I wanted more than artifacts. I hoped to see a ghost or something magical. My hopes picked up one evening in my sixteenth year. Walking past the horse pasture near the bus stop, I witnessed a profound supernatural sight. Later, I convinced myself it had been a dream. But every day since then began with a faint memory, a longing for the same.

Such it was on the Saturday of my last performance. The tour bus arrived slightly late, maybe because the day was warm and green, the dawning of spring, and the restless stirring I felt inside was not my own, but a collective unease about the state of Naudiz. I dressed as always, pulling a light-blue cotton dress over my corset and petticoat, which I then covered with a clean white pinafore, still slightly damp, a plain white bonnet, and my dirty boots. I was ashamed of the caked dirt on their soles and worn laces, but new ones couldn't be afforded. At the chipped mirror over my bedroom bureau, I braided my long red-brown hair, cleaned my face, opened the top drawer, and removed the jar of facial tinting cream that Esme's mother had bought with LUSH credits. It had been a birthday gift to me, a secret one. In *Cherish the Past*, we weren't to use modern products, especially those stamped LUSH. I applied the cream lightly, just enough for an even skin tone. I had a flitting idea that Gareth Teague might show up.

Lastly came my name card, which I pinned to the left pinafore strap.

Isla Kiehl, it said in my own printed handwriting, *Cherish the Past, House 1: Pre-Civil War*.

I found walnut muffins in our kitchen and took two with me to my post outside the barn, where Papa had already set up the wooden spinning wheel, stool, basket of roving, and—kindly—a stoneware jug of apple juice.

The spinning wheel sat outside the barn for the visitors'

convenience. They had only a short time to tour our farm before going to my best friend Esme's family farm, also known as *House 2: Post-Civil War*, so we positioned ourselves in easy-to-see spots. Papa was inside the house with a teapot, sitting in the library beside the oil lamp, his current almanac open on the hickory desk one of our ancestors had built by hand. My brother Perrin, dressed in suspenders and a limp-brimmed leather hat, was a few yards off from me, waiting in the potato field with the tilling equipment and the wagon. The mules were hitched to the wagon rails should any visitors wish to ride up and down the muddy rows.

Perrin waved. "Morning!"

"Where's your name card?" I shouted, sitting on the stool to split a muffin.

He just shrugged and took a bristle brush to a mule's backside.

The cards didn't matter, really. I only wore mine because, if Gareth would show up, I wanted him to learn my name in case he didn't know it. We knew each other only through long looks exchanged at assemblies or those uncommon occasions when we found ourselves on the town bus together. There had never been a chance to speak, but I was determined it should happen. I was running out of time; Archie Thimm would soon ask Papa for my hand and, without another suitor, I would have no reason to refuse.

Finishing the muffin, I watched the tour bus rumble down the dirt lane. It halted at the stone hitching post near Perrin's workshop and the door swung open for a group of eight visitors, the typical crowd of older Citizens in pastel pinks, yellows, and blues —the standard shades for retirees. There was a small child in black knee pants, a blonde boy, who clutched the hand of his grandmother.

Gareth Teague had not come, of course—how could he afford to spare any LUSH credits he may have earned? There was no time to regard the disappointment; the guests were heading toward me, stepping carefully into the tall grass.

"Welcome to the Kiehl family farm." I motioned the small

group toward my spinning stand. "I'm Isla Kiehl, a direct descendant of Effort Kiehl, a Mennonite farmer known for his precise meteorological record-keeping. My papa will show you great-great-grandpa's old record books later, but first, let me show you how women folk of the 1800s spun their roving into yarn."

The crowd was silent and respectful, watching with fascination as I fed a clump of rough roving into the spindle and pumped the pedal, pulling out a long purple-gray strand. Once I had spun a few yards, I wound the fiber into a small skein and handed it to the little boy.

"Thank you," he said. "And how old are you?"

"Interesting you should ask me that," I replied. "I just became eighteen three days ago."

The boy smiled. "You're pretty."

His grandmother ran her fingers over the skein. "A strange texture," she remarked. "Your sheep must have very wiry coats. And are they purple?"

"There are no sheep here, missus. They died out from a virus despite our best attempts. This roving comes from a plant we call cheather, a versatile shrub discovered in this area just a few years ago." I pointed the crowd toward Perrin. "And if you'll step over this way, my older brother, Perrin Kiehl, will show you the potato mounds. You can ride the wagon if you like. Afterward, walk over to the house to see the wood-burning stove, antique furniture, bed quilts, and the library of historical reference manuals. Papa will give you each a batch of homemade paper to take home. On your way out, stop here again to watch me clean our clothes with a washboard."

"Paper," the little boy screamed, jumping up and down. "I want paper!"

"Very well," said the grandmother. "Let's ride the wagon first."

The group strolled off for Perrin's lesson on potato farming, peering into the wagon, petting the mules, and raising their hands to ask questions. One man turned away from the group to gaze up at our windmill in wonder. Touring *Cherish the Past* was something many Citizens wished to do, but most couldn't afford the admission until their older years.

I sat down with the second muffin as the tour group broke into pairs for wagon rides. Once done, they filed toward our farmhouse, where Papa would greet them at the back door, showing them the old iron stove, stone fireplace, and washroom. From there they would enter the front parlor and meet the Kiehl family through a gallery of framed photographs arranged on the wall. The oldest photo was of great-great-great Grandpa Casper; the most recent was my older sister Hollis, who would be sitting beside me at the moment had she not run away with a bad girl from town and then killed herself.

The group would then enter the library and sit on the tufted sofa and wooden benches as Papa took out the most ancient of almanacs to present a few delicate pages of weather predictions, dating back five centuries.

"And the tradition continues today, my friends," Papa always said with a gesture toward the strewn papers and ink bottles on his desk, "with my own work. Next year's almanac, for the year 2152, is currently in my production. The predictions will be aptly sent to the Polity's Library of Ages and archived in this room indefinitely."

Sometimes I laughed when I heard him speak these words so calmly. Even though he agreed with their primary philosophies, Papa often admonished the Polity for their "bloody lies" about continent contraction. Instead of the floods they often talked about, he believed in a long-ago war. I didn't understand his conflict. What difference did it make to us now? I was forced by birth to live in the past, but I was more excited by the future and longed to shape mine in many different ways.

"If you'd like to look around, you may," Papa said to the tourists. "You have a few minutes before the bus takes you on to the next stop."

The guests would pull out the more modern almanacs, the ones from the 2000s filled with vibrant advertisements for places that no longer existed—bowling alleys and diners, tanning salons, plumbing companies, and astrologers. My great-grandparents had earned most of their income from producing them, building a mill a few miles off to print the pages and covers. The almanac business soon overtook farming, which allowed our family land to rest and recover. It was now more beautiful and bountiful than any other acreage in the quadrant.

Static crackled from the tour bus intercom system.

"Attention, tourists." The recorded voice was crisp and friendly through the speakers. "It's now time to exit stop number one. You have three minutes to re-board. This bus will be leaving in five minutes. You have three minutes to re-board." The headlights flashed three times—my cue to pull the wooden washboard and metal washtub from the barn. I used the secret rubber water hose on the side of the utility shed for hot water and added a drop of standardized dish detergent purchased from the commissary. No one would notice I wasn't using lye soap as they did in 1856, the year we were supposed to be living in. With the washboard lying against one side of the tub, I sat on my knees to scrub one of my pinafores—I only had two and they were always soiled. The guests filtered out the front door, some lingering on the porch to smell the blooming peonies on the bush planted by great-great-Grandma Ruth Alice. Most just gave a friendly wave as they passed by, not too interested in my hand-washing process.

"An honor to meet you, young miss." The man who'd liked the windmill drifted over. "What happens at the next stop?"

"Stop number two is Post-Civil War," I told him. "You'll see a water wheel, a tailoring studio, and learn how to churn butter with a wooden stick. My friend Esme will give you a cup of fresh apple juice—they make it there," I said, pointing to my stoneware jug. "And it's truly delicious, even when it's off-season."

"And after that?"

I told him about the remaining three stops. He'd visit a turn-of-the-century horse farm; the 1920's swine and dairy ranch owned by the Thimm family, where he'd taste a slice of smoked bacon; and—finally—a 1980's country villa to walk the mile-long grape vineyard, leaving with a pint bottle of grape juice.

"Seems that much of history is missing," the man mused, wandering away. "Well, good day."

The bus started its ignition and the guests boarded through the narrow twin doors, the little boy flapping his paper pad into the wind. There were enough seats that each person could have had two, but they chose to cluster together near the front. As the bus lunged forward, I noticed its gray paint was chipped and fading around the window panes.

Papa and Perrin joined me at the hitching post, where we smiled and waved with enthusiasm until the coach faded into a cloud of dust at the end of the road, turning out of sight.

"Zasha," Papa said, using his pet name for me, "why is your face so beige? Clean it up before Vespers this evening. Perrin, get the ponies washed and ready, will you?"

"You got it, Pops."

Heavy with dread, I did ask as Papa asked, cleaning my face in my bedroom washbasin and heating the iron to press my formal clothes—a grey dress, white pinafore, and black bonnet.

A few hours later, Perrin strapped the ponies to the cart and the three of us rode the three miles to the center of Naudiz, hitching the cart near the water fountain and walking single-file down the rock steps to the outdoor amphitheater. Vespers was held monthly, an observation of what Mother Cordish called "our most deeply held morals and faith, those values binding the present to the past."

We were to sit in the front row as always. Perrin and Papa stood back, following the rule that women and girls go before men and boys. Unfortunately, my seat was directly beside Archie Thimm. How I would have preferred Esme, but she was further down, safely at the end of the aisle. Archie smiled and attempted to catch my eyes, which I avoided. Still, I tried to remain pleasant, sitting with perfect posture and trying not to think of how he smelled like bacon grease. After all, it wasn't his fault his family owned a pig farm. The Cordishes soon appeared on the stage, three sons and four daughters with their mother in the middle. Their flat expressions told me they were disappointed with how few Citizens were in the audience.

Mother Cordish, dressed in a plain navy-blue dress, raised her arms and began the service. She was a very old woman, so old that her voice barely emerged, but hearing her words wasn't necessary. We all knew what she said, that she condemned technology and the use of science for anything other than curing the many diseases and viruses around us. She spoke of the old days, nodding to the first-row families of *Cherish the Past*, and the simple, virtuous ways of living that preserved the earth's resources and kept our bodies and souls pure.

As she spoke, there was a restlessness in the thin crowd. A group of women whispered gossip and allowed their children to pass toys around. The Cordish children observed, neutral and emotionless, as their mother had finished her litanies. At that point, we all stood and observed a moment of silence, listening to the evening sounds of the woods around us. It was my favorite part of Vespers, so still and somber that I was able to forget Archie beside me and focus only on the calls of the words in the trees. In the silence I could hear up the hill where the towns-people were milling about, having chosen shopping at the market or commissary over attending the service. They would be settling in for the evening, I knew, cooking meals and gathering together. Some of them would watch television, trading ancient tapes and discs among each other. Despite Mother Cordish's disdain for technology, she tolerated its use among the townspeople because it was needed for community-wide announcements.

As the moment of silence concluded, I heard a shuffling at the wood's edge, followed by a tickle of laughter.

"Hold them," Mother Cordish demanded. "Heretics!"

A pair of guards who'd been standing in the back jumped up and rushed into the woods.

The interruption put an end to the ceremony. As we began to

filter out, Archie escorted me up the stairs and started up a conversation.

"Who was that, laughing at us from the brush?" Seven years older than me, he had an egg-shaped head and dark eyebrows that resembled fuzzy worms. Although I avoided him when possible, he'd sometimes corner me at the commissary and attempt to lay out plans for dates or picnics. He'd once asked my older sister to marry him, but she'd run away shortly afterward. Still without a wife, he was seeking my court.

"Maybe a small gang," I said. "I encounter that kind at school, so brash and daring in how they speak out against us."

"That's terrible," Archie replied. He tended to spit when he spoke, so I turned around and caught Esme's eye. She immediately understood. "Some can't fathom the consequences of bad manners, can they?" Archie continued. "I imagine Mother Cordish will prosecute them properly. Now, tell me, Isla, how it is that you look so lovely tonight?"

"She always looks lovely, Cousin Archie," Esme said, forcing her way between us.

"But—" Archie stammered, his face falling into its flabby lines. He had no choice but to allow her to take his place, as any other action would be abhorrently ungracious. "But—"

"Good night, Archie," I said.

After Esme and I stepped from the shadowed woods and onto the well-lit street, I thanked her for coming to my aid. "He was about to invite me for a picnic, I believe."

Esme laughed. "He's my darling cousin, but even I don't want a picnic with him. Now, remember to return a favor when I need one, won't you?"

"Of course," I said. What could Esme want from me that I wouldn't want to give her? We were as close as sisters, having grown up together on adjacent farms. We shared so many memories it was almost at times like we were the same person. "I would do anything for you, as always. Ride back with us, won't you? Perrin will drop you off."

"Not tonight." She used her body to shield me from Archie, who was pulling dangerously close, as I boarded our cart. Papa was already seated, holding a hand over his eyes against the overhead street light. Like Mother Cordish, he disliked electricity. "My mother has some ideas for a new dress. Come by tomorrow and I'll show you the sketches."

"If I can. If not, at school on Monday."

Perrin roused the ponies and we were off. I turned to wave goodbye to Esme, keeping my bonnet low to hide my face from Archie, who was still looking my way. My friend stood back and smiled, so neat and poised in her perfectly pressed pinafore and gown.

It was true, there was nothing I wouldn't do for her.

CHAPTER 2

*T*he next week, I prepared for an exam that would raise my status from adult child to full Citizen and earn an ability to travel around the quadrant. Alone in my room at night, I often dreamed about seeing the mountains and the gray-green Raidho River that divided Naudiz from the rest of the quadrant. And there were cities on the other side, some of them ancient, others reconstructed, the streets lined with museums and shops. They could only be accessed with an automobile, and only those with special stations were allowed to drive.

The only such person I knew personally was my teacher, Ms. Hardin. She was the teacher for all areas of Naudiz, which included the town as well as the farming zones. Earlier in the year, she'd introduced our class to a girl visiting from the Center for Research on Ecological and Intellectual Advancement—the CREIA—an institution known for its vast library and creative research laboratories. Hundreds of young women from around the quadrant went to their recruitment ceremony every year, but only a few were selected to stay for the teacher certification training program.

"At the CREIA, all girls selected for the long program are

expected to complete an extensive course of study," the girl had said from behind Ms. Hardin's wooden desk.

I'd been transfixed by her clothing, a blouse in the deepest crimson I'd ever seen, a slim black skirt, and boots that reached her knees. The girl's face was broad and sensuous, full lips and dark eyelashes, and her neck was thin and delicate, so pale that the veins beneath were visible in the afternoon light.

"And we offer many programs," she'd said, looking over to me and Esme. "You can choose to study a topic that interests you, one that you may teach later."

"You could learn to teach something too," Esme whispered to me.

Ms. Hardin glanced over and held a finger to her lips.

When I daydreamed about my future, I was never in my corset and petticoats but in modern clothes like Ms. Hardin wore. I loved our farm and all the animals, but I often thought of leaving for a while to try my luck in town or in one of the cities. Esme was set on being a teacher, but I found the role too limiting. I wanted to have children someday, but only if I loved the person I married. That person was definitely not Archie Thimm.

After the girl finished speaking, Ms. Hardin let us go up to meet her.

"Will we see you again if we come to the ceremony?" Esme asked.

The girl turned to gather her things and my eye was drawn to a strange spot in her skin, a patch of ink that appeared when she slid a bag over one shoulder. Although I couldn't see the entire shape, it seemed the same as the LUSH certification seal, the mark of goods that were above-average in quality or exceptionally hard to obtain. But I'd never before seen the stamp on anyone's body, so doubted my observation. More likely it was another stamp or seal I didn't know of.

"I'm afraid I won't be there," she told Esme. "You see, my role is to travel from school to school throughout the quadrant, explaining to girls like you what we offer at the CREIA. As you know, only the best are taken in. Finding that best requires an extensive search. I have to run off now, girls. Hope to see you soon."

Traveling around in a car alone and visiting schools was an impossible fantasy to me. It seemed that the CREIA was a place of hidden opportunities.

Esme was also captivated, going on about the things we'd see and do if we went. The CREIA housed the Library of Ages, a collection of books and media from history, and it was also where Papa's almanacs were stored. How peculiar it would be to see them in a completely different place—I was the only person in our family who could even think of such a thing because the CREIA only admitted girls.

"The library is larger than our fields, Isla," she reminded me once we were on the bus home. "Filled with many important stories and poems we haven't read in school."

"What kind of stories?" I asked. As usual, she was more knowledgeable than me about the world; some of this perception came from having a television hidden in her bedroom closet.

"Such as a series called *Harry Potter*. It's about a boy who became a wizard. The whole world was influenced by this tale," she claimed. "That's just one story out of so many. I've heard also of a novel called *To Kill a Mockingbird,* which is very beautiful, the type of story that makes you cry but feel better at the same time. And so many more—romances and crime stories and detective mysteries."

"I do want to see the CREIA," I admitted. "But I'd prefer not to become a teacher and give up marriage and children. Not for all the LUSH in the world would I do that." The white-haired Mother Cordish held firm that all teachers should dedicate themselves fully to the profession, so, just as in the very old times, they weren't permitted to have families.

Esme laughed and pulled a pair of gloves over her smooth hands. She wasn't required to work often at her farm chores like I was. Her mother, a seamstress, preferred her to stay inside and study.

"Don't worry, Isla," she said, gently condescending. "They will hardly pick you, especially if you do poorly on their tests. They'll have hundreds, even thousands, of candidates to review. With your misfortunate past, you will likely be sent home with the first group of rejects." She flipped her long braid to one side and turned to me with urgency. "But please try your best to score well on the Citizen test. I need you to come with me. Without you, I'll be terrified and lonely."

I knew she was manipulating my decision. Throughout our lifetime of friendship, I'd learned that Esme thought mainly of the moment at hand, often failing to consider how her actions impacted others. She was up and down in her moods and could lose her temper in an instant. But she was immensely proud of her intellect and would lament for hours if she underscored on an exam. She had very little interest in boys and had long ago laughed away the proposition of marrying my brother Perrin and merging our farms together.

"Perrin is a slave to his ambitions," she'd said many times. "We are incompatible."

Perhaps she was right. Perrin's mind was entirely focused on developing new formulas with the cheather seeds he'd discovered in the hidden lot several years before, developing and deriving extracts to cure the range of sicknesses around Naudiz and throughout the quadrant. He ignored the girls who tried to get his attention. I knew he'd never recovered from my mother's long illness and slow death. By curing others, I suspected he eased his own inner pain.

I couldn't blame Esme for not wanting to pair with my preoccupied brother because I was firmly set against matching with her cousin Archie.

"So you will come?" she persisted.

"Maybe. I suppose even if I was selected to be a teacher, I could always change my mind and excuse myself to leave. But what would I wear to the ceremony?" I knew we were expected to dress up in our very best clothes, but I only had hand-me-downs from my mother and sister.

"I'll ask my mother to make you a dress. We'll take your measurements soon."

The bus driver, Staris, steered to the roadside and opened the door for us.

"Good night, my beauties," he said as we descended the narrow steps to the gravel road, holding up our skirts to avoid dirt and mud. We didn't heed his flirtatious remark—he was a wild character, harmless enough, with unevenly cut hair and a broad, greasy face. Sometimes when I was the only passenger, which happened often on Sundays when I was taking cats to town for delivery, Staris would pull out a battered box of illegal music tapes and play them on a device hidden in his dashboard. I liked the haunting voices and the complicated rhythms of the ancient recordings. They would linger in my mind afterward, sometimes for days and days.

After Esme and I parted at the bus stop's bench, I walked down the road home a few yards and stopped to visit with the two old dappled horses who grazed inside the fenced pasture owned by one of our *Cherish* neighbors. The neighbors were inattentive and lazy, leaving the horses out at all hours, often in the cold with little to feed upon. The two beasts lived together like a married couple—the wife smaller and more blonde than the husband, who was thick and gray. They trotted over to eat the sack of wild carrots I'd brought for them, a ritual that occurred with each bus trip to and from town. Their fondness was so deep they allowed me to brush the long bangs from their spotted foreheads and gaze into their black eyes.

"Should I leave you for a spell?" I asked them. "And take a small adventure to the CREIA?"

The husband snorted and they both ran off toward the setting sun, hooves thumping soundly into the moist dirt. It was early in May and their field was sprouting with fresh clover and grass.

"You will miss my carrots," I called out, folding the empty sack into the satchel I carried back and forth to school. Inside was an item I'd hidden in the lining. One of my classmates, Marta Klein, had given me a case of eyeshadow she'd bought at the LUSH market but didn't like on herself. In exchange, I'd promised to bring her a bag of onions. The eyeshadow fascinated me and I couldn't wait to try it on. Cosmetics weren't allowed in *Cherish*, but since no one was closely monitoring us, I took the occasional dare.

Walking home in the dim evening, I saw lamps flickering through the windows of my brother's workshop. There were patients inside, I assumed, sick Citizens from the quadrant who'd heard of Perrin Kiehl and the indigo syrup that healed wounds, viruses, moods, and maybe even cancer. My brother never took tokens for the cheather syrup, only trades, because he cared more for the Citizens than for his own wellbeing and wealth advancement. A law passed by the Polity many years before my mother died had decided against treating illnesses with science and technology. All such resources went instead into modeling human DNA to be fully resistant to illness. I'd heard many people complain the Polity was playing like a god, dismissing death and suffering for an ideal that could never be, but there was no means to send such complaints over the peaked crest separating us from Peorth, the only city in the quadrant that conducted acts of state.

I crossed the long brick path to the workshop door, opening it quietly. Inside was a man with pocked cheeks and a dark beard standing with a woman, plainly dressed with her hair tucked into a loose cotton hat. Between them was a blanketed figure, a child maybe, propped in a wooden chair. My brother was on one knee, his intelligent face flickering in the lamplight, looking beneath the hood that covered the child's head.

"You really can't help?" the woman asked. "I heard that your syrup could cure even the worst of conditions."

"Not this. No, not this." Perrin stood up. "I'm sorry you traveled so far, my friends. You can take some tincture home as my gift. Use it as you will."

I slid behind the cluttered table, catching his gaze over the mess of bottles and plant stems. The child cried—a thin, slobbering cry—and I saw a pair of small hands reach for the woman, who covered them with the jacket fold. The man looked at me, suspicious.

"My sister," Perrin explained, motioning me toward them.

"I'm Isla," I said.

"We call her Zasha at times," Perrin added. "Our mother was Russian."

I wondered why he mentioned my pet name but sensed he was trying to send the couple out with light conversation. The child kept on with its odd crying. Curious, I stepped into their circle, thinking I might help my brother set them out the door. The child again reached forward with both arms and the hood fell away from his face.

I gasped—the little boy was without eyes, stretches of pale, smooth skin bulging over the empty sockets in his skull. Oddly, I felt that he could see and understand my horror. The tiny rosebud mouth, perfectly formed under two flattened nostrils, opened into a thin, shrill scream.

"Darling," the mother said, pulling up the hood and pulling the child into her arms. "Shhh, quiet."

"I'm sorry," I said, horrified at myself. "I didn't expect to see—"

"No one does," she snapped, caressing the child's blond curls.

"We'll be on our way now," the man said. "If there is no help for us here, we must move on. There's a surgeon in Ironcove we can see next."

Still shuddering from the child's tragic deformity, I focused on the parents instead, placing them as ordinary folk. A bright-green symbol shaped like a tree on the man's jacket pocket told me he worked as a laborer of the land in some way, perhaps building houses or opening up the new roads. His wife wore a blue dress made from standard quadrant cotton cloth. It was sold at the marketplace for a token a yard, each yard stamped at the selvage with the name of the mill that produced it. The curve of the collar confirmed also that she'd used one of the three standard dress patterns made available to married women, cutting the pieces out at home to sew at a rented station at the warm-weather market.

"Take this with you," Perrin said, handing her a bottle of tincture. "You can use it for more common ailments, like fevers or cramps. Injuries even. Pour a few drops into water. And should you consider another child someday, it could possibly aid conception."

She took the bottle and handed it off to her husband, arranging the little boy in a body sling. The family left, silent and sullen, the child sniffing and crying out the door.

I ached for them, all three of them. What would it have been like, I wondered, to birth what others saw as a mutant, even a monster? That she obviously loved the baby made my heart cry. I also worried—what if such a thing happened to *me*?

"A tragic shame," Perrin said, watching them through the square window over his squat white stove. The stove, rigged to operate with corn fuel, had been a find from a house in the old lot, carried with Papa's help out from a white trailer. "These deformities are happening more often now. It seems to get worse every year. A few days ago I saw a baby without arms."

"I wish I'd not gasped so loudly," I said. "But without *eyes*? The sight was so ... unnatural."

"I hope it's an isolated case." My brother moved the chair under a bench littered with glass vials and jars filled with dried leaves, some encased inside crudely sewn pockets of muslin and floating in colored fluids. He was always working on new strains, trying to make his cheather even more powerful. Sometimes he locked our barn cats into cages, infusing his test tinctures in their water and food before breeding them together and documenting the results. He'd found that when the cats lounged and played in the cheather field, they took an ample amount of pollen into their coats. When such a cat purred while sitting in the lap of a sick person, rapid healing could occur. Perhaps the dandruff drifted into the sick one's lungs or perhaps the cats' calming presence fortified them with a confidence that assured a cure. Either way, it worked well and we reserved the cats for the very sickest of the sick, using them as supplements to the tincture. One of the new kittens, a gray tabby named Aura, had proven a more effective healer than any cat we'd ever had on the farm.

"Where is Aura tonight?" I asked.

"I have her harnessed to an apple tree. Let's go get her now, Zasha. I must also carry in the sack of blossoms I picked earlier today."

We blew out the lamps, closed the workshop door, and stepped into the chirping darkness. Dozens of blackbirds rummaged in the tree branches, flocks that had flown in from a warmer climate on the other side of the Raidho River. Papa was tracking the migration with his usual methods, writing notes in ledgers with leaky fountain pens even though better pens were all over the house. He preferred the old-fashioned ways of the Mennonites, the religious clan our great-grandparents had come from, and berated Perrin and me for too often dismissing our heritage.

The young cat had pulled her rope out to the furthest point possible, almost to the edge of the vegetable garden, her neck tight against the harness. She was a strong, solid feline with silver stripes, tall pointed ears, and a powerful purr. In the sunlight, the pupils of her melon-green eyes shrunk to tiny crescents that curved in like phases of the early moon. She was loving and sweet in spite of her ominous appearance, and I dreaded that Perrin would soon cage her for a long experiment he had in mind.

"She's the only cheather cat left on the farm," I reminded as he untied the rope. "All the others are out on missions. And I'll soon be gone for a few days to the CREIA ceremony, so I won't be able to help with her."

"I promise to spoil her with cream and cold water, so put the concern out of your mind. And why would you go to that place when you're needed here? You could watch over the experiment yourself, help me record metrics and improve the latest strain. Isn't that a job more worthy than whatever that schoolteacher tempts you with?"

He slid Aura from his arms into mine and I held her tightly, enjoying the delicious warmth of her purring body as my brother gathered the burlap sack of blossoming apple branches he'd pruned from the tree earlier in the afternoon, the white and pink petals shining like shells as he carefully arranged them inside the fabric case. They were to go to a funeral in the morning, for an old friend of Papa's who'd died of a heart attack.

"If only Papa had known," I said, scratching Aura behind the ears. "We could have helped."

"Cheather can't help what arrives without warning."

"And kills so quickly."

We heard a sound coming from the lot, its origin way past the pines—a thud followed by a gurgling that sounded like human voices. A cold tickle of wind blew, and I felt a twinge of trepidation.

"Did you hear that?"

Perrin hoisted the bundle of apple blossoms over a shoulder. "Likely just a falling branch. Rats, maybe. Come on, let's go in. There's supper on the stove."

I followed him to the house, still clutching Aura, entering to the salty smell of butter and boiling potatoes. Papa was in the library, oil lamps burning, flipping through his paperwork. Once Aura was in the pantry with her bed and a bowl of food, I sat for a few moments by the wood stove and looked out into the evening, listening again for the mysterious sound, but heard only insects and a few lonely birds looking for mates.

Over dinner, I told Papa and Perrin the details about my trip to CREIA.

"I'll acquire LUSH credits just for participating in the ceremony," I told them. Since the trip was viewed as a public service, every girl would receive at least one hundred, Ms. Hardin had said. Enough for some new clothes, boots, and maybe even a bit of jewelry. I had only one necklace, a silver heirloom locket that held a small photo of one of my female ancestors. Since they all looked similar, I wasn't sure who the blurry, somber face belonged to. Even so, I wore it every day.

"What's the value of this?" Papa asked. "What can you buy with LUSH that's worth the trouble and the risk? Bright fabric? Tall shoes? Make-up for your skin? You can't wear such things here, Isla, so LUSH is nothing to you. Accept your position— there are many who envy the fresh food we eat and the nature all around us."

"But there's much that can't be envied, Papa," I argued. "There are no boys to marry, and we live without electricity. We must model the clothing of another time, and I'm tired of petticoats and bonnets and being laughed at behind my back. I want to *go* on a field trip instead of live in one."

Papa looked into the lantern flame, his face pensive. I knew he was weighing my request, considering possibilities. Finally, he spoke.

"If you are so restless, then proceed with the journey. Sadly, you are right that the marriage options for you are limited here in Naudiz. It might be that—"

Perrin interrupted. "But there are no boys at this place either, Pops. It's all girls."

Papa looked over at me and I nodded. It was true. I wanted to kick Perrin in the shin for trying to usurp my wish, but in my heart I knew he was trying to protect me.

"As I was saying," Papa continued, "a trip across the river could be a healthy adventure for a young girl like you. When you return, you might better appreciate what you have." The flame inside the lamp's glass trembled, casting licks of amber and green onto his graying beard. "But do not take items of value with you, such as the heirloom locket around your neck. And don't speak about what we do that isn't seen. Mother Cordish and her Polity know only that cheather is for paper and roving, nothing else."

"Yes, Papa. Of course. And—"

"Say nothing about Perrin's work or the things we've taken from the old lot. Keep your sentences simple and without elaboration when they question you."

I was about to assure him that I would say nothing about our occasional cheating to anyone at the CREIA, that above all else I would shield him, Perrin, and all the animals on the farm with my life, but he was already shuffling away to the library, shoulders sloped.

I looked down, worried.

"Don't despair about the future," my brother said, cutting a large slice of berry pie. "There is much happening lately and Papa is concerned that we won't sustain the farm as he did. He'll be anxious until you come home."

"I still want to go. This is a chance to see what lies on the other side of the river."

Perrin smiled and fell into thought as he ate the pie. After a few moments, he spoke again. "Since you must go, please note the landscape there so you can tell us about it when you return. Take paper along and write down what you see growing from the ground and what the weather is like."

"Of course I'll take paper," I said. "If only I could take a cat, but I'm sure that's not allowed. What is it about the landscape that makes you curious?"

"I have a theory," he said, picking up a knife for another slice. "Diversification."

"What do you mean? Don't eat the entire pie, please. Save some for my breakfast in the morning."

He cut a sliver and slid the pie in my direction. "The rest is yours. I think that diversification could make cheather stronger. It's a simple theory—when a plant grows in unfamiliar terrain, it must strengthen in order to survive. No different from us, really. Becoming strong means suffering for it."

"Understandable," I said. "And that's exactly why I want to go —being away from home will build my character. But I can't take cheather with me. They would find it strange."

"Of course not. But I must tell you," my brother lowered his voice, "I recently knew a girl who went to the CREIA for this same spectacle you're attending. She was very pretty and smart. After she left, I never saw her again."

"Perhaps she was selected for the teacher training. Or just moved away to get married."

"Maybe. But maybe something else happened to her. Promise to be careful and watch out for traps."

"I promise," I said, my heart warming to my brother's concern for me.

"Good night." He stood and stretched his long limbs, brushing his long bangs from his eyes. In bright sunlight, they were nearly navy blue. Many girls thought Esme was irrational for refusing to pair with the most handsome man in Naudiz, but I knew that he cared little for her erratic disposition and tendency to judge everyone and everything she knew.

"Good night."

In my room, I collapsed on my bed and closed my eyes. The corset underneath my dress was tight after so many hours, so I pulled off my shirtwaist and loosened the lace. The cosmetic case Marta had given me that afternoon at school fell from my pocket, landing on the mattress upside down.

Stamped on the bottom with the blurry blue LUSH seal, the case was molded from stiff white paper—two sharp-edged planes held together with miniature metal hinges. But it was the inscription on the front that I found most fascinating—a strange girl's name imprinted in glossy gold lacquer. The scripted lettering implied she claimed credit not only for the case itself, but also its color and design, its hinges, and the eye powders inside. That she could even claim me should I apply the powder to my eyelids. I ran my fingertips over the lettering.

Ashleen.

The name felt harsh and crude when whispered in the cold air of my bedroom.

I thought of the girl who'd come to class, the one with the stamp on her skin. There had been a hesitant tension in her face and body, I remembered, as though she held a formidable memory away from us. Was the mark I saw a symbol of this repressed stigma? I began to feel fearful but willed it away, reminding myself that the girl had been friendly, nice, and in good health.

The make-up case held two small square trays of glittering powder—one gray, the other pale pink—that sparkled in the yellow light of the battery-operated lamp on my night table. A groove inside the case had once held a small application brush, I assumed, but it was missing. Perhaps Marta had kept it or forgotten to slip it back inside. The powders themselves appeared untouched. Although I was tired enough to fall asleep, the temptation to apply them was impossible to resist.

Standing at my bureau, I hung the lamp overhead and used one finger to streak the gray powder onto both eyelids, standing back to consider how the deep tone made my eyes look more green instead of hazel. But in the next second I was overcome with an overpowering sense of trepidation, a foreboding concern for the future as the mirror's reflection morphed. The girl in the mirror—who was me, but a sinister and brutalized version of me—appeared to convulse and clutch her throat, eyes bulging. Shocked, I stepped back in fright and crouched to the floor.

Be sensible, Isla. It's just you and only you.

Trembling, I reasoned with myself. There were many reasons for the gruesome sight. The mirror was old, the eyeshadow was artificially dark. The lamplight was yellow and ominous. I was very tired and my imagination was often too active. I grounded myself in the normalcy of the night, listening to Papa's slippered steps going up the stairs, the cooing of owls and wood creatures out the window, the light breeze across my bare shoulders.

I stood up and dared to look in the mirror again.

The reflection in the mirror was as it had always been, the me

I'd always known. Pulling off my corset and heavy skirt, I wet a rag in my washbasin and rubbed the color away from my eyelids. I then stomped the make-up case with one foot, breaking the hinges, and buried it in my trash pail.

Drifting off to sleep that night I had a subtle sense of someone watching me from a point beyond reality. I hoped my mother and sister were hovering around, that they had come to protect me from the force of the inevitable and the unknown. But my dreams told something different, and I woke the next morning with the uncomfortable sense that what I'd seen in the mirror had been a message of sorts.

Or perhaps a warning.

CHAPTER 3

"Why didn't you wear your eyeshadow today?" Marta said during lunch break the following afternoon. "You said you couldn't wait."

"I just didn't like it, Marta. But I brought your onions anyway. They're on the front bench inside."

"I prefer your face without cosmetics," Esme countered. "Eyeshadow is for loose girls."

"Maybe you think so," Marta replied. "But many girls wear it. And thank you for the onions, Isla. My mother will be so happy to use them in her bread and beans."

The three of us were sitting on a hilltop outside the school building, taking in the sun and fresh air before Ms. Hardin called us in for the Citizen exam. The day was lovely, cloudless, and the air smelled like warming earth. From our spot beneath a willow tree, veiled with a wave of blooming branches, we had a view of the school's front entrance where a group of young men had gathered. Most of them wore the yellow suit of the soybean factory in the valley, but a few were in the green suit of the concrete mill down the road. They clustered near the door, peering through the window panes, strolling up and down the walk, spreading mud and dirt with their boots. I leaned forward

for a closer look at one of the yellow suits. It was Gareth
Teague.

"What is *he* doing here?" I asked.

The recess attendant came out, calling us back to the classroom. Esme and Marta stood up and brushed leaves from their
clothes.

"He could be here for the exam," Marta said, adjusting the belt
of her button-down dress. She lived in the town condominiums,
the ones that Papa often berated as sad cement boxes, with her
mother and two younger sisters. Their father, red-haired like
Marta, had been killed in a hurricane when she was a small child. I
often saw her mother outside the blood bank, waiting in line to
donate plasma to science and earn a few tokens. "Maybe he didn't
pass last year and has come for another chance."

"Gareth Teague didn't pass? That seems unlikely," I said. "I
heard he's very intelligent and savvy about so many things."

"Hardly," Esme said as we passed through the branches,
revealing ourselves in the bright sun. "You're impressed by his
appearance and imagine a brilliance he doesn't possess."

I pulled on my bonnet and tied it under my chin. Already
Gareth had spotted me on the hill and was holding my eyes with
his own. The bonnet could cloak my face enough that the others
wouldn't notice my reciprocation.

"I agree he's very handsome," Marta said. "But brusque at
times. Come on, let's go down."

Ms. Hardin emerged from the school building, small and slight
in her tailored black skirt and spotlessly white ruffled blouse, platinum hair held back with reading glasses propped on her head.
The boys gathered around her, keeping a respectful distance as
she counted them with a pencil.

"We will see," she was saying as we scurried by. "But I doubt
there are enough test packets for all of you."

I didn't dare peek around the brim of my bonnet when passing
Gareth but looked closely at the toes of his boots, the only part of
him I could observe without raising Esme's annoyance. In the

classroom, I sat between Marta and Esme at the front of the room as the boys filed into the back, waiting as Ms. Hardin distributed the tests to each student. The exam questions were contained inside a battered and faded red envelope, the front sticker signed by the students of years previous who'd read the same pages and answered the same questions. The Polity never updated the new Citizen test—it was the same every year, since even Papa was a school child. The final score wasn't calculated on the quality of the accuracy of the answers or the quality of the essay responses, but on the teacher's assessment of the student his or herself. I had no fear that Ms. Hardin would allow me to move from child to full Citizen—she wanted for all of us elder girls to visit the CREIA, which was not possible without a Citizen registration card—but I worried that she would again refuse to let Gareth pass, casting his fate as a soybean worker for life.

Ms. Hardin stood in front of the class, looking over the rows of hopeful students. Those sitting near me were unusually quiet and obedient, but I was aware of a rustling in the back of the room.

"There weren't enough packets," someone whispered.

Turning, I caught sight of Gareth and the other boys leaving the room. My heart turned to stone, but I turned back and forced myself to pay attention.

"All of those with packets may now begin," Ms. Hardin said, eyes lingering on the group going out the door. "You have the rest of the day to complete the test. Be completely silent and do your very best work. When you are finished with the exam, bring it up to me and exit the building. I'll announce the results as soon as possible. Are there any questions?" She sat on a blue-painted chair beside the wooden desk.

Everyone in the class was silent and without questions. Outside, the sun moved behind a cloud and the packet on my desk darkened from pale red to a sick shade of dead blood. Esme opened her test book and the rest of us followed her lead.

The first section of the exam asked for the correct answers to

a few dozen math questions followed by a few dozen science questions. After completing them with confidence, I moved onto the
biology section. The pages in this section were whiter and cleaner
than the others, as though they'd only recently been stapled into
the book.

*True or false: A human female can be born with eggs that are not
her own.*

I hesitated, knowing that *false* was technically the correct
answer, but that one of the Polity's current projects—the program
called UniKind—was a mission to develop composite humans,
each one created through DNA fused together in a laboratory. It
could be that such composites, the females, were designed to be
born with eggs not their own. But how was that possible? I circled
True and went on, completing the biology section and moving on
to Quadrant and Continental History, the final portion of the
test. By then, I was hungry and tired and felt sad that Gareth had
been turned away.

*On your own paper, write an essay of two pages describing the four
main reasons for continent contraction.*

Esme was already well into the essay, writing thoughtfully in
her perfectly proportionate round script. Smoothing out a pad of
paper I'd brought from home, speckled with the pulp of the
cheather plant, I began to write, knowing by memory what to say
in each paragraph. The four reasons for continent extraction were
known to everyone, repeated often at state ceremonies, in the
newscast, and in the literature we read in school. Reminding
myself that I'd probably never again have to write such an essay, I
took a deep breath and gathered enough will to compose the
details in the best manner possible.

As the afternoon retreated into blue dusk, I wrote the things
that Mother Cordish and her league of Polity taught—about the
vile chemicals our ancestors used in building their civilizations of
plastic, about how those plastics decayed into particles that cont-
aminated the oceans and caused viruses and cancers like the one
that killed my mother when I was a small child. I wrote about the

uncontrollable floods, sinkholes, earthquakes, and wildfires that flattened cities and killed millions. Papa would have shaken his head at my words—he didn't agree with the long-held truth that it was only the toxins from plastic that caused the ocean to swallow the continent at its edges. It was not the whole story, he claimed.

"There was a war, Isla," he said. "A chemical war among the old countries that in turn set off Mother Nature's war against all of us. The Cordishes deny the truth so we will live in harmony, but the great suffering that occurred should be recognized and documented. These chemicals are lingering in our ecosystem and they are morphing, causing the sickness and deformities we see. They think their new DNA will solve the problem, but at what cost to us who are made the old way?"

He may have been correct, but I did not refer to a chemical war in my essay because the Polity denied that one had occurred. Placing a period at the end of my final sentence, I closed the book and carried it to Ms. Hardin, adding it to the stack. Esme was still writing as I left the classroom alone and strolled into the twilight. The commissary was open for a bit longer and Perrin had asked me to bring home a new broom for his workshop, so I turned toward the tall wood-shingled building. Reaching the main floor required a long flight of steps, but I'd hardly lifted my skirt when a whisper came from the recess under the porch.

"Isla," a voice said. "Can you see me? Over here."

It was Gareth, still in his work suit, hiding under the staircase. "In here," he said, moving toward me. "Don't worry, it's safe. Just be aware of the rocks and pebbles."

I hesitated only for a second before taking his hand and stepping into the stony blackness where we faced each other. I'd never been so close to him before, had only observed him during assemblies and at the bus stop. Already I was panicked that the shoppers above heard our murmurings and would come down to peer in the secret pocket where Gareth and I stood.

"So you *do* know my name," I said.

"Of course. Of course, I do. I know all about you and think of you often. I was hoping you would walk this way after the exam."

We smiled and moved closer, just inches of space between us.

"What happened today?" I asked, taking in the curve of Gareth's face, the shape of his eyebrows, etching his face to memory. In the darkness, it was as though he was made of colored powder and a firm touch could make him disappear. Still, the light was enough to reveal the deep olive-green of his eyes. "Did you come for the exam? To retake it?"

"That's what everyone may think, but it's not true. I passed the exam two years ago, long before Patricia Hardin became the teacher. I only joined with the failed boys to see you, Isla. I must tell you a piece of news—I'm leaving Naudiz in the morning."

I was crushed. He'd stopped me only to say farewell.

"But why?"

"I have more to do than this town will allow," Gareth said. "I'm capable of much more than picking beans, and I refuse to breathe through a mask all day long, but there are no jobs here. I'm going to Raidho to join with a rogue team—they are pulling up treasures and artifacts from the water, Isla. They need strong men like me who can dive and swim. Can you understand? You must try to get out too, and I want you to follow me there." He took hold of my forearms, pulling me closer. "I've heard troubling things about the farm where you live. The Polity may terminate the tour bus because Seranack could send in spies to take that land as his own. Already Citizens are fearful about asking for tickets."

I remembered the *Cherish* tour group of the previous Saturday. So small—only eight people. Papa had to be told this news immediately.

But Gareth's hands were velvet in my own. "I feel the same way, about wanting more," I admitted, thinking of the traveling role held by the girl with the stamp on her shoulder. "So I understand you. But who is Seranack? He can't be one of the Cordishes?" Mother Cordish had seven children, all of them named after religious figures, who were referred to as Upper Polity. Everyone who worked beneath them in service, like Ms. Hardin, was Lower Polity.

"Seranack is a brute from another quadrant who's trying to usurp the Cordish reign. He's gaining station through bombs and brutality, gathering some of our Lower Polity into an armed brigade. If he wins, he would do little to help us, Isla, perhaps make the living standards even tighter."

"I didn't know about this," I said, uneasy. Gareth's claims made me anxious, but at the same time I was suspicious. He was still a stranger and could be making up outrageous ideas to manipulate me.

"Why would you?" Gareth asked. "You live in a much different place than most of us. No one is inflicting standards on what you wear or eat, who you can love and where you can go. You aren't forced to wake every morning in a spiritless cement tenement."

The wooden steps above us thundered with the weight of two Citizens coming out of the commissary with parcels, their motion activating the safety light in the tree above.

"Mother Cordish is very ill," he continued. "She's always been of low intelligence. She's hardly capable of organizing against him, and will die soon. Seranack is much stronger than her dull and slow-minded children and he's already set up command in the downtown section of Peorth. The one good thing is that the rules in the city are relaxed while they busy themselves with their scheme."

"You're wrong about me, Gareth. I am forced to live by standards too. They are different than yours, but they are there. And I must go now," I whispered, gathering up my skirts, "to tell my family what you've reported. I'm sorry that you are leaving, but I understand. I'm leaving myself in a short time. With Ms. Hardin, in fact. She's taking a few girls to the CREIA."

But he would not let me leave.

"Tell me one thing," he said, pulling me into him. "Tell me you'll think of me often, and wish I were nearby."

Before I could speak, Gareth crushed his lips against mine, his tongue probing my mouth. I squirmed like an animal, but his hands held firm at my waist. Suffocating, I pushed him away. "You ass," I said, shaking with rage. "How dare you assault me here?"

Above us, the shop was closing. I heard the clicking of boot heels on the wood as patrons came out, the door squeaking on its hinges, washing Gareth's face in the white safety light.

"I'm sorry," he said, clearly regretful. "I thought—I'm sorry. It's just, I think of you so often. And the corset you wear makes your body so appealing. Every boy is looking at you, Isla. You and Esme, more you, but her too. It's difficult to ignore the comely way your body is shaped."

My face burned in humiliation. I picked up my skirts and moved around him, but he caught me by one elbow, gently pulling me back.

"Please," he whispered desperately. "Just kiss me one time, here and now. We might never have the chance again."

My thoughts spun and I nearly reconsidered. I'd longed for the chance to be so close to Gareth, had imagined the excitement of meeting him in this secretive way, but the moment lived wasn't as dreamed. Above us, the shopkeeper locked the doors and came down the stairs, keys jingling in the pocket of her black dress, walking out to the darkness like a ghost. We watched her form fade into the fog and stinging insects.

"I have to go," I said when she was far off. "Please step aside. The bus is coming soon and it's the last route of the night."

Gareth stood aside to clear my passage, waving one hand like a gentleman. "I'll remember you fondly," he said.

But as I tried to pass, he caught my arm again.

"One last thing, Isla. Be wary of Ms. Hardin. She's an instrument of the Lower Polity, maybe even Seranack, held under rule by threats. I am certain of it. There is no good to come by following along with her ideas. She's a liar, don't you know?"

"So you say." I shrugged.

"Haven't you heard the rumor about her? She has a daughter hidden in a small town around here."

I paused, remembering I'd heard the rumor from Marta Klein, who had heard it from her mother. A long time ago, they said, Ms. Hardin was seen at a bus station with a little girl at her side. But there were many reasons why she could have a child with her, I thought, a niece perhaps.

"You could be right," I admitted. "But I will decide the affairs of my own life, thank you."

The wind whipped around me, snapping the dry ends of the tree as I finally pulled away from him.

"Goodbye, Isla," he called.

I didn't reply, rushing to the bus stop without the broom I'd come for. Sitting on the bench alone and shriveled, I was washed with regret that my romantic fantasies had been so skewed, that I'd been consumed by a rough and unmannered ogre. The kind suitor in my dreams, the one who would save me from Archie Thimm, did not exist, at least not in the world I was now living. With my bonnet pulled tight, I sat in the waving darkness, nauseated from the worry and weight of Gareth's warnings and my injured hopes, until the bus came rumbling down the road.

CHAPTER 4

*P*errin was often reminding me of the miserable life I'd have if I left home for town like our sister did. Our farm provided fresh food and offered space for long walks through the woods. Without it, there would be no cats to pet or breed, no goat's milk, no long afternoons swinging in the hammock tied between two mammoth oak trees or any other such leisure. Without an income, I could wind up as an Unsaved—a person without a home or security of any kind, left to certain death by disease or starvation.

"Better to be a spinster here than leave for town," Perrin once advised. "Even better, marry Archie Thimm and have your own farm. He's a little old and cock-eyed, but nice enough. He would treat you well. Fate is cruel, sister."

After the bus dropped me off and I fed the two horses their carrots, petting them in the darkness, I went directly to my brother's workshop to tell him about the warnings I'd received from Gareth.

The workshop was lit, I found, but he wasn't inside. Since he'd irresponsibly left the oil lamps burning, I put down my satchel and occupied myself by visiting Aura, now locked inside a large cage in a far corner of the room. She purred and nibbled my fingertip through the slats, and I was about to lift her out for some time in my lap when Perrin shot through the door, his face pulled in panic.

"What is it?" I asked.

"There's—" He stopped, breathing hard, supporting himself with one hand on the large table in the center of the room, knocking a wooden bowl of cheather pods to the floor. "There's someone, or something, out there." Perrin gestured toward the open door. "Outside, past the field, I think a trailer has been occupied. Whoever it is must have come in from the opposite side, on the logging road. That was the sound we heard last night."

"Calm down, won't you? Maybe it's just a rat like you said, or a nest of them."

"Only if rats wash their clothes and hang them from tree branches. She had a dress drying in the wind. And—" He hesitated. "Underthings, you know, like a girl wears. A brassiere."

"She?"

"It seems so, yes, although I haven't seen her."

I looked down at the spilled cheather pods, my mind turning through possibilities. No one besides us dared venture into the crumbling village of trailers and old houses behind our field. Except for Polity, very few outside *Cherish the Past* even knew of its existence. After three generations, there was nothing valuable inside the old structures—we'd long ago pulled the wiring from the walls and lifted the glass from the windows, snuck out the stoves and pillaged the cabinets for dishes and silverware.

"I'm not sure what to make of it," Perrin went on. "Or what to do. Should we confront her?"

"Let's be on guard," I told him. "I was given a warning tonight. A boy in town, Gareth Teague, told me that a leader named Seranack who may reside in Peorth is gathering power and wants to claim our land. That may be why the tours are so thin."

"I've heard of these crazy rumors," Perrin said, turning his back to me to wash a vial in the sink. "But our farm is under contract with the Cordishes and cannot be dissembled. The terms were negotiated long ago to repay the debt they accumulated for using our land as storage. Your friend is telling you conspiracies."

"Maybe, but—" I bent down to sweep up the spilled cheather pods, holding them in the pocket of my pinafore and then dumping them on the table. Inside each shiny, copper-brown pod, most smaller than my index finger, lay hundreds of fluffy seeds. "Gareth seemed certain of this."

"*Gareth* doesn't know humdiddle," Perrin said. "This farm is ours forever."

Together, we extinguished the lamps and walked to the house where we found Papa putting out a pot of bean soup. Over dinner, Perrin declared his suspicion that someone was living in one of the abandoned trailers. I added what Gareth had told me about the tours, and Papa laughed.

"The Polity couldn't be less interested in our remote land and all the litter in the lot," he said. "And the tours have been fading out for some time now. Truthfully, would you care if they stopped? I can certainly find better things to do on Saturdays." Behind him, the fireplace crackled and hissed.

"I suppose," I said. But inside, I still feared that Gareth knew things my father and brother weren't aware of. Life in town was lively. People gossiped and exchanged information with one another. We had only each other and the animals.

"As for the intruder," Papa went on. "It's likely an Unsaved looking for a place to die. Leave her be tonight and we'll investigate in the morning."

But I was curious about the unwelcome guest. After the dishes were cleaned, I slipped out the back door to loiter near the apple tree. The cheather field stretched before me, ripples of unturned earth and dark valleys reaching into the jagged strip of pines. The moon draped the roofs of the nearest empty houses and trailers, but I didn't see the garments hanging in the breeze as my brother had. Maybe she was already gone, having cleaned her clothes and taken a rest.

I sat on the stoop and tried to enjoy the peaceful evening, but my mind was restless. With school nearly complete and no boy to preoccupy my thoughts, I could think only about the CREIA and what it would be like there. But was it right to leave Papa and Perrin when there could be danger brewing, as Gareth had said? There was a hoot owl in a far-off tree—a light-brown mound quivering on a thick branch. I silently asked him if I should stay home or indulge in my excitement about traveling with Ms. Hardin and the others. We were due to leave in two days. The owl eventually emitted a long and ominous call, so pure and eerie I felt hair rise on my skin, but it was hardly an answer.

I crossed the back garden, determined to see if the intruder was still in the trailer. Keeping my figure low, I hiked to the old lot and soon spotted a round beam in the blackness—it was the electric light Perrin had seen. Moving closer, I made out the clothesline, a folding table, and a work basket placed nearby. There was a vibrant spirit in the way the place had been tidied up, a sense of purpose, pride, and ownership. The person inside the trailer was not an Unsaved, I knew, and she was not afraid of us. I only wondered if we should fear her instead. Turning, I walked briskly back to the house.

Papa was waiting for me at the back door when I emerged from the garden. The sight of him so saggy and sad and tired, coveralls torn at the knees, seemed to answer the question the owl did not. My heart withered in resignation.

"Zasha, why are you wandering around in the darkness? Come inside now. Will you become like your sister?"

Above us, the night sky was fogged with glittering stars and a brilliant moon just shy of completion.

"No, Papa. I was just out looking for any cheather cats, maybe that gray one, Isaac, who ran away—Aura is the only one left here and she's becoming so lonely."

"Yes, I remember that old Tom you called Isaac," Papa said, wrapping one arm around me and leading me in. "What a grifter he was, that tabby."

"Give me your coveralls later." We crossed the threshold into the kitchen, which smelled of soap and tea. "I'll darn the holes for you."

"Good daughter. What would I do without you?"

So it seemed my question was decided. The next day, I decided then, I would reject Ms. Hardin's invitation to the CREIA. And if Archie came by soon, I would find something to like about him and encourage his proposal. I would protect and care for Papa, the farm, the cats, and make sure Perrin turned off the oil lamps every night. Our farm would carry on for another turn of time and one day I would die a contented soul who had made the proper decisions, sacrificing herself for the greater good. With such thoughts rambling along, I turned down the covers of my bed and closed my eyes, pushing away the doubt and despair of knowing my deflated heart would soon repair itself, my sensibilities would submerge, and that I could not deny the alluring draw of a love yet to be discovered.

CHAPTER 5

"Your name?" Mr. Schultz asked as I sat on the stool and faced the camera lens.

"Isla Kiehl."

Earlier that morning, Ms. Hardin had returned the exam booklets—each one stamped with the "PASSED" seal—to the four elder girls in our class and sent us to the identity station to be photographed. Each girl was to sit straight on a wooden stool and look directly into the lens without smiling. She should then turn for a profile portrait. We would get two copies of each shot, one pair for Ms. Hardin and the other pair to keep. I planned to give mine to Papa.

Mr. Schultz smiled beneath his white mustache. "A Kiehl, you are. I remember your older sister, always out with that Combs girl." He looked down at the camera and clicked the shutter. "Go downstairs to the front booth for your duplicates and identification card. They'll be ready in a minute or two. And tell me, please, how is your sister these days? It's been a long time since I've seen her. Is she still in Naudiz or has she gone off for something better?"

"No. No, she isn't." I was surprised Mr. Schultz didn't know my sister was dead. "You probably won't see Hollis again. Not ever." I left it at that, rising and leaving him perplexed behind his camera.

The other girls from class had gathered outside in a small group—we were officially adults and it was time to celebrate. The identification card allowed all Citizen benefits: the chance to celebrate holidays, have two children, go to a final school if accepted, get married, and receive honor upon death. But there were exceptions and exclusions for special assignments. Esme guessed that the CREIA had more assignments than the teacher training program, and I mentioned the girl who traveled around to talk to us.

"Maybe that, but there's more. Ms. Hardin said we might also be considered for UniKind," Esme said.

"Why would we want that?" Marta asked. "I heard they steal all the eggs out of a girl's body and leave nothing for her to use later. I don't want any part of getting old before my time, even if it means coming back home and being bored."

"UniKind is just a DNA experiment," Esme claimed. "They likely only need a little of your DNA, maybe just one of the eggs from your fallopian tubes, and they analyze it to see if you have traits they are collecting."

"Collecting for what purpose?" I asked, remembering the strange question on the Citizen exam. I suspected she didn't know as much about UniKind as she seemed to. Whenever Esme wanted to know something but couldn't figure it out, she made up things based on the facts she had. I'd been holding off on telling her that I wouldn't be going with them to the CREIA.

"I'm sure it's a good reason," she said. "We better go now. The bus is on the way. Let's go back to school and empty our desks."

"I doubt I'll be chosen," Marta remarked on our way to the stop. "They probably don't want girls with red hair and fair skin." She flicked one of her chestnut-colored braids over a bony shoulder.

"They don't mind your hair color," Esme said. "And you have red undertones, not red hair. Anyhow, it won't make a difference because they can choose a DNA sequence for hair or skin color from another strand. They kept Ada Baker for the second round, and she had red hair. Really red."

"I don't remember her," Marta replied.

"How do they select the final group of girls?" This came from Leslie Snyr, who had come along with us. I knew little about her even though we'd been in school together for most of our lives. Just as Marta, she lived with her parents in the cement condominiums in town, but she was seldom cheerful. Most often, she went around alone, her slumped shoulders covered with a limp cardigan sweater, her dull brown curls held back with a cotton band. She was always clean and neat, but her plain features and the awkward, uncertain way she moved and spoke put her insecurities on display.

"Once we arrive at the CREIA, we'll participate in a ceremony," Esme told Leslie. "A formal ceremony requiring us to look our very best. During the procession, a panel of judges will review our academic dossiers and choose the most appealing young women to stay for a prolonged time. Do you have a dress to wear?"

"Not really," Leslie said.

Esme and I had been working on our ceremony dresses for many weeks. Sewn by her mother, they were hanging on a rack at her house. I considered releasing my secret by telling Leslie that she could take my dress since she didn't have one, but at that moment the bus arrived.

We got off at the school building and went in to clean our desks. Mine was stuffed full of random items accumulated over the year. Among the mix of things was an old white sweater with pearl buttons, a tiny bottle of cheather tincture that I'd used to calm down before exams, a toothbrush and toothpaste, a hairbrush, many pens, pencils, and a pad of paper from Papa's supply. I was about to leave when a card drifted from my desk to the floor. I picked it up and smiled at the faded photo of a large fish on one side. *Greetings from Sea World*, it said. I'd found it in the old lot inside a metal box hanging lopsided next to the front door of a crumbling shack. Months earlier, I'd brought it in to show the smallest children and forgotten to take it back home.

With our satchels packed, Esme and I boarded the bus back home. Since it was nearly noon, the vehicle was full of Citizens on their way to errands and their second-shift jobs around town or in the soybean processing factory, making it bothersome to find a standing place. I found it strange to be riding so early in the day, but with school complete, I was officially an adult with no claims on my time. When the bus arrived at our stop, the spitting bits of gravel caused the horses to run off when Staris opened the doors for us.

"I should wait a few minutes for them to return," I said to Esme.

"I'll wait with you," she offered. "It feels thrilling to be out early in the day." She smoothed her dark braid and adjusted the bones of her corset through an embroidered bodice. "The sun is up high and the sky is marvelous."

"Come on now!" I called and waved to the horses. The beautiful beasts were together in a far-off corner of the pasture, snorting and chewing grass; above them, the sky was streaked with a curving rainbow prism.

"What is that, I wonder?" I said, pointing to a lilting cloud of gray smoke rising beside the wondrous arc. "It's nearby."

"Looks like a fire," she said. "Is your brother cooking his queer potions again?"

I squinted, assessing the density of the blackness. "If so, it's quite a pungent batch."

"Just as the plant itself," she said. "How you ingest that repelling tincture, I don't understand. The formula makes me dizzy and unable to walk without tripping into things."

"You wouldn't care about such matters if you were ill and needed its medicine."

"I doubt I'd ever get so desperate." She fiddled with her

bonnet. "Goodness, it's hot out here," she said. "Let's go to my house for a while. We can cool off and let Mother see you in the new dress. She worked so hard on the neckline, you know. You owe her a final glimpse."

I agreed, thinking that, once we were there, I could explain that I'd be excusing myself from the field trip to the CREIA. On the way back home, I'd stop to give the horses their carrots.

"Just for a while," I agreed.

As it was, a while became a very long time.

Esme's family farm—a half-mile off from the bus stop—was distinguished by an old, rusted water wheel latched to one side of the weathered barn. Because her father had died many years ago, they didn't work their fields or hire out the labor. The land grew untilled except for hundreds of apple trees in the back orchard, which were pressed into cider during tour performances. They sold jugfuls for several tokens each. Her mother's dressmaking business was supplementary income, one quite enriching because many women desired couture attire made by hand.

My long gown was hanging in the upstairs sewing studio, so beautiful I nearly regretted that I wouldn't present myself to the judges at the CREIA after all. An intense shade of blue-lavender, the dress had a flowing silk skirt made from many thin tiers of fabric. The neckline was trimmed with tiny pearls and the sleeves flowed from the shoulders like loose flower petals.

"Isn't it stunning?" Esme asked. Her own dress was equally beautiful: a fitted bodice of sparkling green sequins attached to a magnificent skirt made from billowing organza of the same color. "And aren't you overjoyed we will be out of Civil War drabbery for once? If we are asked to stay for the second round, Ms. Hardin said, we might be given school uniforms to wear. Modern skirts and sweaters, perhaps, and no corsets!"

I sat on a chair beside an opened window, looking down on the cider stand, feeling I could no longer put off telling her what I'd decided.

"Please listen—I've decided not to go to the CREIA after all. It's not right to leave Papa and Perrin alone." Esme's face fell in shock, but I rambled on. "If I were chosen to stay, who would take my chores such as breeding the cheather cats or canning tomatoes? I so wish I could wear my dress, but I'll give it to Leslie instead."

Esme stomped one foot onto the wood floor, shaking forth a blast of dust. "You can't back out now, Isla. It's far too late." The sparking anger in her dark eyes shook my soul.

"But I can't go—I'm worried."

"About what?"

I confessed my meeting with Gareth, his warning about Seranack and the possibility that Ms. Hardin had unknown motives.

"You imagine things," Esme said, scowling. She flung open the sewing box, refusing to look at me. "I should have known," she muttered, hunting through the supplies, "that you would turn into a puddle for your brother and father."

"That's not why."

"Why then?"

"I told you. They need me more—"

At that moment, the humming sound of a car came from up the road. Out the window, a dark-blue sedan—a standard automobile for workers of the Lower Polity—turned in slowly and stopped on the bare patch of lawn beneath us. I caught sight of the driver's silver-blond hair, cut straight around her head like a scarecrow's. The door opened and she stepped out, smoothing out her tailored black suit and raising one hand to shield the sun from her eyes as she looked around.

"It's Ms. Hardin," I said, heart quickening. "Why is she here?"

Esme leaned out the window to wave. "Hello there!"

Our teacher spotted us, smiled, and returned the wave. "Hello, girls. I'm glad to find the two of you together," she called. "We must leave for the CREIA tonight instead of tomorrow. Road construction is planned for the morning and we must avoid the chaos to arrive promptly."

Downstairs, we gathered in the front parlor, where I explained to Ms. Hardin that I'd decided against leaving, exaggerating the details for impact. "My papa is—he's old, not so much in his body, but in his mind. And since my older sister Hollis ran away and was killed when she was my age, he's in a panic that something bad will happen to me."

Esme was rushing around, bringing down her satchel and the formal dress, now folded and tied up in muslin. I was pleased she was occupied with packing the car and too concerned with herself to fume about my announcement. I'd slip away with a quick good-bye, a quick hug, and best wishes. Parting with her would feel sad, but it was likely we would see each other again soon.

"Maybe I could talk to your father," Ms. Hardin suggested, pulling back the window curtain to watch Esme. "I could explain how the process works and give him an understanding of how attending the ceremony will benefit you."

"That's a kind offer, and I'm so sorry that I've created inconvenience, but it's not just Papa holding me at home. The decision is my own, you see. Although the CREIA seems interesting and the experience unforgettable, for me it's not the best choice to leave right now."

Mustering the courage to meet my teacher's questioning gaze —her slanted eyes were intensely light blue and thickly outlined with make-up—I stood up to retrieve my wilted bonnet and school bag from a side table.

"I'll say goodbye to Esme now and walk home. The afternoon is hot as an oven already."

"Isla, don't be silly," Ms. Hardin said. "There's no need to walk home when I have a car right outside. Sit in the back seat and I'll drop you off. I promise not a word to your papa."

I thought of the horses and how they would miss their carrots and refused Ms. Hardin's kindness, but once outside at the car, Esme convinced me to accept.

"You can see those horses any old day," she said. "But how often do you have the chance to ride in a car?"

Ms. Hardin was already behind the steering wheel, adjusting the fold-down window blind. The dashboard before her was a spectacle of knobs, colorful dials, and buttons, so I leaned in for a closer look. I'd never been inside a car before and was curious about how the instruments worked and why so many meters and measurements were necessary just to travel from one place to another.

"It feels like you're floating on a cloud, not at all like a bumpy bus ride," Ms. Hardin explained. "I regret now that I never took you girls out after class. Come on now, Isla, and get in the back seat. Once the ignition is on, I'll activate the fan and you can enjoy the cool air as we ride."

"I suppose Perrin would like to hear about how the vehicle operates," I said, dropping my bag into the back and folding myself into the covered bench behind the front seat where Esme was sitting. She'd said goodbye to her mother privately in the house and her cheeks were crimson, her eyes full of tears. If I were to ride with her a little distance, perhaps it would help her regain the composure she needed to show Ms. Hardin her inner strength.

"It's a shame for your first ride to be so short," Ms. Hardin said, adjusting a lever on the steering wheel that moved us backward. "You should come along with us to pick up Leslie and Marta. There's room enough for the three of you back there, and then I'll take you home on the way out."

"Wouldn't that keep you longer?"

"Not if I circle around," my teacher said. "I know a shortcut."

I settled into the comfortable seat and accepted a water canteen Esme handed to me. I'd seen similar canteens at the market. The hard, round vessel was covered with canvas, the opening secured with a tight plastic screw.

"Take a drink," Esme said as the car turned onto the road. "The water is very cold. Ms. Hardin put ice inside and it's so refreshing."

I carefully unthreaded the screw, trying not to splash the car's clean leather seats or the lap of my pinafore, and took a long drink of the cold fluid. Outside, the landscape rushed, trapped in the frame of the car window, a blur of spring-green earth melting into the powder-blue sky. We passed the bus stop so quickly that I had to turn around to catch a glimpse of the married couple galloping through the pasture, the rainbow arc still glimmering above them. Ms. Hardin adjusted the dashboard vents to release more cool air. Esme unwound her hair from the long braid she always wore, allowing the strands to blow and whip around her head.

"I'll be so happy to take these cumbersome clothes off once we get to the CREIA," she said, taking another drink from the canteen and passing it back to me again.

"Drink a little more, but leave some for Marta and Leslie," Ms. Hardin said, catching my eyes in her rearview mirror.

I took another few sips and returned the canteen to Esme, who stored it in a closed box embedded in the car's front panel. Once Marta and Leslie were picked up, their bags stored in the trunk, the four of us shared the rest of the water, leaving not even a trickle. Our conversation was as light-hearted and free as the day itself, and I found myself feeling liberated from restraints I hadn't even known were in place. The car powered down the road, its fueled energy vibrating through the seats, the dashboard wind fan sending Esme's dark locks back like strands of silky flax. My fingers and toes grew numb and cold, but a pleasant warmness spread out through my torso and into my neck and cheeks. There was nothing much to be concerned about, I thought, relaxing into the seat without a care that Marta's slumbering body was so closely pressed into me.

Out the window, the sun was shrinking into the hard line separating sky from earth, and it occurred to me that we'd been on the journey for a long while, that Ms. Hardin hadn't taken the shortcut to take me home, but also that it didn't matter, really, if I were to go home. At that moment, I was happy enough where I was. Closing my eyes, I allowed the last shred of worry to merge with the blissful inertia of travel and soon fell asleep.

PART II
THE CREIA

CHAPTER 6

arta pressed her elbow into my thigh. "Wake up, Isla. We're here."

I'd been dreaming my hair had been cut short with dull scissors. A mirror in the dream reflected a sickly version of me, jagged tufts sticking out straight from an exposed scalp.

"We're where?"

"Wake up. Here's your bag."

It was morning, dawn, and we had arrived at a pretty place of brick buildings draped with blossoming purple flowers. The wind passing through the car's window was warm, smelled of salt, and the sun flicked through a shelter of gnarled oak trees.

"Slide out of the car, girls," Ms. Hardin said, waving us out to a winding brick driveway.

Sluggish, I pushed out. My mind was thick and groggy, my lips and tongue severely parched. All I could think of was Papa and Perrin frantically searching for me.

"I'm so thirsty," Marta complained. "How long were we riding? I feel as though I slept for such a long, long time. And why are you still here, Isla? I thought you weren't coming with us."

"Come on now, girls," Ms. Hardin said, short and crisp. "Marta, brush the lint from your blouse. Isla, let me take a look at your rumpled clothes. We'll be meeting the head teacher soon—let's smooth them out." She took my elbow, steering me away from the others. She sensed my confusion, taking my hands in hers.

I flinched away and forced her into eye contact. "This is the CREIA, isn't it? You've tricked me into coming here."

"Shhh, don't panic. I tried to wake you, Isla, but road construction was blocking the way back to your farm. It was impossible to cross. You were sleeping so deeply, too deep to rouse. It must be all the hard work you do, and the warm sun—the car's hum can be so relaxing. I had to slap myself to alertness at times."

Liar!

Gareth had been right—our teacher was a conniving spy. There was no road construction near our farm and never had been, not in my lifetime, but I thought it best to pretend I believed her. She was a proud woman, insistent that her ways were correct. In class, she'd always taught us to argue the most powerful point of logic, leaving emotion aside.

"But I must go back," I told her. "My papa needs help with cooking and chores, and my brother often neglects his stove and lamps. Without me, he could set a fire. There was even a cloud of smoke when I left. Esme and I spotted it right before you arrived."

"I didn't notice a fire or any smoke on the way out." Ms. Hardin's tone was resolute as a judge's gavel, but she seemed taken aback by the information. Her eyes grew thoughtful. "If it were a serious flame, smoke would have been evident from my view of the road, and I saw no such thing. I'm sure your family is fine without you, Isla. Look around—wouldn't you like to stay and enjoy the events?"

Looking about, I saw the group around us expanding from the driveway into the brick courtyard, which was artfully paved with stones and centered with a large six-pointed star. The girls around me were happy and excited, too awed at the spectacular scenery to gape at Esme and me in our old-fashioned attire. I, too, was soon drawn in by a range of blue mountains in the distance, stony peaks rising into white vapor. My heart lifted at the sight, so beautiful in the balmy morning.

"You're here now, having come such a long way, so try to enjoy yourself," Ms. Hardin urged, placing a hand on my shoulder and turning me in with the others. "Now stay still for a moment and I'll tie the back of your pinafore."

Beyond the brick buildings was a spiked black iron fence against a forest of evergreen trees. Esme caught my eye and smiled, partially apologetic. Some of the girls were wandering around, circling into a garden of lilies where—they shouted out—there was a very tame squirrel. A brick structure across the courtyard was four stories high, every window covered. Every so often, a curtain panel trembled. A driver took Ms. Hardin's car away through a gate that surrounded a garage; shortly after, we heard a bell ringing.

"The ladies are coming out now," Ms. Hardin said. "Come together, girls, and stand near me."

The building's door soon opened for three women. One carried a national flag, another held a hammered copper bowl on a tray. The woman between them, tall and thin, walked with her hands free. All three wore long white gowns with straight skirts slit modestly on the left side. The centermost woman walked ahead of the rest and circled through the group to shake hands with the teachers who'd just arrived. When reaching Ms. Hardin, she smiled as though greeting a dear friend. The sleeves of her gown, I noticed, ended just above her knobby wrists. I saw a marking on the left—a character from an ancient alphabet, so white and light it nearly glowed.

She raised one hand, stepping back to gain our attention. "Welcome to the CREIA," she said. "Perhaps you have thought of coming here for many years, or perhaps you have just now come to understand our role in promoting advanced ecology and research. Either way, your presence here is a gift to us. You are one of the first groups to arrive for the ceremony. We expect two more rounds of participants late tonight."

Some of the girls put down their bags, shielding their eyes against the sunlight.

"I am Rielle," she continued. "Your head teacher." She considered us with black-brown eyes, large and languid like a hound's; her eyebrows were thick, high, and perfectly arched. From the side, her profile revealed a long nose and a sharp chin. Her brown curls were brushed straight down to tame them, her face clean of make-up, yet smooth and evenly toned. She was slightly younger than the women at her side, I noted.

"We've brought some water." Rielle gestured to the white-haired woman beside her. "Take a sip and follow us into the dormitory."

The woman holding the copper bowl stood to the side as Rielle and the flag bearer turned back to the brick hall to glide up the steps. One by one, each member of our group stopped at the bowl for a drink. When it was my turn, I pushed my hair back and aimed my hands toward the bowl. The water was nearly gone, but I was able to get a few teaspoons onto my tongue. The liquid was extremely cold, but other than that, it had no unusual taste or quality. The water-gifter did not smile at me or speak, but I felt her eyes traveling over my face.

Once Esme and I entered the dormitory's cool and dim hallway, the attendants asked us to choose a bedroom. We agreed on one facing the northeastern portion of the courtyard because the sunshine coursed through the curtains, giving the walls a soft warm light. There were two small iron beds, a sink and mirror, and a gray cotton rug between the beds. We divided the four drawers of a carved wooden dresser between us—hers on top and mine on the bottom because I didn't mind stooping. Inside the drawers, we learned after pulling on the green glass knobs, were nightgowns and CREIA uniforms. Esme was excited that we already had the uniforms, but I was angry that she seemed not to care about my abduction.

"Why didn't you stop her from stealing me away?" I accused, sitting hard on the bed. My pinafore was wilted, so I folded it into my bag. A few cheather pods clung to the inside of both pockets, I noticed. "Papa and Perrin must be frantic about where I am."

"I fell asleep before I even knew," Esme claimed. She hung our dresses on two hooks anchored to the back of the door. She ran her hands over the wrinkles and fluffed out the skirts.

"And why did you bring both dresses if you thought I wasn't coming as I said?"

Esme laughed at my accusation. "Of course I brought both. To give myself a choice and a spare. Besides, you said Leslie could have your dress. Now she will never know you thought that way, and you can wear the dress after all. You're here now, so indulge yourself, Isla. You're a full Citizen and can make your own way. Perrin and your papa will gradually assume you came with us and just didn't have a chance to let them know." She sat on the bed beside me, her face drawn and churning. "Did you see there's a television here?" she asked. "It's in a big room full of sofas and benches. Let's go see it."

I thought of the beauty of the mountain range. And there was the dress hanging on the door, so perfectly sewn and pressed, its silk shimmering like butterfly wings—an irresistible lure.

"I'm so hesitant to stay," I said, my will weakening with the thought that Gareth could have been wrong about everything he told me. He was, after all, a brusque stranger who'd cornered me under a staircase. "Maybe I could, but only if I can send a note to Papa."

"Of course you can. Let's go see the TV."

We went down the hall to the parlor. I'd never seen such a large television before.

"It's as big as a table," I said.

The electrical cord was plugged into the wall, but no one could locate the power button or a wand for control. It sat silent, a thin black plastic box.

"If the screen would only come on, we could talk to our families," said a girl I didn't know. She kneeled in front of the screen, cupped her mouth in her hands, and shouted, "Hi Mommy!"

"It probably doesn't work," said Marta. She had brushed her long red hair and tied it back neatly.

Leslie was with her, exhibiting more presence than usual, explaining that Ms. Hardin had brought her a dress from a stock kept on the CREIA campus. "It's very pretty," she said. "Pure white with a pink belt."

Esme waved us to a corner of the lounge, where she had found a few heavy books with colorful pictures on the front and inside. She read the titles out loud to the group: *The Scarlet Letter, Jane Eyre, Naked Lunch*. But the inside of the books wasn't printed in words. Instead, the pages were punched with tiny raised dots in various formations, one of which was the sideways "T" I'd seen on Rielle's wrist.

Esme was clearly disappointed that she wouldn't be able to read the books, and sneezed from the dust we'd brought up by opening them. I tried to help by looking inside every book we could find in hope one would offer printed language, but they were all the same. Eventually we sat with the others and traded stories long into the afternoon. For dinner, we were served from a long cart pushed into the hallway by an attendant in a gray dress. We ate the bland meal quietly and returned to our rooms.

Ms. Hardin knocked on our door and pulled me aside. "I was able to contact your family through the wire," she said, whispering thickly. "A man from town will deliver a message to your father tonight."

"Thank you, Ms. Hardin." I looked down at the flat cotton rug on the floor. I didn't completely trust her words, but there seemed nothing I could do. Esme and I dressed silently into the long nightgowns we pulled from the dresser drawers and slid into the small beds. A bell rang and, shortly after, the lights went out.

My sleep that night was troubled and light. The night tumbled into a deep hum, the dark stillness circled me like a flock of bleating crows. I woke, heart pounding, at a very early hour in the morning, my senses tuned to a crackle in the air and my stomach uneasy with nausea. A nightmare had jolted me awake, but it raced away before I could remember, a speeding train far, far off in the fog.

~

In the morning, we weren't to put on our ceremony dresses, the morning attendant said, but uniforms from the dresser—knee-length skirts made from light-brown cloth, a button-down shirt in the same color, knee socks, and canvas boots. After dressing, Esme and I stood together at the mirror and registered that, for the first time in our lives, we wouldn't attract attention with corsets, bonnets, and dresses so long they dragged in the dirt.

"I feel peculiar with my torso so free," Esme said, turning sideways to look at her stomach.

"We'll expand like sponges without the bones holding us in place," I said.

"Still, let's wear our corsets to the ceremony later," Esme suggested as we walked out and met the others in the lounge. "Our dresses were designed for them. If we don't have a corset on, the shaping will be strange."

"If you want," I said, but my thoughts were with Papa and Perrin. Had they received the message yet from Ms. Hardin? The anxiety came at me again as I wondered if the message had ever been sent at all.

We walked in a single-file line across the courtyard to a long, blue-painted building on the other side of the squirrel park. The rising sun observed us, bleeding peach and amber rays into the mist over the mountains, dark in the distance. In the dining hall, an attendant directed us to sit at a long table. There were so many girls on the bench that I was uncomfortably close to the person next to me, a sweaty blonde. The room had the smell of rubber mats and cleaning fluid.

"There are so many of us," Esme murmured to me.

There were at least twenty rows of benched tables. With two tables in each row and about fifteen girls at each table, I estimated that nearly six hundred young women would be participating in the ceremony later in the day. Seeing how much competition there was, I relaxed a bit. The chances of being picked were obviously slim. There were many attractive girls among us and likely many of them were also very smart and accomplished. Two tables away sat a black-haired girl with sharp cheekbones, deep green eyes, and porcelain skin. She resembled a China doll, and her deep burgundy suit and button-up boots made it seem more so, but she had a shy demeanor and kept her gaze on the table, where she was folding and refolding her napkin.

"She's *very* striking," Esme observed.

I didn't have the chance to respond. Rielle entered the hall with her two attendants and the crowd fell silent to watch the trio travel through the center row and take their places at a table under the screened windows. There were gasps when the screens overhead suddenly transformed into close-ups of their faces. I noticed that Ms. Hardin's face was on one of the screens—she was sitting at the head table. Esme also noticed, and we shot each other a glance.

Everyone watched as Rielle smiled and began to speak, her voice carrying over the room. "Good morning, everyone," she said.

Some of the girls responded with loud shouts and cheers.

"Welcome to your ceremony day," Rielle continued. "Most of you will be leaving later tonight, but don't let that keep you from appreciating this experience. It should remain a lifelong memory. If you are turned away, don't consider it a rejection of yourself. Only girls with a particular set of qualities are invited to stay, and the set of qualities changes from year to year."

She paused to take a sip from her glass. Every girl in the room watched her put the glass down, some so excited they could barely sit still in their chairs.

"After our meal, return to your rooms to prepare. Put on your special dresses and your shoes. It should be very warm out, so leave all jackets and sweaters in the dormitory. Once you have been turned out from the circle, immediately return to your room to gather your things. The buses will run in two shifts, with all efforts directed to sending you home by the morning." She paused and held both hands out to the sides. "These are your judges," she told us. "I will be judging, too, of course."

Rielle then motioned to a petite young woman at the very end of the table. The screen adjusted so we could see her small round face as she stood up.

"I'm Cistine," she told us. "Your ceremony hostess."

The cheerful enthusiasm in the room shifted into uncertain curiosity.

"Yes," she said, "I am a composite."

I realized she was born out of the UniKind Project. I had never seen a DNA composite before and was surprised how small she was. And her features, although symmetrical—were not especially pretty or beautiful, just plain. Her skin was the beige-brown color of the clay we dug from the ground when making bricks, her eyes were deep-set, and her blondish-brown hair completely straight. I noticed Ms. Hardin looking at Cistine with pride; it was the same look she gave me and Esme in class when we got an answer correct.

"I'm twenty-one years old," she said, "and I was one of the very first composites ever born." She then explained that composite humans are designed on a smaller scale than natural humans because smaller people waste less of the Earth's natural resources. "We eat less, drink less, and don't take up as much space," she said. "Our environmental footprint is smaller because we live shorter lives and are sterilized to control population growth. We're designed to sustain nature, not consume it. In most ways, though, I'm exactly like all of you."

This comment caused Rielle, Ms. Hardin, and the other judges to smile with amusement.

"Cistine is humble," Rielle said, her voice amplified through the cafeteria. "She's much more intelligent than any of us. Last year, she designed and helped build a water distribution system that extracts moisture from the atmosphere, transports it into a filtering pump, and delivers it to our tanks."

We applauded, but I wasn't impressed by the water system. Back home, we engineered the farm in many clever manners. We made solar panels from bottles taken from the city refuse, used a windmill that generated electricity for the workshop and barn, and watered the fields with a soaker system made of rubber tubing. Perrin had built his lab from old parts he'd gotten at the salvage market and the abandoned lot.

Cistine sat down as Rielle continued. "Before we eat, I want to thank every one of you for participating today. Should you be chosen for the teacher training or the UniKind program, your sacrifice will aid in producing future generations of composite humans designed to perpetuate our planet and direct the evolution of humanity. Our children, the composites, are designed with small appetites, large minds, and are naturally inclined against violence toward people and the animal kingdom. With each new generation, terrible diseases like cancer, arthritis, and multiple sclerosis are less likely to occur. With genetic control, we eliminate physical abnormalities, retardation, and many strains of mental illness."

She paused and slid on a pair of eyeglasses. "And did I mention nearsightedness?" she said.

There was a confused pause before we realized she meant this as a joke. Ms. Hardin and the other judges applauded and openly laughed, so we did too.

"And, now," Rielle said, "it's time for breakfast. Enjoy it."

Soon, plates of food arrived. Everyone was hungry and happy to begin, but I found my mind stuck on one thought: What had Cistine meant by *sacrifice?*

CHAPTER 7

*B*reakfast was not enjoyable, Esme complained as we walked back to our room to get ready.

"Was that *oatmeal?*" she asked.

"I think so."

The "oatmeal" had been a sticky blob of gritty nuggets served in a ceramic cup. A saucer beside it offered a cube of white cheese, a pat of butter, and a boiled egg cut into quarters.

"We're going to starve all day. Did you bring anything from home we can eat? I have a bag of walnuts."

"How could I bring food when I didn't expect to be here?"

Esme didn't answer my question.

When we arrived at the dorm, we found that the other girls on the floor had gathered in the lounge to spread out fruit and bread brought from home. There was even a jar of blackberry jam. We divided the food evenly among ourselves and ate silently from the sofas and benches.

"Personally, I hope I am not among those chosen today," said Marta, breaking the silence. "I much prefer the food at home and I already miss everyone." She chewed the last of her bread and bit her bottom lip wistfully. "Plus, I have a boyfriend," she announced. "And he's anxious to see me come back home."

"Who?" Esme asked. "I've never seen you with a boyfriend."

"He's just a boy from our block," she said. "Andy. You don't know him."

Ms. Hardin came in, clapping her hands. "Time to get ready, girls. The ceremony starts soon. Go get into your dresses and come back for my approval. If your hair is long, you must wear it up or back in braids. I want to see your faces and so do the other judges."

The group slowly filtered out. Someone had left a smoked sausage sitting out with the food crumbs. Sealed in wax paper, I'd seen similar fare at the commissary but never had enough tokens to purchase one. When no one was looking, I picked it up and tucked it under my blouse before returning to the room, where I found Esme sad and slumped on her bed, a hairbrush in the lap of her uniform skirt.

"Maybe this place isn't what I expected," she said, her eyes shiny with tears. Behind her, our dresses hung on the closet door. The late morning sunlight crept in, exposing bits of dirt and colored threads in the gray cotton rug. "I used to think the prettiest girls would win. Or the smartest. Now it seems without logic."

"Do you think," I sat on my bed and began working the tangles from my hair, "that the selection could be determined for a reason we don't understand? Ms. Hardin seems very familiar with the people here. And she's one of the judges, a fact we didn't know until this morning."

"Why didn't she tell us that before?" Esme whispered. The question hung between us, lingering until an abrupt knock on the door caused us both to jump. "And what did they say about UniKind? I didn't—"

"Girls, are you dressed?" Ms. Hardin called. "Meet us in the lounge when you're ready, and hurry."

Esme dressed in her green gown and I in my lavender one, forgetting any worries for a moment to enjoy how the skirt swung out when I walked. The lacy hemline brushed the floor with such a sweep I had to lift it an inch with my hands as I went to the lounge with Esme, where we sat at a round table cluttered with hair styling instruments and make-up cases. Ms. Hardin braided my hair into a crown and fastened it with a barrette borrowed from Marta. As she worked, I noticed there were many cases on the table with the golden *Ashleen* inscription on the front and LUSH stamp on the bottom. I remembered the night I'd applied shadow from an exact case and shook off the chilling memory.

"Keep still. A smart and enterprising young lady, Ashleen is," Ms. Hardin said, noticing how I'd observed the make-up cases. With a curling rod, she spun the loose hair around my face into wispy curls. "Pick a color for your eyes and one for your lips."

"Ashleen is a real person?" Leslie asked. "I thought she was just the name of the cosmetics company."

"Of course she's real. And if you're lucky enough to make it through the first round, you might even get to see her," Ms. Hardin said, moving away from me to run one hand through Esme's hair. "Now, don't tell anyone I told you so—it's a secret Rielle passed on to me this morning. Goodness, your hair is so thick and coarse, like a pony's mane."

Her words made me miss the married couple, the horses at home. Without my carrots each day, would they feel abandoned? I remembered also that Aura was locked in a cage and would be lonely without my visits, that Papa's clothes were not yet darned as I promised, and that Perrin wouldn't have my help with cooking and chores. It was important to get back as soon as possible, which meant ensuring a rejection at the upcoming ceremony. I selected a garish shade of yellow from the eyeshadow cases, smearing it onto my lids, and applied a ghostly pale pink shade for my lips. There was no mirror around to check my appearance, so I sat back and tried not to think of the anxiety sitting like a sore in my stomach.

Eventually, the lounge became busy as more candidates entered to use the supplies on the table. It appeared that most girls, like us, had arrived at the CREIA with a teacher from their locale who handled their appearance and coached them on how to walk, smile, and stand with good posture during the ceremony. Some of the girls were too poor to buy custom dresses and had sewn together their attire using scrap fabrics and random trims to embellish ordinary gowns from the commissary. But many others wore elegant LUSH dresses adorned with sequins and crystals. When they inquired about our own lovely gowns, Esme and I explained they had been made by her mother, who had special access to materials as the seamstress in *Cherish the Past*. Most of the girls hadn't heard of *Cherish* and didn't know we usually lived in a reenactment of the 1800s.

"Your mother could make an entire line to sell at the LUSH market," a strong-boned girl said to Esme. She introduced herself as Sorrel and appeared to be smart and bookish. I noticed two electronic mechanisms tucked into each of her ears, partly hidden by her light-brown hair. They were hearing aids, she explained; without them, she was completely deaf. But when they were in, she could hear as well as anyone else.

Ms. Hardin led us from the building in a single-file line. The sky was hot, wavering with heat, and the walk to the ceremony site was long. Sweat trickled down my back. Passing through to a corridor of greenhouses and solar panels, we continued down a narrow asphalt lane and across a bridge suspended over a quiet road. Eventually, we came to the edge of a green grove and Ms. Hardin held a finger to her lips.

"Quiet," she whispered.

One by one, we went down a steep mossy staircase cut into a hillside and descended into a valley. In its center was a water fountain made of elaborately carved and sculpted gray stone. The water cascaded from a faceted sphere and tumbled down to its bowl in a rhythmic whooshing melody. The girls who'd arrived ahead of us had encircled the fountain and we joined them. Since there were hundreds of us, the circle had grown many yards away from the water, so far off that I could barely make out the figures of Rielle, Cistine, and the other judges. We waited for what seemed like an hour as the circle was completed by arriving groups of girls. By the time Rielle turned on the microphone set on the paved space next to the fountain, I was sweaty, hungry, and more than ready to be excused. My feet and ankles ached and the high neck of my dress choked my throat. A glance at Esme, who had somehow wound up about five girls down from me, confirmed that she was as hot and tired as I was. But she held herself tall and, by the way she took in the sight, I knew her earlier misery had lifted.

"Good afternoon," Rielle began.

The only sound was the water and the rustling of the trees around us. Someone coughed.

"Today we will select about thirty girls to stay here for observation. If you are selected, you will receive a certificate and a gift. The gift is yours to keep even if you are not ultimately selected for the teacher certification program or as a DNA donor to UniKind."

I looked over to Esme—it was now certain that the CREIA was selecting for UniKind donors during the ceremony. She didn't see my glance but appeared unstirred by the statement.

"When Cistine raises her hand, move with the circle in a clockwise direction." Rielle pointed toward the mountains in the distance, indicating it as the proper direction. "As you walk, the judges will pull some of you into an inner circle. If selected, continue to walk clockwise. Girls who are not selected will be escorted away."

Cistine raised her hand and the circle shuffled into motion. The damp earth clung to my thin shoes as I took careful, tense steps at a pace much slower than natural to me. Back home, Papa and Perrin made jokes about how quickly I walked. All those miles to and from the bus stop and town had built strength in my legs and ankles, but now the strength was aching to manifest and I had to restrain it. Overhead was the *caw-caw* sound of some big white birds that might have been eagles, but I didn't look up, keeping my focus on the girl in front of me. It was Sorrel, the one who wore hearing aids. Her broad silhouette gradually etched itself into my vision.

The walk went on for a stretch of time. The outer circle thinned and the inner circle developed. My heart quickened in hope that I'd soon be escorted away. Some girls had already been pulled out and sent off—I could hear them rustling up the stairs leading from the valley. I was about to take a glance to see who was leaving. Was it Esme? But then there was a tap on my shoulder. Cistine smiled and gestured me into the inner circle. I crossed in and noticed that Esme was there too. We didn't dare speak, but I kept my eyes on her green dress's trailing hem.

We walked and walked. The fountain at the center of the circle gushed a spectacular flow of water. How I longed to go over and scoop some up into my hands and swallow a long drink. I became aware that yet another inner circle had been formed and that girls in the first inner circle were leaving. I walked and walked until Cistine tapped again and pulled me into the new group. The girl in front of me was the beautiful tall brunette I'd noticed in the cafeteria that morning. She wore a dark-blue taffeta gown with a slit down the left side. It was attractive on her body, but poorly constructed; the back seams of the dress were pulling apart. They hadn't been stitched properly, maybe even sewn by hand.

The fatigue intensified as the walking continued. The sky had become cloudy, transforming the hot day into a gray, cool stillness. Just as before, the circle I walked in thinned as a new, smaller circle formed inside it. Surely I would be eliminated this round, I thought. Soon I'd be climbing the stairs out, hungry and exhausted, but free. I'd go back to the room, find my bag, and maybe pry open the stolen sausage before boarding the bus back home. Tomorrow I'd be sitting at our pocked dining table to tell Papa and Perrin about the campus with its lovely architecture and horrible food.

But there was another tap on my shoulder. This time, Cistine draped her arm over my shoulder and led me to within a foot of the fountain.

"Stay here," she whispered in my ear. Her breath smelled flowery.

There was rustling behind me. The other girls in the inner circle had been sent off.

It was over.

"Each of you who face the fountain is invited to stay with us," Rielle said into her microphone. "Relax and look around."

About thirty of us were standing in the chosen circle. I couldn't see everyone because the fountain blocked half the group, but I saw that Esme was still there. She shot me a confident glance and I gave her a weak smile that hid the panicked beating of my heart. I didn't want the judges to know I wasn't happy about being selected.

There were other girls I recognized. The tall brunette was there, as was Sorrel. And one who was a great surprise: It was Leslie Snyr, our classmate in the borrowed dress. Her eyes were uncertain and filled with tears.

"Congratulations, cadets," Rielle said. The mic crackled with her words. "The judges have seen special qualities in each one of you."

Cistine traveled around the fountain to hand each of us a certificate and a small, thick envelope. The certificate was nothing much—just an elaborately bordered sheet with a seal at the bottom.

"Your names will be inscribed later," Rielle said. "And please open your envelopes."

Inside was a 100,000 LUSH token. Some of the girls gasped.

The heavy silver coin gleamed in my palm. With this much, I could buy meat and cream and as much chocolate as we wanted. Papa could go to the river before he was too old to travel. And I wanted new boots, some stockings and ribbons, anything that could be hidden under my skirts. I'd never had a single LUSH credit, much less

100,000 of them, and my mind was scrambling with the possibilities. I wondered, how much was it to get a car? It occurred to me that Ms. Hardin must have used LUSH to get her dark-blue sedan, and I wondered how she'd acquired such wealth. Most likely, a car was more than what I now held in my hand, but the token still teased me.

"Please take a drink from the fountain before leaving," Rielle said. "And when you return to campus, go to the cafeteria for dinner instead of back to the dormitory."

I imagined the dormitory was bustling with girls getting ready to leave and the buses were lining up to return them home. Aching with despair, I stepped toward the fountain. Why had I done a good enough job to be chosen? Apparently, my unflattering make-up choices hadn't been effective enough to deter the judges. I should have been more sloppy and stupid about everything. But it seemed vital to play along and act as though I'd wanted to stay and was overjoyed at being selected.

The other girls were crouching at the rim of the cement bowl to scoop the water into their hands, drinking with vigor. It had been hours since we'd had any refreshment. I slipped the token back into its envelope, held it tightly in my armpit, and stooped down to the bowl, cupping my hands to catch a stream coming from the faceted sphere. It was difficult to get enough water with just my hands, but there were no vessels to drink from. Like the other girls, I slurped as much as possible and held my face into the splattering droplets, breathing the moisture that smelled slightly of lemon balm.

"Time's up," Cistine said. We were led away from the fountain, wiping our faces and burping up air bubbles. The long walk back wasn't as rough since our parched throats and mouths had been relieved. And I wasn't as hungry, either. Esme and I climbed the stairs from the valley, crossed the bridge, and resumed the trampled path back to the CREIA campus.

During the journey, we spoke to the tall brunette.

"I'm Hannah," she said after we introduced ourselves. Up close, she wasn't quite as pretty as she'd seemed from far away.

Her green eyes were slightly crossed and her front teeth were chipped. Her speech was oddly lilted with an accent I couldn't place.

Hannah told us she'd grown up high in the mountains. There was no school there, but she'd been called to the ceremony by a midwife who'd come to help her mother birth one of her many younger siblings. Their entire family had lived in seclusion for generations in a cabin that had no electricity. They had goats, a small pasture for farming, and a tiny solar radio. If she was happy about being chosen, I wasn't sure. She seemed like someone who could be happy no matter where she was.

"I'm so excited to be here," she said. "For so long I've dreamed of seeing the world beyond our mountain where we have nothing."

"How did you get your dress?" I asked as we approached the campus. I could see the low yellow lights of the cafeteria ahead.

"The midwife helped me," Hannah replied. "She brought the fabric from a town market and we cut out the pieces with a razor. It took a long time to sew them. I unwound a spool of twine and used the strands as thread."

That explained the loose seams. Not that it mattered any longer—at lunch, Rielle told us that we would be wearing uniforms during our stay. We were also moving into new bedrooms, she said. Each girl would have a roommate, just as before, and Esme and I were paired up again. Sorrel was rooming with Leslie; and Hannah's roommate was a girl named Robin, one of only six of the chosen thirty with a skin tone classified as "taupe."

While we were eating dinner, we heard the released girls out in the courtyard laughing and shouting. A bus arrived, sputtered to a stop, then rushed away after a few minutes. Marta Klein and the others were returning to life as they'd always known it. Meanwhile, Esme and I had crossed into the place of legend and rumor.

With rosy cheeks and glistening eyes, Esme was already well

into the lunch tray that held a bowl of broth, three yellow carrots, and a block of soy cake.

"This food is delicious," she remarked.

"It isn't bad," said Sorrel. "I like it."

I sipped a spoonful of broth and savored the salty tang. "It's good."

I was reminded of a young chicken we'd roasted at the farm earlier in the year, one that had baked slowly inside a net of thyme, basted with butter. With it, we'd had large potatoes cut into halves and covered with mushroom gravy. The heartiness of that meal seemed captured in the thin cafeteria broth, as if I had pulled the memory from a forgotten place to enjoy it all over again.

Our new room was in a one-story building sitting near a row of identical silver-sided flat-roofed barns. Through the long rows of windows, I saw people in white coats working inside, their heads covered with blue paper caps. I assumed they were scientists of some level, perhaps the very team working on UniKind, splicing DNA into composites like Cistine. Outside each barn sat a squat silver tank with a yellow hose running from the top through a porthole in a door marked *Do Not Enter*.

Ms. Hardin gathered all thirty of us in the lounge, where we sat on carpeted crates arranged in a square. There was another blank television in one corner.

"Congratulations on your advancement." Our teacher sat on a crate and smiled directly at me and Esme. "Your official role as cadets is to learn as much as you can from the teachers and libraries, but please stay away from the lab you walked past on the way in here. The lab is a dangerous place and it's not at all intended for tours or even short visits."

"Why is it dangerous?" Robin asked.

Ms. Hardin seemed amused. "The scientists are working with

very strong chemicals and tools, some that have been under development for decades, long before continent contraction. As a precaution, the CREIA secures this area with deterrents meant to scare you away. If you see any spiders, for example, it simply means you are in a private place and should immediately leave," she said. "The spiders look venomous, but they aren't real. They are a special project the CREIA has been working on for a long time. Remember, this is an innovative research facility. These spiders are holograms and cannot hurt you, so don't panic. Just take them as a sign to move to a different location."

Sorrel asked to see one, but Ms. Hardin said she couldn't do that.

"The spiders appear on their own when it's necessary," she said, standing up. "Let's go now to your rooms. We've already brought your things in and you have the rest of the evening to unpack and get settled. You'll be here for a few weeks, at the very least."

A few weeks? My heart dropped, but I reminded myself of the importance of pretending not to care.

Later that night, just after Esme and I had put on our nightgowns and sat on her bed to knit with some wool skeins and wooden needles they'd given us, Ms. Hardin knocked on our door and came inside. When we stood to greet her, she pulled us into a tight embrace, stroking our hair. While it felt odd to feel the touch of a woman's hand on my body, I found it very difficult to pull away. With my eyes planted on the carpeted floor, I imagined a wavering of colors—blue, pink, green—that reminded me of the rainbow arc I saw the day we left home. It was in this illusion that I focused until Ms. Hardin broke the grasp.

"Esme and Isla, the bus is waiting and I have to return to town to manage our school." She gave us a reassuring smile. "I'm so proud of you both. I have faith in you girls, more faith than you can even know. As soon as I get home, I'll explain to your families where you are and why. And Isla, I'll ask your father about the smoke you mentioned."

"And please tell him that—" Once again, the words were hard to arrange, but I crudely thrust them out. "Tell him that I will be home soon, very likely, and ask my brother to care for my cat Aura."

"Of course I will."

I should have been sad and scared, after all, Ms. Hardin was our last connection to home, but I felt nothing akin to sadness watching her leave the room and close the door—just a neutral sense that things were progressing as they should.

"I wonder when we'll see her again," Esme said flatly.

We turned to one another. Searching my friend's dark eyes, I thought I saw something swimming there, something I remembered. A sentence arrived on the tip of my tongue, clusters of memory trying to emerge into speech. But the sentence could not come forth. Instead, I said, "I don't care much, do you?"

Esme tossed her braid and stretched out on her bed. "I don't," she said. "I don't care at all about seeing Ms. Hardin again. I don't care if I see anyone again, or if I go home. I want to stay here."

CHAPTER 8

The new room was slightly larger than the first one we'd been given, and it had a private bathroom, high ceiling, and a storage shelf running along three walls. There was a tall narrow window with white curtains centered in a wall overlooking the courtyard. Its thick, cloudy glass pane was embedded in the frame and impossible to open. The closet and dresser were packed with clothing, towels, and low-standard toiletries—toothpaste, soap, and menstrual pads made of cotton fabric. Esme and I were given two uniform dresses each—dark-blue sheaths with blue shell buttons down the front and white rounded collars. The wardrobe supply also included fourteen identical navy-blue knee-high socks made of stiff cotton, which we pooled into the upper of two small drawers built into the table between our twin beds. I removed a stack of underwear from a small cardboard box and used it to store small items from my bag—the cheather pods and tincture, the old card with the photograph on the front, my pad of paper, and the 100,000 LUSH tokens.

The heavy door to the room, which auto-locked when closed, was marked with a number "17." It was one of twenty rooms in the building, each one occupied by a pair of girls who had been invited to stay. The day after Ms. Hardin left, we were called to an orientation by Cistine, the composite. She poured small cups of water and asked if we had any questions.

"What should we do with our clothes from home?" Leslie asked.

"Just put them away in the closet. You'll need them again if you aren't selected to stay here. Also make sure that you always wear all parts of your uniform, including the head kerchiefs and boots. I see that all of you are still wearing your own shoes, but you should be wearing the CREIA footwear." She pointed to the canvas boots on her tiny feet. The laces, a shade darker than the tan fabric, crisscrossed up and tied just above her ankles. "When we are done here, go back to your room and put them on. You'll find them on the top shelf."

"How did you know our sizes?" I asked.

"Your teacher gave us that information when she submitted your dossier."

Cistine went on to explain that we were welcome to tour the campus during our break times, but that we should always keep away from the laboratory. Soon we would be given assignments to keep us busy during the day. But every so often, she said, we would be called away from our assignments to the central building.

"It is here where you will be tested by the elder teachers and staff. The results of your tests will determine if you qualify for the teacher certification program. If not, it's possible—but not likely —you could still qualify for UniKind DNA extraction. You could even be chosen for both, but that happens to very few."

DNA extraction was painless, Cistine said, but afterward it would be impossible to have children. There was a tight feeling in my chest at the thought of never becoming a mother, and I shifted my body to allow a few deep breaths. Some of the others looked at me, conflicted in the same way. Why hadn't we been told about this possibility ahead of time?

"It doesn't bother me at all," Esme said, noticing the unsettled quiver among the group. "I would be happy to donate."

Cistine smiled at Esme and went on, speaking words to comfort us. "Remember that—if chosen—you'll be contributing to a collective DNA project, which means the composites are in part descended from you. In that way, they are your offspring. If you're curious, take a few minutes after breakfast tomorrow to walk past inside the children's building and the playground. That's where the current generation of composite children are living."

The thought of children living near us stirred the group to smile and relax a little. We fell into a friendly conversation, sharing stories about our lives at home. It was during this conversation that I began to miss Marta, who had been sent back without a last word to us. But the pang of worry was eased with a cup of cold water, which Cistine was pouring at our request. It seemed the more I drank, the more I wanted, but she eventually stood up with the empty pitcher in one hand and declared the orientation over.

"Off to your rooms, cadets," she said, smoothing her long thin hair. "The herald will ring at five in the morning."

I slept deeply that night; the morning bell coming just as the light emerged behind the white curtains. Esme took a shower first, using all the hot water. As a result, the light trickle of my own shower was barely warm. I dried off with the issued bath towel, dressed in the uniform, and walked to breakfast with girls in identical attire. It felt strange to look like everyone else, but the equality was also liberating. I walked with even steps even though the canvas boots pinched my toes into uncomfortable points. The air smelled like salt and algae, but the river was blocked by the mountain view.

Esme was having trouble with the dark-blue scarf we were supposed to wear over our hair. While we were standing in line waiting to enter the dining area through a set of double doors, I helped her knot it tightly so it wouldn't slip loose, creating a pocket that allowed the long waves to fall down her back.

"It's giving me a headache," she said. "And these boots are painful. I almost want to dress in our old clothes instead of these, even the corset."

"Come with me, Esme," Cistine said, coming up to us. "I'll take you to the wardrobe closet and we'll find a better scarf for your thick hair."

Looking around while waiting for her return, I saw that everyone on the campus wore some version of the uniform, and that a hierarchy was apparent. The older women who often accompanied Rielle wore white dresses with narrow blue belts, while the younger women wore light blue dresses with narrow white belts. All the women were teachers of some kind, except for those who served the food. They wore pale gray dresses with black belts, and I noticed that some of them were very beautiful. I didn't see any men from the science lab in the cafeteria with us, but I had seen several in the courtyard on the walk over.

The breakfast trays came out on carts wheeled by the pretty women—called "Grays"—who stood at the foot of each table and passed down the meals: three slices of apple, three triangles of cheese, and a tiny biscuit. The tray also held a small plastic cup that was soon filled with water by the gray-dressed women walking around with pitchers. I was thirsty and drank the water immediately, but the cup wasn't refilled.

The hall was hazy with morning sun and the chatter coming from the tables seemed to encase the vast room. At an adjacent table was a group of five girls dressed in dark-blue, cadets like us. I didn't recognize them but noticed that they weren't wearing the required head wraps. One of the girls had long blond hair, the color of new corn kernels. When they stood up to leave after the meal was over, I was surprised to see they weren't wearing the issued stiff canvas boots, but a variety of different shoes—I saw sneakers, Mary Janes, even a pair of sandals.

"She's the daughter of the mayor of Peorth," Esme whispered.

"Who?"

"The one with long blond hair."

"How do you know that?"

"Cistine told me while we were looking for my new headscarf."

I kept my eyes low as I watched her slender form disappear through the arched doorway, the other unknown girls following behind like ladies in waiting. None of them had been in the ceremony, so I assumed they were a special group.

After breakfast, we went to an auditorium and watched a long dull movie about the origins of the alphabet and numerical system. I tried to pay attention, but my mind wandered and I studied the crowd of girls around me. The blonde girl and her friends weren't in attendance, but I spotted both Sorrel and Hannah in a nearby row. Like me, they were bored by the film— Hannah was examining her fingernails and Sorrel was staring at the floor. Esme held her gaze on the screen, determined to pay attention.

During the mandatory free time after lunch, I went alone to a spot under a large tree and sat cross-legged in a broad patch of grass where the robust breeze coming off the mountains carried the flowery scents of late spring. Leaning back against the tree trunk, I watched the sunlight weave itself into the rocky range and flitter over the tops of the evergreen trees. I imagined myself at the very top of the mountains. If only I could climb up there and stand with my arms spread into the sky, a watercolor of purple, pink, and green-blue.

My daydream was slashed by a scream in the courtyard—a loud, chilling scream followed by deep choking gasps and yet another scream. Although reluctant to end my break, I stood up and went to see what had happened. A cadet was outside our dormitory, obviously terrorized. Huddled into the little alley separating our building from the lab, she had her arms wrapped around herself.

"Just a spider," one of the older teachers said, running toward her. "She must have wandered too near the laboratory door."

Soon a group of teachers and Grays circled the distressed cadet. The girl inhaled and exhaled through a paper bag to slow her panicked breath, and her roommate found a cool cloth for her forehead. By the time we were due back in the classroom for a geology lesson, she was apologizing to everyone who had helped her.

"How stupid of me to drift away from all of you," she said, eyes emotionless and glassy. "From now on, I will better heed the rules."

Lying awake in bed that night, I stroked the locket still around my neck, thinking of home where we had plenty of bugs and spiders. I smiled at the memory of lifting crickets from the kitchen floor with a sheet of Papa's paper and gently releasing them into the grass. It seemed like such a long time ago that I had lived there, the memory already pale and strained, almost too painful to pull forward into my mind. I became aware of the sounds drifting around in the hallway outside—the Grays cleaning the floors and bringing in water from the main hall, lining up paper cups for us to drink from first thing in the morning.

With each morning herald that first week, Esme and I would drink our water, shower, dress, and eat breakfast in the bright cafeteria. Afterward, we sat through lessons and educational movies. Then there was lunch and free time before a few more hours in the classroom or the private hall for testing. The tests were usually painless, but not always. The worst one required the doctor—a hollow-eyed man in a white coat—to cut a piece of skin from the back of my shoulder. The cut burned and stung and was in an unreachable place. Esme and I changed each other's bandages in silence before going to bed that night. In another test, we were ordered to shut our eyes for a long time and answer questions about the intensity of light behind our lids. There wasn't a right or wrong score for any of the tests, but our results were recorded.

We were also interviewed by some of the older teachers. In one interview, I explained that my mother had died of cancer.

"And what about your older sister?" the teacher asked.

"She ran away," I confessed under the dim light of the interview room. A small stone fountain sitting on a table in the corner gurgled with reassurance. "She had a friend who convinced her to leave us. And then she changed."

"In what way?"

I tried to pull a memory of Hollis from my mind, but very little came. "My papa said she lost her mind. One night, she jumped off a bridge."

"Which bridge? There is no bridge in Naudiz." The teacher spoke crisply. "It's a landlocked town. Did your sister travel somewhere far away?"

"She must have," I said, frustrated I couldn't remember more.

Late one afternoon, the cadets were gathered in the gymnasium, where we pulled out foam mats and formed a circle with Rielle and Cistine in the center. The windows were open and a breeze flitted in and out. It was a quiet day, the only sounds coming from the dormitory where the composite children lived. Like the older women and Rielle, they wore white uniforms. On this night, I could hear them laughing and tossing a ball around in the field, a fact that seemed to bother Rielle. She got up and closed the window before returning to her place, where she sat cross-legged.

"Cadets," she said in a controlled voice that echoed against the walls. "You've been here for some time now, and it's time we discuss your futures."

The blonde girl and her friends, the ones who'd arrived ahead of us and who were still violating the uniform rules, were also in the circle. Usually, they kept to themselves and interacted only with each other—Esme and I had come to call them the "aloof ones." They seemed to have grown up together and, in the evenings, they often sat in the lounge with the doors closed and watched shows on the television set. They knew how to turn it on, but they never shared the secret with the rest of us. When watching, they would whisper, giggle, and sometimes erupt into loud laughter. In our circle, however, they sat upright with solemn expressions. I'd been told their names but had forgotten all but one. The mayor's daughter, the tall blonde with a turned-up nose and thick jaw, was called "Ashleen."

"Many of you have told me how much you have enriched your intellect by living here." Rielle looked down at her hands, eyelashes half-moons on her pale freckled cheeks. "In the upcoming days, decisions will be made about which of you will have the opportunity to stay. We wish it could be all of you, but as you know, there is limited space for housing. The chance to be part of our community is an honor assigned only to a few."

Sorrel raised her hand. "If we aren't chosen to stay, will we go home?"

Rielle smiled. "Of course," she said. "Of course you will go home."

Cistine cleared her throat and spoke up. "We brought all of you here tonight for this sharing circle because we want to know how you're feeling."

"Yes," Rielle said. "And if you would like to be one of the ones to leave the CREIA, we'd like to take that wish into consideration."

I fidgeted through the seconds of heavy silence, thinking. I knew that, at one time, I had wanted to go home desperately. But I no longer understood that desire. The anxieties and worries rattling around in my mind had evaporated, as had the need to return to what used to be "home." The girls around me appeared to have a similar stance; no one said a word about wanting to leave.

Hannah raised her hand. Since we'd arrived, the stains on her teeth had been erased and her eyes didn't appear crossed. With her hair tucked away from her face with the uniform scarf, her high strong cheekbones and full lips brought out her enviable beauty.

"I don't want to leave," she said. "But I must share something —about my family."

Rielle gave an encouraging nod.

"What would you like to tell us?" Cistine asked. Beneath the tinted gymnasium light, the composite's eyes were light blue-green.

Hannah spoke tonelessly. "My parents—and my brother too—they're agitators who disagree with the standardization and efficiency clauses."

There were a few gasps throughout the circle; Ashleen looked over, amused. Her friends sat up straight and glanced at one another.

Rielle raised a hand. "Calm down," she ordered, then smiled tightly at Hannah. "Your confession is appreciated." She looked around the circle. "Anyone else? Tell us anything about your home that doesn't seem right to you. We want to know."

Esme caught my eye, encouraging in an accusatory sort of way. Should I speak up about Perrin's cheather experiments? Although outside the rules of *Cherish the Past*, his workshop wasn't necessarily illegal. Still, I remembered Papa's warning about keeping the real purpose of cheather a secret. And since cheather served the good purpose of helping the sick recover, there was no reason to discuss it with Rielle or anyone else.

Robin raised her hand and then spoke without being called on. "I know there's a girl among us who isn't honest." She pointed a finger at Sorrel, who had lost weight since arrival. She was much thinner than the chubby girl who had walked in front of me during the May ceremony. With our attention on her, Sorrel contracted her chest as if to disappear, eyes down.

"She throws her water away," Robin claimed. "In the morning and at every meal. Pours it into her napkin and tosses it out into the trash can."

"Is that true?" Rielle's question was hard, with *true* sharply enunciated.

"I haven't been thirsty," Sorrel said.

It seemed strange, I thought, that Sorrel would throw her water away. I was always so thirsty that I drank mine immediately whenever and wherever it was offered. Maybe she was trying to lose weight and imagined that dehydrating herself would help.

"You're lying," Robin lashed. "You know you're lying."

The aloof girls smiled in amusement.

"Enough with this," Rielle said, standing. "Our circle time is over. Sorrel and Hannah remain with me. You also, Robin. The rest of you go to your rooms for the evening."

On the way out, I walked behind Ashleen and her group of followers. She smelled sweet, like lilacs, and her shiny black leather shoes squeaked as she walked.

A girl named Breea brushed my shoulder, reaching over to tap Ashleen's with a loud "Excuse me?"

Blond hair flipped as Ashleen turned around to face us. Her followers stopped moving forward and the line behind me grew into a flock—one large group of girls facing a much smaller one. It was the first time that any of us had been so close to them.

Breea cleared her throat. "Could you please explain how to turn on the television?" she asked. "There are many hours where it sits silently while you are at your lessons."

"Lessons?" Ashleen glanced sideways at her friends. One of them suppressed a giggle but composed herself quickly.

Breea took a small backward step. "Well, yes. Anyway, the television? Would you describe how it works? I'm awfully curious."

"The television doesn't belong to you," Ashleen said, speaking first to Breea and then to the rest of us. Her eyes landed on me for a moment and I felt a frozen chill in my chest. "It's not yours." Chin high, she seemed to speak to a point beyond us, as though we weren't present.

Breea pressed on. "I didn't think it was mine, or ours. But it's in the lounge and we use everything else in the lounge."

A few girls nodded. "I have a TV at home," someone mentioned.

Ashleen's group whispered with each other, conferring as though they had come across a sick animal lying in the road and were forced to do something about it. Personally, I didn't care much about the television, but I knew it was a concern for others. Some of the girls, like Breea, hadn't found a hobby or intellectual interest as Esme had found Latin and I had found knitting.

I might have walked away at that moment, circled the group and gone through the doors, but I was taken in by Ashleen and her blond hair, smooth and polished like wood. Her lips were sculpted with a color slightly darker than her porcelain skin, her eyes darkened to display the deep blue of her irises. If it weren't for the broad jaw that formed her face into a block shape, she could have been one of the water nymphs in the print that Esme had recently taped to our wall. It had been a gift from her classics teacher.

The group broke their huddle and Ashleen spoke again.

"Please let us pass," she said. "We're running behind schedule and must get through. If you'd like, we'll turn the television on for you tomorrow night after dinner."

Breea's courage wilted in light of the unexpected compromise. Deflated, she slunk away and we reformed the line. With Ashleen and her friends at the head, we passed through the doors and into the square in silence.

CHAPTER 9

*I*n addition to Latin, Esme was learning to read the strange textured formatting some of the library books were printed in.

"It's called Braille," she said as we walked to breakfast one morning. The mountains in the distance were edged with heavy blue clouds and the courtyard was under the cloak of light fog. "Every letter in the alphabet is represented by a set of dots arranged in a specific way. After memorizing the pattern, you read them with your fingertips."

"That sounds so slow," I said.

"It's very slow. But you can get better at it with practice. It's a good way to read because of the time it takes. It's not possible to skim and you must pay attention to every word and sentence. And it's worth the trouble because the Braille books are the most interesting ones. Rielle said they were converted so only the most learned could understand our history—the *real* history of North America before continent extraction."

"Yes, but the same kind of history is printed in Papa's almanacs," I reminded her.

"The history I'm learning is beyond the common things you see in the almanacs. There are treatises and laws in the Braille books that explain how our quadrants were named and the Polity organized, and what led them to standardize all goods except LUSH."

"What are the reasons?"

"I can't say. Learning the books is part of my assignment here, and I took a promise to keep the contents to myself. But I will tell you that I'm certain there was a war, a worst kind of war that destroyed the systems providing water and electricity. Crowds of Citizens, children even, were doused with poisonous chemicals. And there were two sides—one using chemicals to kill, the other creating healing chemicals that countered the deadly kind."

"That's very similar to Papa's ideas," I said. "He has even said that cheather may have been made in a laboratory, designed as an antidote to poisons like the one you describe."

"I shouldn't say much more," Esme said, nodding to a scene across the courtyard, "but look over there."

Through the fog, I saw a bus parked near the edge of the courtyard. Around it was a cluster of girls waiting to board—the aloof girls. Ashleen was handing her suitcase to a driver, who stored it in a storage compartment built into the vehicle's side panel.

"They aren't wearing their uniforms," Esme observed.

"They never really wore them."

I slowed my steps to watch each girl deliver her luggage to the driver. He looked familiar to me—tall and lean with dark hair cut unevenly above his eyebrows. He might have sensed my stare and shot me a look across the ten or so yards of space separating us. With a better view of his face, I recognized him as the man who had played illegal music during one of my trips back home from town.

What was his name? I couldn't remember.

"Come on," Esme urged. "Don't dawdle. I want to get our usual seats."

We didn't need to worry about our seats being taken—the cafeteria wasn't as crowded as it normally was. The table often occupied by Ashleen and her friends was empty, so we took it for ourselves. Leslie came over and we ate and drank without commenting on the now-missing cadets. Yet I noticed that Sorrel and Hannah were not in the cafeteria either.

Over lunch, we discussed the classes we were taking. Esme was learning to read the Braille texts. These classes were taught by Rielle and some of the other highly esteemed teachers, and they met for long periods in a small room in the library, continuing long into the night.

"The stained-glass windows are so beautiful," Esme said. "When the sun is shining, the colored rays fall over our books."

I asked Leslie about her schedule and learned she was caring for the composite children in the mind development center, teaching their lessons, preparing their meals, and monitoring them during recess.

"We spent all day yesterday building a castle from wooden blocks," she said. "It's as tall as I am. And they have a bubble-making machine that's very messy, but fun to play with."

I'd seen the children up close the day before for the first time. They looked like normal children, but smaller with a more diverse set of skin tones and hair colors and textures than was natural. A few had extraordinary vision, Leslie said, and could see for miles.

"I only wish they weren't so difficult to look after," she said, swallowing down her cup of water and nibbling an apple slice. "We can't get too harsh, even when they hit and bite us." She showed us a dark-red crescent-shaped indentation on the inside of her forearm.

"That's very deep," I said. Leslie didn't mention caring for any infants, so I assumed the newborns lived somewhere else and were brought in when they were old enough to be without their mothers.

But who *were* their mothers?

"Yes, deep and painful. I was given some antibiotics for it." She changed the subject. "What are you doing for your assignment, Isla?"

My assignment, I told her, was in the weaving studio where I was learning to operate looms as large as tractors. They were constructed on many pieces of wood and bolted together with steel brackets. I liked working in the airy loft with the other weaving students and the quiet, pleasant teachers. Sometimes they would bring in a small pot of herbal tea and we'd sit together for a break with our headscarves off and enjoy the breeze passing through the barred windows. They taught us how to knit a variety of stitches, smiling at me kindly when I passed by the others in the skill, wood needles flying.

"And the looms have hundreds of tiny wire loops," I continued. "It takes hours to get even a few inches."

There were smaller looms, too; they were used to make rugs like the one in our dormitory room. Some of the teachers also made rag rugs from worn clothing, but I hadn't tried that yet.

"It sounds so fun and creative," Leslie said. "I wish I were in there with you." She scratched the bite on her arm and shook her empty cup as though wishing for more. "The composite children are sometimes so sour and ill-mannered."

Esme leaned away from us to look over to the head table where Rielle and the other teachers sat together in a closed group, speaking to each other in hushed tones.

"Weaving is enjoyable work," I went on. "But I wish the yarns and threads had more color. Everything is white, gray, or beige." I hadn't asked why we didn't color the fibers with dye, but I assumed there was a good reason. Still, I couldn't help but envision the beautiful rugs and cloth we could make with better dye baths.

We didn't have any tests to take or movies to watch that day, so after breakfast, I walked alone to the studio. I took my time, strolling through the crowded courtyard and appreciating that I'd finally broken in the canvas boots enough that they didn't pinch my toes anymore. The bus had departed and the exit gates were closed. Ashleen and her circle of friends were gone, probably miles and miles away, but later, after my weaving hours were over,

I found they'd left a surprise in the TV room. Not only was the television turned on for us as they'd promised, on a table was a pile of paper cases holding eyeshadows and blushes—free samples. Each case was printed with the name "Ashleen" in gold script letters.

I picked up a case of eyeshadow—pearl pink and soft gray— and turned it over to view the LUSH stamp on the back. The memory of my own case and the night I'd seen the brutalized version of myself in the mirror emerged with a forceful flip. I was suddenly warm and sweaty, blood speeding through my veins. Why had it never occurred to me—or to any of us—I wondered, that the *Ashleen* on the case and the one among us were the same?

But the question, so piercing at first, soon quelled into a flitting thought and drifted far from my mind.

Back in the room that evening, while Esme was at a lesson, I rested against the wall with a thin bed pillow behind my back to finish a sweater I'd been knitting. The cotton yarn, provided by the weaving studio, had been spun by hand on a wooden spinning wheel. In this raw state, it was the shade of cooked oats. As I knitted, I envisioned the beautiful color the sweater could be if soaked in a dye pot for an hour or two. A warm pink, a sugary brown, maybe even a deep crimson. I could use the left-behind make-up for dye, melting the pigments into a colored bath. But I'd need at least two gallons of hot water and a cup of salt, and that was difficult to find.

After shaping the neckline and decreasing to the final stitch, I released the sweater from the needles, folded it on top of the bed, and stood to gaze out the window. The sun was sinking into the mountaintops and the courtyard below was nearly empty. Only a few girls sat on the library steps with sketchbooks. My abdomen was aching and cramping because my menstrual cycle had begun an hour earlier. At home, I might have laid down with a towel wrapped around a hot iron, but there were no such irons at the CREIA.

I pulled the cheather tincture from the box, swallowed down a few drops, then circled the room to draw the relaxing medicine into my bloodstream. The eyeshadow case from Ashleen was on the dresser, and I turned it in my hands while pacing. The herb soon rerouted my thoughts to the question I'd encountered in the television lounge: why had none of us understood that Ashleen and *Ashleen* were the same person?

Some ingredient, an odorless and tasteless infusion, had numbed our emotions and passions, dispelling any resistance to the rules and procedures of the CREIA.

Could it be the water?

I thought of Sorrel, the girl with the hearing aids. I'd not seen or heard anything about her since the day Robin made the accusation in the sharing circle. Where was Sorrel now? And was beautiful Hannah with her? I hadn't seen her since that day either. The day before, I'd found a basket in the weaving room filled with colored and patterned fabric ripped into long strips. I'd stopped and looked closely because it was unusual to see colored textiles lying about. My eye was drawn to a rich deep blue, a crinkly taffeta begging for my touch. I pulled it from the heap, enjoying the way it slid luxuriously against the other fibers. When it was about halfway out, I stopped with panic.

The taffeta strip, although ripped and ragged on one edge, had at one time been sewn with cotton thread. The irregular, awkward stitches had come from Hannah's hand.

"Cadet, what are you peering at?" One of the teachers had come up to snatch the strip away. "You aren't to snoop around in this area. Go back to your loom." She gathered the basket into her arms and left me standing alone.

As the cheather fueled my cells, I worried the effect would expire before I could apply sensors to all the fearful questions around us. I buried the tincture in my brassiere and searched the cardboard box for the cheather seeds, which I wrapped in paper

and placed against my skin, holding the small package in place
with my belt.

What was it that Perrin had said?

Diversify. Spread the seeds to make them stronger.

And I remembered the name of the bus driver, too.

Staris.

Without another thought, I rushed from our room into the
singing evening. The best time to plant seeds was at dusk, Papa
always said. Moving under the drape of the blossoming trees, I
took a jagged path toward the squirrel park where the delicate
moonlight lay on cleared spots of earth. Opening the pods one by
one, I buried the tiny flecks into the ground, covering them with
a thin layer of soil. There were hundreds more seeds than available land; walking back to the room, I blew the feathery bits into
the air with the wish that each would settle in a fortuitous place.

A group of cadets burst out of the library, Esme among them,
and I pushed forward to return more quickly to the room. But
when walking the alley between our building and the science lab, I
was distracted by the glassy shimmer of a water tank sitting
outside one of the laboratory doors. In the dim light, the DO
NOT TRESPASS sign wasn't as bright and noticeable as it was in
the day. As usual, a yellow hose running through a port in the
window was submerged in the tank, and I was curious if it was
sucking water in or pushing it out, so I moved closer to take a
cautious peek. The calming influence of the cheather, still
coursing in my blood, might have set me at ease when I should
have instead been timid, or not looked into the wavering gray
at all.

In a blinding flash and sizzle of chemical smoke, two round
black eyes sprung from the tank and met my own with a frenetic
grip. Convulsing in fear, I resisted the powerful urge to latch into
the black beads and muffled the scream rising from my throat.
The insect—as large as my clasped hands—glowed and moved in
the water with such smooth motions I couldn't help but keep my
eyes on its many segments, even as I backed off. The spider began

to whirl, so fast it was a blur, and rose in a fan of water and sinewy tendons, aiming to fly at my head. A will stronger than any I'd ever possessed pushed me to the ground, where I cowered with my hands on my head, whimpering softly, waiting for the blow.

But nothing happened.

Just a hologram, Ms. Hardin had said. *Remember.*

I listened to the activity in the buildings around me as the teachers and cadets prepared for the bedtime herald. I needed urgently to get back inside before the doors locked, so I built the courage to stand up on my shaky legs and run from the alley, keeping my steps soft on the stone drive. Once I was out of the light of the laboratories, darkness swallowed my vision and my steps were blind and lopsided. I only hoped I wasn't running directly into danger.

"Stop right there."

I collided with a white form, a small woman who took a tight grip on my forearm. She dragged me under a brick arch leading into the teachers' quarters. In the queasy light of a post, I saw it was Rielle herself.

"Stand back against the wall," she commanded, holding my eyes with such authority I once again began to tremble. "Do not move."

The headmistress surveyed me up and down, scrutinizing every inch of my attire, my face and hair. I stood with my body straight and tense, willing my heart to slow so she couldn't sense my fear.

"You are guilty of three uniform violations, cadet. And you are roaming outside of hours. What have you been doing? And what is your name?" She stepped closer, hovering within inches, the lines of her thin face drawn by shadows.

Somehow I found a voice to answer: "I'm Isla Kiehl, and I apologize for my violations. I was excused from the nightly events because of menstrual pain, and I was simply out taking a walk. Time got away from me, and it became dark. I was rushing in just now—" Pausing for breath, I gauged by the stewing in her eyes that my claims were not acceptable. Still, I wasn't certain she was angry; instead, she was perhaps intrigued by my rebellion.

"I believe I know you," she said. "You're one of Patricia Hardin's girls. Isla, yes. You came in with Esme."

"Yes, Esme is my roommate here and we grew up together in a tour called *Cherish the Past*. Ms. Hardin was our teacher in Naudiz." I found it worrisome that she so easily knew Esme's name. Could it be an advantage to know her, and to associate with Ms. Hardin? Or would that be a certain strike?

"*Cherish the Past*—it's a Polity farm project from long ago. I heard—" Rielle stopped before finishing the sentence.

"Please let me return to my room, Ms. Rielle," I begged. "Esme will be wondering where I am."

At this, a knowing smile cracked Rielle's veneer. "As it happens, Esme is moving from your room into our main house tonight. She has been selected for the UniKind program."

The raw courage that had been holding me in place dissolved. I fell back into the wall to support my weakening knees. "Already? She was ... selected? Does that mean the rest of us will go home?"

"Questions, questions. Now is not the time." Rielle stood back and assessed me again as though turning through options. "You are an appealing girl, Isla, and despite your poor attitude toward the rules, I want you also to stay with us at the CREIA. It so happens there's an opening among the Grays and you can begin your training tomorrow. Return to your room now for one last night. In the morning, report to the cafeteria and Cistine will outfit you appropriately and take you to the bunker."

My heart fell, but I nodded and obeyed, holding my eyes down as she guided me onto the walk. Back in the room, I found that Esme's bed was cleared off and her things were missing from the closet. She'd left a note on the dresser.

Dear Isla,
I will explain later. Very happily yours,
Esme

Of course she was happy—she cared nothing about seeing boys again or walking through the woods or eating food from the farm. She had no animals to care for as I had Aura and the horses. She had no love to think of, no wish to become a mother.

The note floated to the floor.

I sat on the bed, using a cadet headscarf to soak up my angry tears. Papa would be so saddened at my fate—a life in a wet cafeteria serving food and cleaning tables when my ancestral destiny was so much more. It was Esme who'd accidentally set the trap on that day she'd lured me back to her house—her and that scheming Ms. Hardin. I stood up and stomped the note with my foot, twisting the paper into the wiry rug. She'd used my paper pad, one of the fifty sheets made from leftover cheather pulp. Remembering the way Papa pressed the paper into bundles to bind one end with careful stitches, I picked up the speckled page and slid it into my satchel. Esme's words could be erased, the paper used again.

The bedtime herald rang and the lights in the hallway clicked off. I'd never slept alone in the room before and laid down with an anxious and heavy heart, tuning into the sweet sound of the crickets bleating on the other side of the window. The moonlight lay on Esme's empty bed, the spread pulled neatly over the thin pillow and pulled to the headboard; despite my anger, I longed for her company. The memory of the holographic spider lingered and intensified when my eyes closed, its beady eyes and synthetic sizzle so close it was as though the sound had infused into my ears, brain, my very soul.

Sleep was impossible.

Rising, I fumbled in the darkness through my satchel, now packed with all I owned. The bottle of cheather tincture was still half-full. With a few drops ingested, I was enough at peace to lie again under the covers and allow sleep to swallow me into an easy dream of walking a rocky path, Aura at my side, for miles and miles. Although my body ached with every step, there was a true sense that freedom lay at the end, that I was traveling inward and outward and not just for myself, but with the burden of all honest people on my shoulders. The dream carried on for what seemed like an eternity, but must have been only the six hours between my retirement and the morning herald.

I woke with a strong sense of resolve, and with a reason to hope.

Out the window, I saw when sitting up, the sky was pregnant with blues, and the rain was already coming down.

Rain.

I knew that, outdoors in the squirrel park and in every spot where a feathery seed had landed, the rain was opening the soil, sinking the cheather beneath a nurturing cloak.

The rain was my gift, I understood, a message that I should not give up. Somewhere, there were forces stronger than Rielle and Ms. Hardin, more powerful than the terror instilled by holograms. The power of nature was stronger than anything else, and it was through nature that I would find my way home.

CHAPTER 10

*T*hat morning, I reported to Cistine. She was in the kitchen working at a small desk.

"Rielle has told me of your appointment to the Grays," she said. "Congratulations on your new position. Many girls would envy the chance you've been given to stay here at the CREIA."

"I was surprised to receive the assignment so quickly," I replied. "And to learn that Esme was selected for UniKind without a ceremony or official announcement as we had before. And I find it regretful that she won't be a teacher as she wished."

"Oh, Esme will have the opportunity to learn and teach because the two programs are concurrent. And sometimes Rielle makes her choices without fanfare." Cistine stood up and handed me a gray headscarf, a notecard, and a small pencil. "Today you and Alise, she's another trainee, can simply watch the Grays do their work. Follow them around as they serve the students and patrons, but don't be a bother. There's a wooden bench in the dish room if you would like to stop and take notes. You can put your satchel there, too. After breakfast, I'll take you both to the nurse for a physical exam. After lunch, you can go to your new room in the staff bunker for a brief break before returning to learn the dinner routine. The number and code for your room are written on the back on your card, so keep it with you."

She led me to the hot dish room, which smelled of soap and soggy food, where Alise was sitting on the edge of the bench. She was a small girl with pink cheeks, slightly younger than me, with silky blond-brown hair and blue eyes that sank into the folds of her lids when she smiled. The imperfection was sweet instead of homely, and with her high cheekbones and pointed chin, she looked like a dairymaid or a cameo portrait. Sitting beside her, I felt a sisterly responsibility as she seemed so innocent and unassuming.

"Isla," she whispered as Cistine turned her back to slide a mat under the sinks. "Why are you here?"

"I was selected for this role as you were."

"Are the rest of the cadets going home?"

Cistine overheard and answered the question for us. "Since only a few girls can stay, the other cadets will be leaving soon," she said, tying her thin hair back with a circle of twine. "You'll have a chance to see them during meals today, so say your goodbyes. Now both of you follow me—I'll show you the food preparation stations. Stand behind the Grays as they work, but watch carefully and record the process. We have many large meals coming up due to some guests arriving soon, so your contributions to the group will be necessary. There is no time to dawdle or daydream. Come along."

I thought of Leslie, so lucky to be among the rejected cadets who would soon be off and returned to their homes and families. I steered my focus to the task of watching the Grays prepare food and also keeping an eye on Alise.

"Where is the water?" she asked me during a moment when all the others were occupied. "I'm so thirsty, aren't you?"

One of the Grays pointed to a small pitcher on a metal table and Alise went to pour two small cups, drinking her own on the way to deliver the other to me. I pretended to take a sip but secretly dumped the cup's contents into a can.

After the meals and visit to the nurse, I went to my new bedroom. Upon entering, I was surprised to find Sorrel sitting on the bed waiting for me. It was early evening, just before dinner, and she wasn't dressed in the gray uniform that I would soon wear, but in a white dress covered by a white apron—a uniform I'd never seen on anyone. Her chestnut hair was shaped into a straight cut ending at her chin; a handkerchief held it away from her intelligent brown eyes. But the most notable difference was a scabbed gash on her left cheek. I was certain it hadn't been there when she'd arrived.

"I work in the laundry," she explained after we broke from a friendly embrace. "Washing, drying, ironing. I've lost more weight from folding endless uniforms and walking up and down the stairs. Some things are better here in this hall—we have fresh fruit in the meeting room, cheese sometimes. But put your bag away quickly. I'm surprised they let you bring it. What do you have inside?"

"Just my old clothes from home." A pang of sadness washed over me at the thought of home, but I remembered my resolve. "And a notebook and a few other things." I didn't mention the old card tucked inside my pad of paper or the cheather tincture. I also had the 100,000 LUSH token and some dried food I'd collected through the weeks.

Sorrel gestured to a set of sliding doors. "There's plenty of room in the closet for you. I have very few garments of my own."

The tiny closet was nearly empty and my bag fit into a space in the upper right corner. There were five empty clothes hangers for the uniform pieces I'd received from Cistine earlier in the day: two gray serving dresses, a long-sleeved white nightgown, and, strangely, a pink satin camisole with delicate lace trim, and a short pink satin robe. I'd also received a package of underwear, two belts, socks, and boots. During my physical examination, the nurse had given me an injection into my left thigh.

The injection worried me. I remembered that Sorrel had been accused of not drinking the water, so I felt secure asking if she knew what kind of substance might have been in the needle.

"Perhaps a hormone?" she guessed. "They didn't do that to me when I came in."

We sat on her bed, facing each other, and she told me what had happened that day in the sharing circle after Rielle had confronted her about disposing the water into the trash.

"I denied doing it, of course. And there was no proof." She touched the scab on her cheek. "But I didn't go without punishment. As you see, I was brutally cut with a sharp knife by one of the guards. After, it was decided that I would be removed from the cadet program to work in the basement laundry center and I've been there ever since. Honestly, it's not so bad. Lonely at times, but I like the clean smell of soap and I admit that ironing helps pass the time. I've gotten very good at it. The interesting thing is that they don't really care if I drink the water or not. All of them are so drugged themselves they hardly think about anything other than their own supply. The more, the better. Since you'll be in the cafeteria, you can have as much as you want."

"I choose not to drink it," I told her. "And I'm going to find a way out of here."

Sorrel said she didn't know what had happened to the beautiful green-eyed Hannah but had a suspicion. "The fourth floor of our building is completely off limits. If you look at it from outside, you'll see there are windows there, on the back side that faces the woods, and an elevator shaft. I think there's a group of girls and women living in those upper rooms. They never come out at day, but perhaps they do at night."

"And what happened to your hearing aids?" I asked.

Sorrel patted one of her ears. "Gone," she replied. "They took them away and promised to return them if I follow the rules and have a good attitude. I only read lips now."

"Who was your roommate before I got here?" I asked, making sure my lips pronounced every syllable.

"Her name was Julia, and she left yesterday—I don't know to where. She had been here quite a long time and was much older than us. I'm so glad you are here, but I'll miss her a little bit because she was very quiet and at peace. She didn't want anything and didn't mind that there are no boys here to flirt with, or that we'll never have children."

A herald chimed in the hall and we walked together to the staff kitchen to eat a dinner of bread with a tasteless bologna spread. I was shown a chore chart and learned that every Thursday night I was responsible for putting dinner together.

My soul began to ache and I found myself understanding Alise's wish to ingest the medicated water. I didn't want to think about where I was and the impossibility of getting out, and a drug to quell the despair would be welcome. But I remembered my revelation from the previous night—somehow, nature would prevail over us and lead me away. I closed my eyes and tried to remember as much as I could about home. Papa's face appeared, eyes sad and very worried.

Dear Papa,

I began composing a message, mentally writing the words by hand in the limited space of a blank card like the one in my bag, foregoing the date as I didn't know any longer what the date was.

Greetings from the CREIA. It is not the place I expected, not at all. But there is much to learn. Esme will be reading many books and learning astronomy. I doubt that either of us will be home again, but I will try. Please forgive me, Papa.

Love, your daughter Isla.

Sorrel and I parted ways in the morning's early hours, she in her white laundry uniform, and me in my gray dress. We first had a hasty breakfast in the kitchen where we ate hard biscuits, leftovers from the cafeteria. Someone stirred a chicory-like drink in a pitcher and poured each of us a cup. The hearty, sour taste was unpleasant, but my hunger was relieved and I felt energetic walking in the darkness to the cafeteria for my first day of work. Cistine guided me into the back kitchen, where I spent a long while slicing soft brown bread onto plates. The plates were transferred to another Gray for boiled egg slices, then to a third Gray for an apple wedge. The plates were lined up on a long aluminium assembly line. On another line were the glasses and silverware we used to set the round tables where everyone ate. The process of preparing the food and dining room took several hours.

Cistine informed Alise and me that the tasks would become even more difficult once the breakfast herald was activated and the teachers began to arrive. We took our positions at the front of the dining hall with our carts loaded, ready to serve.

"Make sure you're all in order and look nice." The composite skimmed her glittering eyes over our uniforms, adjusting belts, ordering one Gray to go wipe her boots in the kitchen. "We have visitors today," she said.

Some of the more experienced Grays nodded and murmured to themselves, glancing at each other knowingly, standing up straight in anticipation and smoothing the hair under their scarves. Alise peered over at me, eyes squinted even more than usual.

"It will be fine," I quietly assured her, even though I needed assurance myself. We were both worried about breaking the glassware or dropping bread onto laps. My heart picked up its pace when the first group arrived, their chairs scraping the floor as they sat down. Esme and Robin sat together near the front. They were both in teacher uniforms and seemed slightly put-off as though an uncertainty had presented itself to them.

I was surprised to see that all of the cadets who'd been chosen at the ceremony were still present. Leslie Snyr and the others filed in and sat together at the back tables, leaving the center section open for the guests, who turned out to be a large group of men and a few women dressed in outsider clothing. I tried not to look at their attire, interesting to me since it had been so long since I'd seen anything but the CREIA uniforms, and concentrated on serving the tables with skill. Even though I despised my role as a servant, I'd decided to do it well in case there was a possibility to move up to a higher position. I'd learned about possible landscaping jobs, tending to the plants and flowers growing in the beds around the buildings. Although the weather could be rough, I thought, the smell of earth and water was preferable to the soggy odors of the CREIA food. The cheather seeds I'd planted had begun to sprout and I'd be able to watch over them.

I wheeled the serving cart through the section Cistine had assigned to me. It was near the center, where the guests were sitting. Delivering plates and pouring beverages wasn't difficult provided the patron allowed room for my arm to reach into the table area. But some of them seemed not to notice my existence, spreading their limbs into every available inch of space and forcing me to catch their gaze and say "Good morning," or "Excuse me, sir."

One such patron was Rielle. Although she usually sat at the head of the room under the screens, she was instead sitting at a table filled with guests, all of them men in cotton shirts and crisp black pants who spoke to one another in low tones. Her thin freckled arms rested over the nook of space where I might have slipped her breakfast plate.

"Please excuse me," I said, trying to catch her attention.

"Good morning, Isla." Rielle didn't seem to mind the interruption. She then considered me in a prominent fashion, introducing me to the table as one of the recently inducted staff. "Please meet Mr. Carr, Mr. Ashan, Mr. Allesso, and Mr. —" She hesitated on the surname of a man with deeply tanned skin and hair clipped so short it was impossible to tell its color. He was thick-boned and muscular in the shoulders, so much that his shirt pulled at the seams.

"Drexin," he said. His mouth was very wide, with thick

rubbery lips the same shade as his skin. I was alarmed by his eyes, flower-blue, and the way they tried to secure a hard lock into my own. "Mr. Drexin."

"Good morning," I said, not sure if I should smile, nod, curtsey, or do nothing. In silence, I served the plates, accidentally brushing against Mr. Drexin's bulky shoulder, relieved to complete the task and move onto another table also filled with male guests who inquired about my name. The same transpired at another table. When I was done with my section and back in the kitchen, I speculated to Alise about who the men were and why they were among us.

"They're members of the new Polity." Alise had heard this bit of information from one of the older Grays.

I remembered Gareth's remarks about the Lower Polity who were following Seranack. Were these men and the few women among them part of that group? Well-guarded by the metal shutters separating the cafeteria kitchen from the dining area, I watched as the guests finished their meals. Gradually, they deposited their dirty dishes on a moving belt that fed them into the water trough and sanitizing machine. Each piece would emerge with a whistle, hot and steaming, for us Grays to stack in the wide shelves until we'd pull them out again for lunch. The men who'd been sitting with Rielle clustered with guests from other tables. Eventually, the large group left together and headed toward the labs. Esme and Robin went out together, their strides shortened by the slower teachers in front of them.

"Grays, take a short break," someone called.

Mine was spent outside on a brick bench near some cheather I'd planted behind a stack of loose bricks. I watched a few nervous birds congregate into a flock, angry chirps and beating wings, and wondered what Papa would record about this day in his almanac. Would he meter the shifts of the clouds over the sun? Or would he be more interested in the density of the bark on the birch trees? And was Perrin caring for Aura as I would? My thoughts circled with the flock now flying into the treetops. I stretched my legs and tried to forget for a few seconds how my trusting spirit had carried me into such misery.

CHAPTER 11

Two days into my work as a Gray, I learned that life was measured in meals. There was breakfast, most challenging because of the early hour and complicated assortment of condiments; lunch, the easiest because hot food wasn't served; and dinner, the longest and messiest, but the beginning of the evening and allowed for an hour of free time. But on my third day, this free hour was possessed by Cistine. She found me sitting in the meeting room, where I was trying to moisturize my chapped hands with a spoon of shortening taken from the kitchen, and demanded that I follow her to the end of the staff bunker hallway and into the elevator that Sorrel had mentioned.

"Mr. Drexin has requested your photograph," she explained once the doors were closed.

I easily recalled Mr. Drexin as the tanned muscular man who'd been sitting at Rielle's table on my first day. That group of guests had not reappeared since morning and I'd assumed they had gone somewhere else to attend to their official affairs. Strangely, the cadets—Leslie included—were still among us and seemed to have no responsibilities other than enjoying books, television, long naps in the dormitory or—when the sun was out—on blanketed grass in the squirrel park. Every so often, we'd hear a scream of terror as one of them explored out-of-bounds and encountered a spider.

"What is the purpose of this photo?" I asked.

"A Gray such as yourself might view his request as an opportunity." Cistine clicked a button on the elevator panel with a miniature index finger and we moved up a floor. "Especially so early on. But I advise against stirring up your hopes too much as several girls are being photographed today."

The door opened into a bright carpeted hallway where we walked beneath a clear ceiling curved over flexible white pipes, turning into a corner foyer that led to a set of double doors. I followed Cistine through the doors and past a bench of waiting girls and noticed that Breea, the cadet who'd once challenged Ashleen, was among them. We stepped into a closet made from bedsheets hanging from a plastic frame.

"You can remove your uniform, hang it, and put on this robe."

The robe she handed me was made of a soft, loopy fabric. The garment was light and liberating, but in my anxiety about what was to come, I could hardly enjoy the feeling. I walked in bare feet to sit in a rotating chair placed before a large mirror. A composite similar in height and appearance to Cistine, but slightly younger—a teenager perhaps—began combing my hair. To my left was a white sheet suspended from the ceiling, held in place with metal wires. A girl I recognized as one of the cadets from the larger group was posing in front of the sheet, her chestnut hair brushed and curled, lips and eyes colored in rose-pink hues, her robe tied at the waist but loose around her shoulders. A free-standing camera without an operator flickered a red light each time she was to assume a different stance.

The composite with the comb turned my chair away from the sight and attacked the tangles in my hair, spraying it with a sweet-smelling fluid. She seemed friendly, introducing herself as Gem.

"What kind of coloring would you prefer?" she asked, bending down so her pointed face was uncomfortably close to mine. "You have lovely eyes—how about amber shadow?"

"What are the photographs used for?" I asked again.

Gem was more forthcoming than Cistine had been. She dabbed my cheeks and forehead with cold, flesh-colored paint. "When a gentleman requests a girl's photograph, it means he is considering an appointment with her. If the photograph appeals to him, you may have the chance to see him privately in a chamber and become close friends. If the visits go well, you could even receive a marriage proposal." She cleared her throat, pulled a slender brush from a collection on her stand, and stroked the bristles into a pan of glittering light-brown shadow. "Now shut your eyes."

The brush was irritating on my eyelid. I dwelled on the word "appointment," and the nervous feeling I'd arrived with transformed into an urgent agitation.

"Hold still," Gem said sharply. "I must paint your lips and the material I'm using will cause them to tingle and prick slightly. It will not hurt, just feel unusual. And your mouth will look very pretty."

The lipstick was thick and stinging.

"Do not rub your lips together or touch your face," she ordered, running her hands over my hair and twisting it lightly at the ends. "Now sit on the bench and wait for your turn."

I joined the other waiting girls and thought of how to make my photos unappealing to Mr. Drexin, who I did not want to see in a private chamber, much less marry. But, before my turn, Cistine gave me a cup of water to drink and my mind was dull and passive throughout the short period I was on the stool.

After I redressed into my uniform and returned to my room, I told Sorrel everything, facing her directly so she could read my lips and understand. The drugged water began to wear away, and because I didn't want to weep or cry, I found a hard place inside myself that temporarily remedied my fear. I assured myself that, somehow, I would not meet Mr. Drexin in intimacy.

Even if refusal meant putting my life at risk.

We fell into silence.

"What could make you laugh right now, Isla?" she finally asked. "Or take your mind away from worry?"

"Things from home," I replied, after a moment's thought. Reaching into my knapsack still hidden in the closet, I pulled out the ancient card I'd found in the old lot and showed it to her. The calming photo of the sunshine over blue waves made me feel better. "I wonder what happened to this place, and why I found it in a box hanging on a house."

"It's a postcard," Sorrel said. "I've heard about this system." She went on to explain that people of the postcard ages had carried on the frivolity for unknown reasons. "Frequent notes to each other were a common practice," she said, "and Citizens of every age and social standing went around with electric boxes in their hands, typing to each other in short sentences. When I was at a school for the deaf once when I was very young, we used a similar kind of toy to write passing thoughts and bits of news."

"If only I could write to Papa and Perrin right now," I said as Sorrel examined the old postcard.

"This message on the back is so faded it can't be read," she observed. "Did you look in the house, too?"

"Yes, there are many relics all through Naudiz and on our farm because Mother Cordish values history and wishes to preserve so many details." I leaned against the wall and stretched out my tired legs. "But only the details that appeal to her. Much of the past is sordid and very profane—my Papa's almanacs show it as so. I was on a bus not long ago and the driver—the same man we have here —played illegal songs saved inside thin plastic cases. The songs were strange and unsettling, but I'd be interested in hearing them again. The voices had a haunting, longing cry inside, and the tones were exciting and complicated." Then I remembered that Sorrel couldn't hear songs without her hearing aids and stopped speaking about them. "Will they ever return your hearing aids?" I asked her.

"Probably not. But I think they're in one of the classrooms, tucked inside a teacher's desk. I wasn't born deaf, you know. A serious fever when I was an infant destroyed the nerves that allow hearing. There was no approval to fix it. My parents could have abandoned me to the Unsaved, but they found a kind doctor."

"My mother was also not approved for help," I told Sorrel. "She had cancer in her breasts. After she died, my brother learned of a plant called cheather that treats illness and heals sicknesses and he cultivated a strong strain. Don't tell anyone, but I've planted it around the buildings and in the squirrel park."

"You did? How brave of you." Sorrel was in awe. "I'll look for it on my walks to the laundry rooms."

"Yes, it's beginning to grow tall. Look for a fibrous plant with sharply pointed leaves. When it's mature, there will be a large purple flower in the center. It's a very pretty blossom, but will release pollen into the air if rustled even slightly, so be wary of it."

"Won't the landscapers pull the cheather out?"

"Maybe, but I was careful to hide it in weedy areas that aren't well-tended. My brother hopes that the plants will go to seed and blow across a wide area. Spreading the breed across miles of land is important to its continuance."

The herald rang through the hall and our lights went out. Talking was impossible as Sorrel couldn't see my words, so we went to bed in silence. I fidgeted under the covers, worried the rubbery-lipped Mr. Drexin would soon be calling me into an upstairs chamber, that Sorrel and I would be separated, that I would never find a way out of the CREIA. And there was always the lingering concern that a wrong turn or glance into a closet or the back of a shelf would conjure one of those horrible holographic spiders. The very memory of my encounter with the seething black and green creature stirred nausea, so I composed a postcard to reclaim my senses.

Dear Gareth, it began. There would be no date as I didn't know it, only that autumn was coming. Outdoors, the trees and bushes were changing colors and the wind picked up force in the evening hours, leading the birds to warmer nests.

You were right. I shouldn't have trusted Ms. Hardin.

Could a postcard be as short as that? There was much more to say, but the words and phrases expressing my despair could not be composed.

～

Esme had changed. During meals, she always sat in the far back at a round table with other young teachers. I thought it was unlike her character that she didn't try to sit within view of Rielle; Esme was always looking for approval from authority and trying to show off her intelligence. But she was disinterested in the lively chatter around her and focused exclusively on her plate, leaving as soon as she was done and walking out alone.

After the fourth breakfast, I caught her at the laundry receptacle.

She was trying to toss in a napkin, but a hanging thread had caught on her uniform placket, stalling her exit as she tried to detach without losing a button. I caught a glimpse of the inside of her wrist where a cryptic mark had been emblazoned, a white slash that symbolized her contribution to UniKind.

"Allow me to help," I said, approaching her. I flicked the thread from her button and slipped the napkin into the chute. From conversations with Sorrel, I knew the chute led to a bin a floor below that would be collected by the laundresses. They would wheel the clumsy, overflowing contraption into the basement of the staff bunker, where the food-stained fabrics would be washed, dried, folded, and sent back into the cafeteria for another round. "You remember me, right? I'm Isla, your old roommate." I looked down at her mark. "Did it hurt? Is that why you're so odd?"

"Go away," she demanded, turning to the empty hall. "There's no requirement we speak to one another."

I snatched the back of her belt, taking a tight hold. She

slapped away my hand and spun around, her dark eyes full of contempt.

"Don't dare touch me again," she snapped.

"Have you lost your compassion?" I accused. "You urged me to come here and brushed off the risk. So now, because of you, I'm working as a servant and a strange man wants to view my photographs."

Esme searched for a careful answer. "It could be worse," she replied, haughty. "Indulge him and enjoy what you could gain. There's nothing for me in those terms."

"What do you mean? Aren't you in astronomy classes now? Aren't you reading Braille books? It seems your sacrifice ought to have—"

"Be quiet. No, I'm assigned to the childcare center." She looked down at the floor. "Maybe in a few years I'll be involved in more interesting work," she said. "But for now, I'm stationed as a nanny."

"Why did they give you such a lowly job? That's for the cadets to do." I remembered the bite mark on Leslie Snyr's arm.

"How you talk—a waitress such as you. Shouldn't you be in the kitchen right now?"

"They won't miss me for a few minutes. The Grays look out for each other. And it's your fault I'm a waitress. I shouldn't have listened to you and all your ideas about how much fun this would be. Or your insistence that I go to your house the day Ms. Hardin tricked me."

"Well, you did, and that's your fault. Now I have to go or I'll be late. The cadets are leaving tonight and I have to learn more child-training routines from them in order to do my job well. I'm hoping to move up to a landscaping position. I'd much rather be outside all day than wiping noses and playing games with a ball."

"You mean the cadets finally get to go home?" The rage in my chest crept up my neck and into my cheeks. "I so want to go home, Esme. Don't you? We have to find a way out of here."

"I doubt there is one," she replied. "And your face has become pink, a very unbecoming pink."

And then my former friend defensively smoothed a wrinkle in her skirt and walked off. I watched her straight, thin frame until it passed through the bright-red double doors of the childcare center. Although I was enraged at her disdain, I held back from rushing after her. In my heart, I knew she was hurting as much as I was.

Yes, the Grays looked out for each other, a truth that raised my spirits as worry grew heavier. After every meal, when all the patrons were gone, we cleaned the dishes and wiped tables—friends bonded in the color of our uniforms and in our fate. As newcomers, Alise and I were taught a repertoire of songs to sing in unison when work was hard and long. The childish melodies were not at all like the one Staris had played on the bus, nor were they similar to the choral instrumentations played on the radio or at ceremonies, but they were catchy and light-hearted and helped time go by.

When I was young and in my prime
I wandered wild and free
There was always a longing in my mind
to follow the call of the sea

Sorrel told me the laundresses didn't get along nearly as well as the Grays did and there was a great deal of quarreling among them every day.

"I just keep to myself and do the chores that others despise," she said. "Like ironing the lab coats, ensuring the belts and plackets are flat and the collars are starched. Each coat takes a great deal of labor. The research scientists are so messy, staining the fabric with blood and chemicals. Sometimes I have to send

coats back into the wash because they haven't been cleaned properly. The washwomen running the cleaning machines are resentful
and lazy and begrudge me every time."

We were in our room on a brief afternoon respite, sitting on
our cots, still dressed in our uniforms for the afternoon shift to
come. The room was overly warm from the gurgling moist heat
coming through the register. I suspected there was mold growing
in the grate and wondered if the spores were affecting our lungs.
The night before, I'd woken from a deep sleep to cough until my
throat was raw.

"Where does the blood come from?" I asked. After seeing the
mark on Esme's wrist, I'd been repressing the scenes my imagination tried to play for me.

"I'm nearly certain they perform surgeries, removing organs
and other parts from older women who aren't considered useful
anymore. Then they use the material to make new organs for
composites who didn't turn out correctly, a common problem."
Sorrel moved forward, brown eyes clouded, and whispered, "That
might be what happened to Julia, the one who was here before
you."

"You mean—they kill the older women?"

"I believe they do, yes."

A somber hush fell between us as we thought about what we'd
lost, what more we could lose, and the infuriating irony that the
remaining cadets—unchosen girls like Leslie who had underper-
formed on every test and proven themselves unremarkable—
would be, within hours, on a bus to return home.

Earlier that morning, Cistine had told me that my
photographs had turned out well and that I was to meet with her
during evening break in the fourth-floor studio for a training
session. I was not to tell anyone about the "opportunity."

"Sorrel," I said, speaking with careful pronunciation so she
could completely understand, "one of the men who visited the
other day, named Mr. Drexin, is thinking of ordering me away
from this room."

"What would that mean?"

"I'm in a panic that I'll be shuttled to an unknown place," I told her, holding back the sudden sting of tears. "Mr. Drexin isn't here today but he'll be arriving soon and I could be held in a chamber alone to wait."

"Who is this man?" She sat back, looking worried.

"I learned a little about him from the Grays this week. He's a founder of the new Polity—the group that supports Seranack—and has a collection of wives throughout his quadrant. Cistine said I should bring the pink camisole and robe with me tonight."

Sorrel and I glanced over to the closet where the lacy garments shimmered like filmy ghosts. "No, you can't let this happen, Isla. You must escape as soon as possible."

"But how? And what about you? I can't leave you here."

"You have a more urgent situation than me. And I have to stay and find my hearing aids because I think I can get to them soon. Also, if you go first, it will give me an incentive to leave someday too." My new friend pressed her hand over mine. "Lean closely and listen," she said. "I have an idea."

CHAPTER 12

The lacy pink lingerie set was small and light, no larger than an ear of corn when rolled up. I slid the garments into a sack and took them with me to the evening work shift, storing the bundle in a high cupboard in the kitchen.

At the order of Rielle, the other Grays and I were preparing a farewell meal for the remaining cadets, who were scheduled to leave on a morning bus. Instead of the usual fare, we used ground chicken liver, stale bread, and dried thyme to make meatballs. The process of scooping the balls onto the baking sheets took nearly two hours, and that was with about twelve Grays working at full speed. A second team cooked pots of noodles on the stovetops, and another sliced bread and spread it with a paste made from fermented onions. The dessert, served only on special occasions, was easy—white grapes in little bowls—but the course added another round of dishes to the clean-up chore.

We sang through the set of work songs. I had learned them all by heart and liked best the one about having a light of your own to shine into the world. And, even though it was slow and sad, I also liked the one about a chariot going home, swinging low. Alise and I labored together at the chicken meatball chore, scooping quietly amidst the chatter and singing clan of Grays. I wasn't supposed to mention my training session with Cistine to anyone, but I told her nevertheless.

"It might happen to you, too," I whispered. Alise was wearing the mandatory cap over her hair, blond ends poking out. "You're very pretty and one of the Polity will summon you soon."

"You really think I could be next?" Her meatballs were turning out perfectly round and her rows were straight on the sheet. From the way her eyes squinted with curiosity, I had the sense she might even be looking forward to the opportunity to meet with a man from the Polity alone in a fourth-floor chamber. Alise loved drinking the water and was always happy to take my share.

"Doesn't the idea upset you?" I asked.

"Not at all. The rooms on the fourth floor might be better than the ones we're in now," she said. "There are windows on that level, and you might be able to see into the treetops. I'd love to look at the birds and the leaves, watch the rain."

"But you might not be living in the room for long." I tried to explain that the men had a great deal of power, but we were called over to the ovens. Once the meatballs browned on one side, they had to be flipped to the other side to even out the crust, and there was no ability to talk because of the concentration required. The dinner hour was soon upon us, which meant distributing the plates and sprinkling each entrée with a seasoned salt stored in tall plastic jars. The meal looked enjoyable and I was hungry, but my job was to serve, not eat.

The cadets soon arrived for the farewell meal and were sitting at the round tables in the center of the dining hall. I served Leslie Snyr, who acknowledged me with a short, curt "thank you" spoken to her plate instead of to my face. Since she was going home, she might have offered to take along a message to Perrin or Papa, or even Ms. Hardin, but she avoided my eyes and carried on a conversation with her tablemates. I was angry that both she and Esme were so unkind, but reminded myself that nature had designed us to survive with instincts that could be selfish and cruel to others. I was no different in my own instincts and, had I been the one going home on the morning bus, might not have worried too much about Leslie's fate if the tides were turned. Once my serving rounds were complete, I took a stand by the trash cans and watched Rielle raise a small glass of water in a toast to the cadets.

"Farewell, my lovely girls," she said into her microphone from the front of the hall, her eyes glossy. "Many bright days are ahead of you. I trust you will always keep the CREIA close in your thoughts and remember from time to time how we helped shape you into the wonderful young ladies sitting before me. I regret so much to send all of you off tomorrow."

The cadets drank their water with enthusiasm, giggling and standing to leave with a lighthearted energy that brought my spirits down. Dreading what was about to transpire in my own existence over the next few hours, I dipped a washcloth into the bucket of warm washing fluid. Just as I began to wipe tables, Cistine emerged from the crush of exiting cadets and waved me over to her.

"No need to clean with the other Grays tonight," she said. "We have many topics to cover in the training, so bring your gowns and follow me. I only have a short time to spend with you."

The rolled-up lingerie set was still in its place. Removing the apron and tucking it beneath my arm, I said a silent goodbye to the moist, salty kitchen and all the Grays who would finish the shift without me, return to their windowless rooms, and wake up before dawn to begin the next cycle of set-up, serving, and cleaning. If all went well with the secret plan I'd made with Sorrel, I'd never see them again.

But only if the plan worked. If not, my future was uncertain and terrifying in ways I couldn't begin to think about.

～

The elevator ride I took with Cistine up to the fourth floor was the beginning of my training, she said. When the car stopped, she showed me how to manage the controls, pressing the "up" and "down" button and speaking the special code into the speakerphone.

"You'll be in residence for an unspecified time," she explained. "Mr. Drexin has an erratic schedule, coming and going according to a timetable determined by his duties. You must always be in the chamber waiting in case he arrives unexpectedly, maybe even late into the evening hours."

"Of course." I nodded earnestly. "I'm very interested to meet with him."

The composite considered me suspiciously, surveying my body for any protrusions or other signs of rebellious intent. The elevator door opened and we began a long walk around the photography studio, now dark and empty, to another hallway leading to an octagon-shaped foyer lit with a beautiful overhanging crystal chandelier that cast flittering rainbows onto the walls and floor. A prism of color hovered on Cistine's right cheekbone as she led me to one of the eight wooden doors and into a high-ceilinged parlor filled with dark furniture. A grand piano sat in one corner—I'd never seen one in person before, only in pictures—and three arched windows reached toward the vaulted ceiling, each one curtained with shimmering brocade panels. Although I was curious to move closer to the drapes and examine how exactly they were woven, Cistine demanded that I follow her through the suite.

She took me into a quiet room with a large bed, corners crisp, and pointed toward a wooden door leading to a dressing room. "Change into your gown and robe," she said. "And put your uniform down the chute."

"Are there any other—"

"You're to wear the gown and robe at all times," she said. "The maid will bring you a new set each morning and make up the bed."

Under the bluish light in the dressing room, I removed my gray uniform and boots and put on the lacy pink camisole, which left my shoulders, legs, and arms exposed to the cold air until I slid on the matching robe and tied it at the waist. The 100,000 token that had been in my uniform bodice was not quite as secure in the camisole's flimsy lace, so I tucked it into the band at the top of my underwear. I placed my worn, dirty boots on a mat on the closet floor, but there were no shoes to wear in the apartment.

The laundry chute was built into the closet's wall, a metal square with panels that folded like fan blades when an illuminated green button was pressed. I placed my uniform, a warm heap of wilted cotton, directly on the blades and observed how the device opened, sucked the garment into a tunnel of darkness, and snapped shut with an efficient click. I tried the button a second time, but the mechanism didn't operate—I surmised the machine had a sensor in place that required a bundle or weight on the blades for activation.

"Enough dawdling," Cistine called out. "I'm in a rush."

"Are there any shoes to wear?" I asked, emerging from the dressing room. "The carpet is soft, but I need to cover my feet in case something sharp falls."

"The maid can bring you some slippers and a make-up kit— ask her in the morning. You have a hairbrush and toothbrush at the sink. Use them often. And keep your lips and face clean and fresh."

There was a small kitchen counter with an ice chest, water pitcher, and a set of four clear glass tumblers. Cistine opened a drawer that released a sweet smell, and I gasped at the bounty of food inside—neatly wrapped packages of butter crackers, nuts, chocolates, chocolate-covered nuts, tins of cheese and sugar wafers. My eyes landed on a small jar of peach preserves; the impulse to open it and spread a cracker with the fruity paste made me realize how deeply hungry I was.

"Try not to gorge yourself," Cistine said, sliding the drawer back into place. "But do eat a few snacks tonight as you've become too thin and could plump up a little. And there's one more thing to see." She led me to a long cabinet in the living area, located an electronic wand, and used it to raise a television from a low console. "Watch what you like," she said, handing it to me. "There are many dull hours for girls on the fourth floor."

The wand was smooth and heavy in my hand, a lure into a portal of glittering colored gems and liquid voices. I'd never had private access to a TV before, but I wouldn't allow the entertaining machine to distract from my plan. "When will Mr. Drexin arrive?" I asked, placing the device on a small low table situated near a long plush dark-blue sofa.

"There is no specific time, not tonight and not ever." Cistine went toward the door with her clipboard, made a note, and rested a small hand on the metal knob. "Remember that you are a servant and should keep your appearance together as though you are having another photograph taken. He could be coming tonight or another night and will arrive without notice to you. I must be on my way now to help the children to bed, so get settled in and speak with the maid in the morning—her name is Katrina —about other supplies you might obtain."

I watched the door click into place, the lock snapping.

All alone in the chamber, I decided to eat a few chocolate-covered nuts and crackers before nightfall. It was unfortunate that I wouldn't be able to take any food with me, but there were no pockets in the pink robe. The windows revealed the deep blue dusk transpiring outside, and I had a segment of time to waste with snacks and television. But how enjoyable could those pleasures be with such a weight of worry on my mind? The crackers and preserves were luscious and I was so hungry and deprived that I devoured the entire package within seconds, moving on to a bag of silky crescent-shaped nuts coated in salt. Once I was so stuffed that I couldn't eat more, I arranged myself on the plush sofa, sitting with my cold feet tucked under my thighs and was about to turn on the television when there was a knock on the door.

My heart dropped.

The knock came again, three soft thumps. Something about its politeness lowered my guard; Mr. Drexin wouldn't knock in such a way unless he was extraordinarily considerate, a quality I doubted he possessed. So I snuck over to the door and pressed my ear to the wood, listening as the knock came again.

"Who's there?"

"Who are you?" It was a female voice, young and friendly.

Hesitant, I fiddled with the lock and opened the door, peeking through a crack.

The green eyes and long dark hair were unmistakable, and I opened the space to let her in. We stood together in the dark shadows of the hallway, speechless at the sight of each other.

My visitor was Hannah, and she was dressed in a long satin gown.

"You're not dead?"

She smiled and strode into my chamber, long skirt trailing, perched on the arm of the sofa and looked around with bemusement. Her eyes were outlined with dark kohl, shaped into catlike slants, her full lips glistening under the light.

"Me, dead? Of course not. I was wondering who the new girl was and thought I'd see for myself. I'd not expected it would be you, Isla." Leaning forward, so close I could smell the lemon scent of her hair, she quietly asked who had requested my photographs.

"A man named Mr. Drexin."

"Drexin? Hmmm, he must be the newcomer. Well, don't worry too much. He probably won't last long."

"What do you mean?"

Hannah glanced toward the ceiling where a security camera's amber detection light flashed, making it clear that she was inhibited from providing specific information. "Some of the Polity travel frequently."

I had a sense she was changing the subject.

"You might not know this," she said, waving a hand toward the window. "But there is more land on the other side of the ocean. The other two quadrants are much larger than ours."

"Are we near the ocean now?"

"I'm not sure, but I know the Polity owns a large ship because I was a guest onboard one evening. You might have that chance too." She stood up and fiddled with the ankle strap on her pointy-toed slipper. "I advise following along with every rule and keeping a cheerful attitude in all situations."

"Situations? I thought I was expecting a marriage proposal."

"Is that what Cistine told you?"

"It's what the hairdresser in the photo studio said."

"Oh, that's Gem. She doesn't know much. The composites look at our role in an innocent fashion that makes sense to them, so listen with doubt. Remember they are unable to breed on their own and don't have urges. Soon I'll introduce you to the other girls on the floor and we'll show you ways to pass the time between appointments and how to bribe the men into bringing you new clothes to wear. These slippers on my feet, this dress—both were given to me."

Her words wavered hesitantly in a way that reminded me of the Hannah I'd met on the first day, the shy Hannah from the country who'd hand-sewn her own dress in hope of a chance to go somewhere in the world.

"I should go back to my chamber now—I'm in chamber six and you're in number two. We are supposed to stay in our rooms at all times, but a few visits are tolerated during the day and sometimes we even have sleepovers." She placed her warm hands over mine. "Do you like wine?"

"Wine? I suppose so."

"It's so delicious," she said. "And helps you relax. I must go now, but I'll be back soon."

"Before you go," I asked, "can you tell me what happened to bring you up here? Did you have photos taken? I never saw my photos, did you?"

"My photos weren't taken because I was brought up on the day I left the circle group where you last saw me. That's the way it happens at times, if Rielle commands it. They gave me the injection that day—it makes your menstrual cycle stop for a month. You'll have another one in a few weeks. Now I better go. Knock three times on the inside of the door if you want to call me, and I'll return when it's possible."

As she turned and flipped her hair to one side, I saw the most curious mark on her body. Just above the knobby top of her spine was the stamp I recognized: LUSH.

In a panic, I rushed to the bathroom and turned around, twisting my head to see into the mirror. There it was, printed on the back of my neck, the stamp I'd seen only at the better goods market, a stamp that had no place on a human body. My body.

LUSH.

I began to tremble, thinking of the girl who'd come to our school. The stamp I'd seen on her was now my own. But where was she now? Wherever it was, I no longer cared to join her.

Sitting at the piano, I watched the sky blacken into the late hours. When even the singing crickets were silent, I prepared for my escape, braiding my hair and tying the robe's belt around my wrist, winding it tightly in case it could be helpful once I landed in the basement. Boots tightly tied, I went to the bathroom to brush my teeth and wondered if I could write Hannah a note before leaving. A pen and a sheet of paper lay on the bureau, a translucent sheet that had a pleasant crinkle sound when folded, but I left the page untouched and waited by the window until the first haze of sunlight appeared on the horizon.

I should have left earlier.

The door clicked and Mr. Drexin walked in without a knock or warning of any kind. We confronted one another in the center of the carpeted room, the light of dawn pulling his eyes into twisted red shadows.

CHAPTER 13

"Good morning," he said. "Isla, is it? Don't shy away." Mr. Drexin stepped closer. "I am a gentleman and an honorable man." He loosened a strap on his torso, removed a revolver from a holster, and set the weapon on a side table. He gestured to the sofa, sprinkled with food crumbs. "Shall we sit and get to know each other? It's been a very long night for me, with many hours in consult with the brigade and a long ride here."

My blood rushed and my mind circled with possible ways to evade his interest. I stood to the side with my eyes down, allowing him to move around and sit on the sofa.

"It's quite dark in here," I said. "There's a lamp beside you."

"Tell me," he said, sitting down and turning on the lamp. "Why is a girl such as yourself dressed in such a ragtag manner? Turn around for me, miss. I'd like a long look at you."

"Please, sir," I said. "While I'm flattered that my pictures pleased you, I plan to withdraw from this program." I remembered the tattoo on the back of my neck and reached for the spot, covering it with my fingertips and stepping back.

Mr. Drexin laughed, a hollow chuckle that tumbled between us. "A withdrawal is not possible, but I find your stubborn innocence quite charming."

"Why has my skin been branded?" I asked, voice quivering. "With the word LUSH, as though my body is a product available for purchase?" But as I spoke the question, I understood through the look of amusement in his eyes that the stamp was an indicator, a claim of status for men like Mr. Drexin. My cheeks burned and I focused my eyes on the carpeting, thinking of how to carry on with my escape plan despite his intrusion.

He relaxed into the sofa, spreading his legs and pulling a small case from the pocket of his jacket. "Come here," he said, coaxing. "There is a way to make this easier for us." He removed his jacket and laid the case in the lining, opening it to reveal a vial and two tiny needles attached to slender glass bulbs. "You will be able to enjoy yourself, miss, and I am looking forward to knowing you better. Come over now," he said, lifting a glass vial from the case. "This relaxant is the best around, very valuable and expensive. Like you." He smiled and rested his eyes on my breasts.

"Like me? You mean you pay for—" I stopped to cover the tremble in my voice. "You paid to come here?"

"LUSH credits, of course. How do you think this place is financed?" Mr. Drexin swept a hand to the window, where the sun was setting into the dark treetops. "Certainly not from the DNA programs. A waste, as I've heard Seranack say, to spend so much on those grimy composites. There's nothing wrong with the human race as it is." He shuffled around in the case for a small rubber ring, attaching it to one of the glass vials before inserting the needle into its opening.

I backed up to the kitchen counter. "This substance you're drawing up … I cannot share it with you," I told him. "But there are many girls here who are of a different mind than me. You could choose one of them instead. I prefer to return to my bunker bedroom with your respect, sir."

Mr. Drexin stood up and moved toward me, the loaded vial in one hand. With the other hand, he tapped my skin just below the collarbone. "I am an honorable man," he said, "but your teasing game is quickly losing its charm. Hold out your arm, miss. This will be quick and painless. You'll soon be thanking me for the experience." He took hold of my left arm, twisting it into an unnatural position.

"Lights," he said, and the bulb above us came on, shining onto the faint blue veins beneath my skin. Drexin held a strong and firm grip on my wrist, preventing circulation as he massaged a point in the crook of my elbow. A vein began to rise out and he aimed the needle for it.

"Stop," I insisted, yanking away with all my force. But I was too late—the needle was already in my skin. The glass vial detached from its seal, falling to the floor.

I stomped it with my boot and the clear fluid seeped out.

I wasn't prepared for the slap that plowed across my cheek, nor the crushing blow that came next. And then there were more blows, so many that Mr. Drexin's form shook at the edges as my eyesight blurred. I covered my face with my hands and sobbed, so strong and deep I couldn't recognize myself. I wanted to hit him unconscious, to slap him back, to scream, but my lungs insisted I breathe deeply to quell the angry tingling under my skin.

"We're on a camera," I managed to say, cowering on the kitchen floor. "Rielle will know what you've done."

Mr. Drexin sneered. "Stupid girl," he said. "Rielle is just a teacher, and she's on drugs herself. The Polity controls the cameras, just as we control you." He raised his hand as if to slap me again, but let his fingers fall softly on my right cheek. "You get another chance because it will be great fun to break you down. So clean up and think about it, because I'll be back soon."

He looked at the needle that still dangled from my arm. "There's likely a bandage around here," I heard him say. "Order one up if not."

The door slammed and I willed my sobs to stop. I had only a few seconds after his exit to find myself and restore the will I needed to deploy the escape plan, but the strength couldn't be mustered and I collapsed on the floor again, writhing with tears.

A segment of the needle remained in my arm, where it stung painfully.

Get up, Isla. Get up.

Papa would say some such thing, I was sure, and it was as though his voice was in my ear. I stood up and took a sharp knife from a kitchen drawer, tucked it into my boot for protection, and scrambled into the bedroom to fling open the closet door.

The electronic button on the laundry chute limited the amount of time the chute door would stay open, so I prevented it from shutting by stuffing a wadded-up blanket into its jaws. The button flashed and the motor churned, but the beeping sound was muffled. I climbed inside, supporting myself with a strong outward clench on the surrounding walls, lightly resting my feet on the blanket.

I closed my eyes, took a breath, and allowed physics to take control.

My feet slammed the blanket through the chute and my body slid into the darkness with just enough space to pass, the cool air whistling. I landed at the expected corner point—Sorrel and I predicted three such junctures on the plans we'd drawn out. With a pivot to the correct side, I fell again through what I suspected was the third floor, turned again and fell through the second and then the first, the air growing warmer and the chute wider with each one. At the final corner point, I took a breath to calm my wildly pounding heart before sliding into the last chute that would —if Sorrel's participation had played out as expected—lead me to land in a bin of dirty dishtowels.

The soft plop and vigorous odor of old food confirmed that I had landed in the basement. There were only minutes to get out before the first laundresses would arrive to begin the morning work. Crawling out, I looked in panic for the bin Sorrel had told me about, locating it exactly where she'd said it would be, near the side door where she'd wheeled it especially for me. Inside, I found my knapsack and a neatly folded and pressed cadet uniform. Quickly, I slid out of my camisole and robe and buried them in the bin, dressing in cadet blue, leaving the skirt half unzipped in my rush to the back door, which Sorrel had left unlocked. Creeping into the dawn, I found a spot under a tree to adjust the uniform, wrap a strip of cotton around my arm, stick the LUSH token in my bodice, hide the knife in the knapsack, pull on socks, and retie the boots. Hoisting the pack onto my shoulders, I took a look back at the dormitory and spoke a silent sentence:

No, Mr. Drexin. You do not control me—I do.

CHAPTER 14

*O*utside the dormitory, the insects sang in eerie unison. The moon above was a round orb in the still-dawning sky. I crept behind the bushes surrounding the courtyard, keeping low. My plan was to get on the bus—how, I wasn't exactly sure yet —and get off when we were close to my town. Since Leslie was one of the girls going home, the bus would be required to stop near Naudiz.

I continued my low crawl toward the garage gate. It was closed, and standing up to open the latch might expose my silhouette to one of the courtyard cameras. But earlier in the week— when checking in on a patch of cheather I'd planted in the squirrel park—I'd seen an area in the back of the fence where two posts failed to connect, leaving about two feet of space. Circling to that spot, I quietly tore away at a bulk of ivy and weeds. The pollen and dust that rose almost caused a sneeze, but with mental force I held it back, crawling across the sidewalk to the garage door and reaching up.

My heart lurched.

In a crackle of ultraviolet energy, a spider skittered across my bare arm and hugged multiple hairy neon-yellow legs onto the latch, spinning a tight nest of blue string around it. As the insect's black eyes sizzled into my own, I choked on a scream, clenching my larynx with both hands to stop myself, emitting just a weak *ugh*. But I was breathing fast and hard and could not turn my eyes away from the spider's penetrating, beady gaze. The insect grew larger and brighter until its translucent orange egg sack burst and bubbled over the door handle. The sickening spray brought up a nauseating rotten odor. I gagged uncontrollably and fell to my knees, scraping them on the pavement.

My throat and sinuses burned in the putrid air. There was no choice—I had to turn around and find a way back to the fourth-floor chamber. I'd endure my fate as Mr. Drexin's abused mistress and allow him to inject my veins with whatever measures promised by the clear fluid.

But something told me to hold still and take a breath, to swallow my bitter saliva, to keep my eyes on the ground and remember—to believe with everything I had—that the spider was not real. It was just a hologram, I remembered. I couldn't and wouldn't allow myself to believe it was real. So I reached up toward the frothy mass of pus that was now quivering in blue strands and refused to look into the center of its eyes.

Just a hologram, I said to myself. *Just a hologram.*

With a shaking hand and thundering heart, I reached for the door handle.

The spider sizzled into an invisible hole, jelly and string skittering on my skin with a cooling energy, soothing like peppermint.

Trembling but relieved, I opened the garage gate and snuck into the ink-black space, tripping over something hard with a loud clang. There were no windows, and even though I could see rows of overhead fluorescents, I didn't dare turn on the switch for fear of inviting another insect my way. The pools of oil on the concrete floor were so thick that rainbow moirés had formed around the edges. I could make out the fuzzy shapes of a tall tool chest, long workbench, and diagnostic machines. Shelves on the walls held plastic jars filled with fluids and oils, springs and coils, and cardboard boxes marked *Electronics*. I looked carefully from a hiding spot in a corner but didn't see the flashing lights or twinkle of security cameras in the ceiling or tucked into the corner beams.

After a short, tense few minutes, I heard the creaking of the gate hinges and the rumble of the bus pulling into the loading zone outside the door. I shrunk into my corner and held completely still as the knob turned and the door opened with a shifting triangle of light. A man in a green mechanic's suit came in with a quick stride and headed for the shelf of automotive fluids.

Staris.

I stood up, cleared my throat, and stepped into the slice of sunlight provided by the partially open door.

He turned, a can of oil in hand, and considered me with amused surprise, taking in the picture of a thin, pale, and terrified girl in a cadet uniform, hand-knitted stockings, canvas boots, and a very full knapsack. I kept my arm flat to hide the wound.

"My beauty," he said. "What are you doing here? And what happened to your face? Has someone beaten you?"

I cleared my throat and spoke with confidence. "I'm Isla from Naudiz, remember? I need a ride home, sir."

"Isla, you are not allowed in this area." Staris waved the air between us with a grease-smudged hand. "Go back to your quarters before someone sees you."

"I can't go back," I told him. "Please, Staris, take me with you on the bus. Let me out when you take Leslie home today."

He took a sideways step to close the door with the toe of one leather boot, casting us into darkness.

"Listen," he murmured, moving closer. "I don't want to get you in trouble, so leave now while you still can." He gestured to the door, encouraging. "The women fare well here. Sometimes officers visit them with gifts."

"I've just been struck by one of them. Please, I'll hide in with the luggage."

Staris set down the oil can and took hold of my arm. In a thin square of seamed sunlight, I saw concern in his eyes. "I can find you a better bandage," he said, "but I can't take you or anyone home." He held my eyes with his. "Understand, the girls getting on my bus today are not going home. They're going to the surrogate center."

Those words—*surrogate center*—dissolved a falsity that had been holding me in place. My knees weakened with uncertainty. "You mean—"

"Yes," he said, pushing me to the door. "They're to be baby incubators. Breeders for the composite program. You don't want to go there, Isla."

Incubators. The realization settled sickly in my stomach, and I felt as though I'd been slapped. With my free hand, I reached into my bodice and pulled out the 100,000 token, holding it out to Staris.

"I'll give you this."

In the darkness, the coin shone like the white moon. I could hear him breathe in, could smell his soap and the oil in his jumpsuit.

"Take it," I urged, holding out the token. "Your payment for my journey out."

Staris took the token, turned it over once in his hand, then dropped it into his shirt pocket. "I shouldn't accept your temptation," he said, somber. "But my wife is very ill and this could help her. I'll drop you off in the city. From there, you're on your own." He took a felt blanket and wrapped me in it, backpack and all, covering me from head to toe in a cocoon-like casing. I was lifted, still rolled, onto his shoulder.

"Don't move," he said, lifting me. "Consider yourself as cargo."

I felt us moving through the garage door and into the daylight, then heard the scrape of a metal hinge and the thumping of an opening door. Staris laid me in the very back of the bus's inset luggage area, pulling away the fabric to expose only my face.

"Don't dare move. Not even slightly," he whispered. "If anyone sees you, we're both dead." He rolled me over so I was facing the inside of the bus.

Eventually, I heard voices outside the bus that indicated some of the girls had arrived. I imagined Leslie Snyr, her curly hair pulled into a tight bun, moving through the aisle. Thumping sounds followed by pressure in the back of my body confirmed that Staris had begun to fill the compartment with luggage. I took in a long deep breath, safe in knowing that I could no longer be seen from the outside. But the weight from the luggage grew heavier, compressing my body inside the metal box. I wondered if I'd suffocate.

Just as it became close to unbearable, the compartment was closed and locked. There were footsteps over me, the sound of the bus engine revving up and bursting into power. A gear shifted and we began to move at a slow speed. There was a breeze coming through the compartment, probably from cracks in the soldering, and my face was kept cool even while the rest of my body was hot from the thick encasement.

Once on its way, the bus bounced, dipped, turned, and sometimes stopped. The luggage and my body slid through the compartment. At times, I was crammed into the corner, folded into the heap of suitcases. At other moments, I could stretch my legs and relish the blood flow. The only constant was the engine vibration trembling through every cell of my flesh and the knowledge that I was suspended only inches above the road. Should the compartment break, I'd be crushed.

During the short stops at road intersections, I could hear the lighthearted tones of the girls above me. There was an occasional giggle or a scurry of footsteps as they went up and down the aisle to visit with each other. That they didn't yet know their fate made me cringe with horror, and I pushed away the picture of them lined up in maternity wards. For the time being, I could do nothing but exist.

I knew we'd reached the final destination when the bus stopped and came to a rumbling rest. There were hard stomps of boots and shoes going down the exit stairs, which seemed to respond to a directive voice that spoke from a point outside the bus. My heart sped madly when the lock to the luggage compartment clicked and the door was flung open, bathing my cave in sunlight. I was as still as a possum as the suitcases and knapsacks were lifted away. I couldn't hear or see anything and didn't know if the girls now had a clue of the fate awaiting them. The silence persisted, broken only by the sound of Staris clearing his throat.

After a long time, the luggage door closed and I heard what I assumed to be his footsteps boarding the bus. The engine shifted and we moved again, reaching a high speed within seconds. This time, I was the only cargo in the compartment. My body slid back and forth with every turn of the steering wheel, the center of my chest sick with vibration. I had to fight off the urge to vomit.

Soon I was in a sweat and decided to struggle out of the felt blanket by kicking my legs until it loosened and I could use my good arm to cling to a metal bar above me. I tried to remember things I loved—the smell of Papa's kitchen in the morning, the comforting rumble of my cats purring, the warm water of our forest brook. And I thought about the future, finding a glint of hope in the fact that I had just exited the surrogate farm without any trouble. Yet the thrill of possible freedom was neutralized by the unknown. Would Mr. Drexin report my absence? And where were we heading now? Staris had said he'd drop me off in the city. How far away were we, and what would I do once I got there?

We finally came to a long stop. A set of footsteps tumbled on the stairs and the door to my compartment opened.

"You must get out, Isla," Staris ordered. "Hurry." He took hold of my still-wrapped feet, pulled me from the compartment, and sat me on the edge.

We were in an underground mechanic's shop. The walls and ground were solid cement, the ceiling supported by metal pillars rising into long, thick beams. We must have come through them and down the ramp to get where we were, a parking area for buses. Besides our bus, there were four others, all empty. I didn't see or hear any people, only the sound of dripping water coming from a sink against a back wall. Beyond the door, yards away, I heard the faint cry of a siren. I became aware of a massive throbbing pulse above and around us.

"Are we in the city?" I asked.

"Yes, the city of Peorth," he said. "Stay here, I'll get you a drink of water."

Shaking off the blanket, I readjusted the knapsack that had been on my shoulders for hours. The walk to the double doors, I noticed, required a steep uphill climb on the metal ramp. Despite the angry cramping in my injured arm, I almost looked forward to it. After hours of lying down, I could have walked for miles. The water Staris brought in a metal cup was a cool ambrosia, and I drank it all in a second with his anxious eyes on me.

"You must be on your way, Isla. My bus is on a schedule that can't be changed without notice from Rielle and the others."

He held out a hand and helped me adjust the straps on my backpack so my injury wasn't irritated by them. Together, we went up the ramp, stopping at the door.

"I'll tell her I found you huddled in cargo and killed you with such venom that delivery of your body was impossible."

I thanked him, thinking how twisted it was to thank someone for such a thing.

"Change your looks so you aren't spotted by anyone who may recognize you," he continued. "The city is full of people, many of them Unsaved, and their desperation puts you at risk."

He opened the door with slow caution.

I followed him outside, blinking in brightness as we faced a parking lot full of black sedans, limousines, and blue cars like the one Ms. Hardin owned. A red bus with dusty windows arrived and began to circle toward us.

"Cripes, it's a crew of Lower Polity," he said. "Run off before they see you."

"But to where?"

"Go." He gently pushed me onto a strip of cement and disappeared behind the door.

I longed to call out, ask him to come back. But the red bus had already parked; from behind the windows, the Polity on board were standing to come out. Panicked, I scurried onto the path and circled the corner, soon finding myself running a downhill path into the city below.

PART III
HOME

CHAPTER 15

I followed the path, keeping my head low. Soon I was at an intersection leading into a road lined with buildings and structures so tall they seemed to brush the clouds. The setting sun rested in their midst, a lemon glow in the pastel watercolor. I was astonished at the beauty of the scene—glistening windows arranged in perfect squares and precise rows, tiny lights inside twinkling and flashing. I kept up my quick pace, drawn to looming constructs before me. Above me wires ran everywhere, up and down, across, sideways, in loops and varying lengths, some connected to poles, others to the buildings themselves. They were for electricity, I surmised, providing light and energy. The air smelled like rust. Eventually, I crossed a long bridge of steel and concrete slabs and beams. Cars passed in both directions; all kinds of cars, not just the long dark-blue and black sedans I'd seen in the underground lot. I walked with a stooped posture to hide the bruises on my face, but my tattered uniform could not be covered.

When the bridge ended, I followed a sidewalk into a park littered with wrappers and cans. People of all ages slept on benches or the worn grassy ground, most of them in filthy clothes, some without shoes. In the center, near a dry fountain, a scraggly, angry man stood on a crate, shouting in a language I didn't know.

Several young boys in blue cotton jumpsuits and canvas boots similar to the ones from the CREIA were playing a game on a patch of cement, kicking a rubber ball into a matrix of chalk-drawn squares. A dignified man with a dark tan and deeply wrinkled skin sat on a bench, holding perfect posture as he read a large page of printed text. His linen pants were limp and frayed at the hem, belted with a nylon rope, and he was without a shirt and shoes.

I dared to raise my face and look around for water.

Four busy streets framed the square, each of them populated with pedestrians and the occasional automobile. There was a store on one corner, a squat, square block building with a hand-painted sign reading Commissary 102. Inside, the store was small and smelled slightly rotten. The clerk, a woman with thin hair and a swollen pocked face, sat at the counter, clipping her fingernails. I asked if there was a bathroom I could use.

"Only for patrons," she said.

I revealed the bandage on my arm. "Please," I said, "I injured myself."

She looked at me with a start, then hesitated. "Oh, I suppose. It's in the back behind the freezer. Keep it clean, will you?"

I walked past a row of canned beans and vegetables; if only I hadn't given all my money to Staris. As it was, I had only a few fractional tokens inside my knapsack.

The bathroom was dark and cramped, but it had a sink that ran a brownish trickle of water. I scooped handfuls to my mouth, slurping quietly. I used the toilet and pulled off everything I was wearing, including the bandage. Washing the blood away, I wrapped a cloth ripped from the bottom of my orange skirt and pulled on stockings I'd knitted in the dormitory. The remaining portion of my skirt covered my thighs and ended just above my knees. The canvas boots I'd been wearing were a problem. Because they were from the CREIA, they could be recognized and mark me a fugitive. But there wasn't a choice.

I washed the knife I'd taken from the kitchen and used it to cut my braids, trimming the strands close to my scalp. Remembering the clerk's request to keep the bathroom clean, I scooped up the thick plaits and stuffed them into the side pocket of my knapsack. Without their weight, my head felt oddly light and I worried the hateful stamp—LUSH—was now fully exposed. I pulled out the stocking cap I'd brought from home, pulling it low on the back of my neck. After another long drink from the faucet, I collected my things and left the bathroom, nodding politely to the clerk as I left.

But she called me back. "Hey, girl," she said.

Apparently, I still looked like a girl, even with short hair.

"Yes, ma'am?"

"You got any ointment for that cut? I can sell you some."

"I only have a few fractionals."

"How many?"

I reached into the bottom of my pack and located three fractional tokens.

"That's enough," she said, taking the coins and passing me a tiny tube of first aid ointment.

It wasn't cheather, but it was better than nothing.

Outside, the park had settled into quiet dimness, the boys and their ball gone, the chalk-drawn square now empty under a streetlight. The fear of being discovered made my heart pound furiously. I walked the cement path, anxiously winding around Unsaved in ragged tunics lounging on sheets of plastic, taped-up cardboards, bedsheets, or nothing at all. In one corner, a group of them had collected around a fire, where they turned a rabbit carcass on a rotisserie made from scrap metal and sticks. One of them was the dignified man I'd seen sitting shirtless on the bench before I'd found the bathroom.

"Young miss," he called to me, "are you lost?"

I stopped but didn't speak. He seemed nice enough.

"We have some bread and tea." Although I was still worried about being recognized, I joined their circle because the aroma of charcoal and rabbit meat stirred a deep hunger. Along with the shirtless man, who introduced himself as Alexander, two old women in headscarves examined me with brittle black eyes. They had a girl with them, about my age, who could not speak.

"She's brain-damaged," they explained as I joined them in front of the fire. "Not born that way," one of the women said hoarsely. "She was electrocuted by Seranack."

Seranack.

Peorth—this was the city he'd overtaken.

The electrocuted girl's name was Sheila, and she had been punished for making bombs. I thought it seemed an odd crime for a young woman, but as the fire crackled, Alexander and the women gave me more details about their world and Sheila's crime began to make sense.

Peorth was embroiled in division and strife, they said. The former mayor—an intelligent old man who'd tried to expose corruption among members of the Lower Polity without success —had been overtaken by Seranack, who'd promised to improve living conditions but had instead made them much worse. Now referred to as the Governor, he lived with his family and followers in a gold skyscraper in a section of downtown off-limits to everyone else.

"It used to be the arts district," Alexander said. "The museum is there, the opera house, and the grand hotels. He has taken complete control of the street with armed barricades."

The rest of the city, including the spot where I was now sitting, was policed by a brigade that issued tickets and violations for any and every contrary action. The electrocuted girl had been building bombs in resistance, but she and many others had been caught, captured, and physically silenced.

"She was released only because she's now inept, a near vegetable," Alexander said. "And there was no one to care for her. Is it so violent where you are from?"

I trusted them enough to explain. "All roles in Naudiz are assigned. We don't have open parks like this one. Anyone caught drifting would be captured and taken away. In my area, there are many empty houses around us brought in from different areas. Each one was supposed to present an era of time, but only ours and a few others are in a condition to greet visitors."

My words set off some discussion among them, one involving the names of people and places I'd never heard of. I was too tired to follow and instead rested my eyes on the flames of the fire, meditating on the shooting sparks and hiss of burning wood.

"What is your name, miss?" Alexander asked.

"Hollis." I gave my sister's name instead of mine to maintain distance. The vagabonds were kind people, but associating with them was dangerous. If a brigade member found me, I could become brain-damaged, too, and I was increasingly worried that the CREIA had sent out an alert about my escape. Somehow, I had to get rid of my canvas boots, the last remnant of my uniform. But the generous hobos feeding me from the already-small portion of bread, water, and smoked rabbit weren't wearing shoes and couldn't trade with me.

"How did you hurt your arm, dear?" one of the old crones asked.

To her, I also lied. "Stabbed by a bus driver. He was trying to kill me, I think."

The group nodded in sympathy. Sheila's eyes sparked at the word "kill."

"Please eat the rest, dear," the woman urged, sliding me a slice of burned bread.

I spent the night in their shelter, an uncomfortable enclave made of sticks and pine boughs. Sucking in a breath, I removed the makeshift bandage I'd wrapped around my wound and used the firelight to squeeze the tiny tube of ointment onto the gash. There wasn't enough ointment for a good treatment, just enough for a thin film in the deepest part of the puncture. Since I had no alternative, I rewrapped my arm in the soiled bandage, tying it into a small, tight knot.

But when I woke in the morning, I had an idea.

After a breakfast generously provided by Alexander, I sat

cross-legged in a secluded spot near the campfire and pulled the ball of yarn from my knapsack. I used it to tie the ends of the of braids I'd cut from my head the day before, wrapping up two neat bundles of long red-brown tufts. Alexander gave me directions to a wig shop he knew about. Before leaving, I took the page of printed text he'd been reading on the bench when I'd first seen him.

"It's the underground newspage," he told me. "Read it and learn more."

At the wig shop, I sold my hair to a withered man for a 100-token piece, enough to buy a new pair of boots. They were cheap boots made from thin black leather with hard, stiff soles molded from recycled plastic. Dark green nylon laces crisscrossed through the silver grommets.

"You want to sell the old ones?" the shoe clerk asked, picking up one of my canvas boots and looking it over curiously. "I'll give you ten."

I took the token and used it at a commissary for a water canteen and a small can of soy hash. Without any of the uniform items on my body, I relaxed a bit and walked openly through the market square, keeping my stocking cap pulled over my hair. The market sold LUSH items, and I was conscious of the stamp on the back of my neck. My collar and hat barely covered it. I realized then that the girl who'd visited us at school had been branded as I had. Somehow, she'd gained enough station to earn her role as a recruiter.

With more money, I would have bought some of the fruit sold at the wobbly tables and some chocolate pieces displayed on a tin tray by a child who barely reached my chin. What I wanted most of all was a slice of ham from a cart in the center. Walking anywhere near it made my mouth water. Hungry, I stopped at a booth filled with turnip greens.

The vendor waved his hands in display of the produce. "Very good choices today," he said. But my eye was drawn to the booth behind him, one selling large rocks, where I saw a girl with long blond hair. She was well-dressed in an embroidered light-green dress, a gold satin purse hanging across her torso, and was surrounded by two similarly dressed girls and a uniformed brigade member. I immediately recognized her as Ashleen, the leader among the girls who had arrived and departed campus before the rest of us. I immersed myself in browsing for the most perfect turnips, keeping my head down, waiting a moment to glance at her in my periphery.

"Do you know that girl?" I asked the man who was selling greens.

"That's Miss Ashleen, Seranack's oldest daughter," the man replied. "She often walks through looking for geodes and perfume."

I hid behind the tarp in panic and watched her browse around, trailed by three friends. A second member of the police brigade had joined their group; he was tall and lean with a gun stored in a shiny holster latched around a leather waist belt. Pedestrians moved aside to let them pass and the chatter of the crowd evaporated into an anxious hush.

The handsome brigade officer hovered near Ashleen as they stopped at an apothecary stand in the LUSH section of the marketplace. She dipped a wooden stick into a vial, sniffed, then held it to his nose. They made funny faces at each other and laughed. I decided to take advantage of their preoccupation and get away as inconspicuously as possible. After quietly thanking the turnip seller, I adjusted my cap and made a tight turn into the crowd. With my eyes on the ground, I didn't know exactly where Ashleen and her entourage had gone, but I didn't dare look up, imagining myself an anonymous bobbing figure in the mix, not attracting attention in any manner.

I was halfway across the square when a bomb exploded.

The market was instantly engulfed in smoke and a blast of intense heat, and a stampede formed—fiery bodies and a screaming, clawing fury.

I crouched on the stony ground, holding in my scream and

protecting my head with my hands as every molecule of space filled with smoke. I shuddered for several seconds. As the smoke lifted, I dared stand with my bag and look over the bloodied core of the crowd, the blackened flesh, sobbing children and—worst of all—a headless corpse, the body of the brain-damaged girl named Sheila. The two old crones who'd shared their meal with me crouched and cried in anguish.

Someone fell on me. We toppled to the ground together, landing on our sides.

It was Alexander, the shirtless man from the square. His face was badly burned, his body so grossly charred I instinctively pushed away and tried to run.

He grabbed my skirt. "Please," he said, spreading open his bloody fingers. "Throw this."

A hand grenade, shaped like a pine cone, wobbled in his palm. I snatched it up, not because of his request but because I feared someone else would take it from him. The square was manic with people running, screaming, and fighting against brigade officers who'd streamed down the hill and into the throng.

Alexander pulled on my skirt, insistent. "Toss it, miss."

His eyes were blinded with blood, his breathing labored. I was about to step over his broad body to tuck the grenade in a hedge or bush when the brigade guard who'd been protecting Ashleen earlier appeared before me, his sculpted face a stern visage in the smoke.

"Move aside," he ordered, hitting me on the shoulder with the heel of one hand and stomping without care on Alexander's abdomen. Just behind him was Ashleen, her embroidered linen dress charred and torn. We recognized each other right away, and her face pulled scornfully.

"Ugh, *you*? Who, how did you—" She saw the grenade in my hand and quickly ducked behind her soldier. "She's the bomber," she accused. "Arrest her now!"

The soldier came at me in a powerful lunge, so forceful I had no choice—I threw the grenade and ran, holding my hands over my ears. I ran through the square like an angry cat, kicking and clawing my way around the pedestrians, caring for nothing except my escape. My boot soles slapped the pavement, the sounds lost in a fresh wave of upset, my muscles charging and fueled with effortless energy. I didn't slow until I again heard the sound of my soles on the rocky path of a side road far from the square.

The neighborhood I'd arrived in was peaceful, eerily empty, and lined with row houses built from crumbling umber-colored stones. I found a dark alley and leaned against the wall, easing my breath and heartbeat. The sun was heavy, its late-afternoon light shining on the rusted gutters overhead.

I was alone, completely and utterly alone.

And I was viewed a criminal, I understood with the deepest, most gripping fear I'd ever known. I closed my eyes and began to weep, reviving the moment in my tortured mind: the grenade, flung from my hand in instinctive defense, the terror on Ashleen's face, so wide-eyed and pale it was nearly tender. And the blast itself, the sound and sight that was now embedded in my soul—the horrible, crackling explosion that was her final second of life.

CHAPTER 16

*I*n the setting sun, I became aware of the river off in the distance and realized that the city was built along a shore. By following the water's flow in the correct direction, I could possibly arrive at the stream that trickled through Naudiz. I didn't risk looking for a map because I had to get out of the city while I could.

The alley where I was hiding led into a maze of side streets, roads, and smaller, darker alleys. I moved like a chess piece, willing method over emotion, and headed toward the water. The city was designed in blocks, with the main streets numbered in binaries and the cross streets with ideographs I didn't understand.

Eventually, I came to a district that had street names—Elm, Jasper, Peony, and Windsor. The cobblestone lanes and shuttered stone buildings, some with stained-glass windows and spires poking from the roofs, led me to guess it was an old district, very old, maybe from even before Papa's time. The Citizens were tucked into shops and cafés, huddled in whispering groups. Probably a warning had been issued after the bomb went off.

At the top of a steep hill, I found a commissary with a sign on the door: *Returning in 12 minutes.* There was no time to wait, and I knew with a heavy heart that I had to resort to thievery. The door was unlocked, so I snuck inside and stole what would fit in the pocket of my knapsack: three tokens from the cash drawer, a few fractional tokens from the counter, a package of crackers and dried meat, a wool cap, a pair of tweezers taped to a round mirror, a bottle of lotion, and a large cotton scarf. I worked quickly to fill my water canteen, fearing the shop owner would come in, but the road outside was empty when I came out. With the new cap covering my head, I walked a normal pace, suspecting that confidence would be my savior.

The sun was fading into gray hues and a cool breeze came off the river, shaking a few yellow-green leaves from the trees. The smells of cooking stews and roasting chickens came out from the softly lit apartments. I passed a dog tied in front of a meat shop. The animal whined and barked sharply, looking over to me with dull, doleful brown eyes. I worried that the mutt would attract attention my way. Walking on, I knew I had to form a plan: remain in the city under a disguise or go home to certain recognition and punishment.

The moon had arrived, an obliging old friend, lighting a path to the shoreline where the leathery smell of soggy wood, fungus, and fish met me. A series of ropes and pillars surrounded a village of shacks and stands, some lit but others empty. At the docks, boats and rafts floated in the murky waves. Further from the shore, stationed at a long dock, was the largest vessel in the port. With three stories joined by spindly staircases, it appeared to be a fishing ship or perhaps a ferry. Three men stood near the dock's edge, dressed in canvas suits and rubber boots up to their knees.

I kept a distance, winding instead into the village toward the tantalizing smell of fish chowder. If only I could find a safe place to rest and a chance to eat. The fear and loneliness of the past two days had brewed into a sense that everything on earth was wretched. The memory of the bombed square came back insistently, eroding my strength. I stood at the river's cusp, separated from the dark water only by a rope, and let the tears come again. I missed them all so much, Papa and Perrin, the cats and the farm.

If I could get back home, even for a night, then I could accept what would become of me.

The moon seemed to pulse with confirmation—*Go home.*

Yes, I would go home.

Somehow.

The silent streets of the village were paved with uneven stones that slowed my pace. The shops and dwellings were tenuous structures, most of them with tin rooftops and charred chimneys. There was a small park that smelled of petrol, likely where the boat crews came for fuel, but it had a bench near a lamppost where I could hide behind a bush to eat my dried meat and crackers. The plump fish and salty flakes were delicious, so delicious I forgot my predicament for a while, lost in the simple act of eating. It was the first meal in months that I'd truly enjoyed. The canteen water was fresh and cold, but I allowed myself only a few sips. I then reclined on the hard bench slats and arranged my knapsack as a head pillow, laying my injured arm across my torso. Sleep came instantly, sucking me into a tunnel of easy amnesia. My dreams somersaulted through scenes of the farm, the CREIA campus, and places I'd never been that were permeated with warm, comforting light. In one dream, I walked alone in a garden of pink roses and entered a circular tower of stones and looked into a kaleidoscope of whirling colors. I was lost in its vortex, bodiless.

The dream, so peaceful and fulfilling, ended when I woke with a start. It was early morning and a brigade soldier, a man with angry red cheeks and shiny lips, was standing over me, jabbing a stick into my ribs.

"Get up, beggar," he shouted, revealing his broken, jagged front teeth. "No sleeping on the benches."

I rose and tried to rush off, but he commanded me to stop. "Where is your identification card?"

Somewhere in the bundle of things I carried was the photo identification card assigned to me before I'd left home. But I couldn't show it to the brigade because my name might appear on a list of fugitives.

"I lost it, sir." I held a hand to my face and looked down. "It fell out of my bag recently and I've been collecting funds for a new one."

The officer ordered me to face him. His tight eyes registered my body and face, taking in my limp, torn clothing and uneven hair.

"You're under arrest," he said. "For loitering and lack of identification."

He removed my knapsack and took hold of my wrists, wrapping them with a titanium tie. My heart sped with panic. I didn't speak or struggle, remembering to remain as though I'd never killed a well-known girl and possibly others, and kept my eyes down.

The cobblestone lane was busy with pedestrians who watched and whispered to each other when we passed. Inside a cinderblock patrol office, the guard motioned for me to sit on a wooden chair in front of a desk occupied by a white-haired man in a tan uniform. I kept my tied hands in my lap as he questioned me, worried that my knapsack could soon be searched by the red-faced guard.

The old man cleared his throat and typed into a machine sitting in front of him. The windows in the office were covered with blinds, each outlined with a frame of light. Outside, the day was going on without me.

I feared I'd never see the sunshine again.

"Your name?" the man asked. His white mustache was greased at the ends, turned up at the corners in points.

"Hollis Kiehl," I lied, also giving him my sister's date of birth and identification number.

"Please stand," he said, yawning and checking his wristwatch.

I stood up and—from the corner of my eye—saw that my knapsack had been placed, unopened, on the bench directly behind me. The guard who'd arrested me was sitting calmly at a desk across the room, writing with a pencil, a coffee mug at his side.

The mustached man pulled a metal tube from a case and flicked a switch to ignite a humming filament inside. A second later, the tube emitted a dull amber glow that crackled when moved even slightly.

"Hold utterly still," the man said, pushing the wooden chair aside and pulling off my cap. "Keep straight and calm; this will not be painful."

I tried to obey, but I was shaking with fear and could barely control the tremble in my legs. The man didn't seem to notice; he ran the lighted rod over the front and back of my body, starting at my boots and ending at my forehead. A few seconds later, the machine on his desk beeped and data appeared on the screen— text and two photos. One was me and the other my sister. I couldn't see them well, but hoped we looked enough alike that the recognition scanner had gotten confused. With my short hair, haunted eyes, and thin, sallow face, I might have looked more like my troubled older sister than myself.

"Well, you're recognized as a Kiehl from Naudiz," he ruminated, squinting into the screen and scratching his temple. "But which one?"

His casual attitude gave me hope. In the eyes of these village police, I was just a beggar from the park, not a criminal on the run.

"I'm Hollis," I insisted. "As I told you."

"But Hollis is dead," he said, reading from the screen. "Deceased seven years ago. The other result is Isla, age eighteen. A resident of the CREIA." He looked intently at my face.

I laughed. "Yes, they do think me dead, sir. Because they prefer it that way. But I'm very much alive, although cast out from the family fortune, of course." I gave a wry smile, inwardly impressed at the believability of my fake story. "My little sister may be at the CREIA, but I'd hardly know as I haven't seen any of my relations since I took off on my own. While I might be a homeless beggar, I'm still healthy and able to feed myself. If you could be so kind as to set me free, I can assure you I will leave your village straight away and never return."

The guard sat in his tattered chair and wiped his brow with a handkerchief. "Whoever you are, you are not to be trusted."

My heart fell as he extracted a rectangle of thin metal from a stack, inserted it into the black machine, and pressed a button that sucked the plate inside. After a short vibration, the metal emerged with a stamped imprint reading "Hollis Kiehl, warranted." My sister's identification number was printed below her name.

"Extend both hands," he ordered, picking up a set of shears.

With a few snips, he removed the titanium tie and replaced it with the imprinted triangle, winding it around my right wrist like a cuff, using a grommet tool to fasten it tightly. The warrant badge was uncomfortable and inflexible, making it difficult to move my hand in a natural manner. I could only be thankful that he hadn't put it on my injured side.

"The cargo freighter will take you downriver to Raidho. From there, take the bus to Central Terminal. Show this to the clerk to board the bus to Naudiz. Once you are there, you are required to go immediately to the court to pay your fine and acquire a hearing date. Do you understand?" He held a tiny recorder to my lips. "Say you understand."

"I understand."

He snapped his fingers at the brigade officer who'd brought me in. "Take her to the ship."

Under his stony gaze, I picked up my bag from the bench, settled it into its familiar place on my back, replaced my stocking cap, and followed the brooding officer out of the station. The orders echoed in my mind: *Ferry, bus, court, fine, hearing.* What would it lead to?

At that moment, however, it didn't matter; it seemed my bad luck had flipped itself around. After all, I had a ticket home.

~

The freighter was parked at the dock where I'd seen the group of fishermen the night before. Painted a deep dark green and stacked with long rows of brightly colored boxes and containers, the ship had a spindly tower topped with a flashing red light in its center story. From a distance, it looked like an enormous insect. I'd never been on a water vessel of any kind, not even a small boat.

"Move quickly, beggar," the guard said. "The ship is about to leave. We don't want you loitering around waiting for the next one."

I picked up my pace to match the guard's long strides and we made it to the freighter just as the crew was about to pull away from land. We stopped a few yards from the bottom of a short staircase leading up to the deck.

"What's this?" a square-faced man wearing a dull brown jump-suit shouted down at us. The patches on his chest and sleeve indicated he was perhaps the captain. He looked me up and down with an even, objective gaze, squinting beneath thick gray eyebrows. "Surely you aren't bringing on a prisoner this late?" A group of men in rubber boots gathered behind him, looking down on me with tired alarm.

"On orders from the brigade station," my guard answered, hesitant beneath the indignant stare of the questioning crew.

"A girl?" the captain asked, incredulous. "And so young?"

So I still looked like a girl despite my terrible hair and sallow complexion. Standing up straighter, I assumed an unthreatening expression.

"Orders from the station," my guard repeated. With a firm push against my back, I was thrust toward the staircase.

"Go up, girl."

I went up the stairs, self-conscious about my skewed appearance. By the time I was at the top, my guard had already turned away to return to his post. He sailed down the path like a marching ant in search of its hill.

"Unbelievable," the captain said, offering his calloused palm to help me on board. "Unbelievable. At the very last minute," he said. "A prisoner."

"My apologies," I replied. "Actually, I'd prefer not to be a prisoner." My legs were unstable on the shaky planks, and I tried not to look past the captain at the miles of blue water beyond us.

"Well, you can't sleep in our cage. There are men in there, bad ones. You hardly look like a prisoner to me. What did you do, girl? Don't tell me now, we must leave port." He pointed to a metal tunnel leading to a black space below the deck. "Go down and wait. I'll send someone for you soon enough."

A cloud of fear lifted as I slunk away and took the dark stairs into the dim, salt-smelling space below. I sat on a small wooden bench and took a sigh of relief as the ship powered up with a vibrating burst and pulled away from shore. Despite the captain's brusque manner, I had sensed kindness in the way he'd pulled me on board.

I spent my first afternoon on the freighter in the lounge, a cold room on the main floor with linoleum flooring and a row of plain plank tables bolted in place. Since I was the only female passenger, the captain had ordered the cook—an old woman with silver-toned eyeglasses—to monitor me. But she was busy preparing meals for the crew, vast pots of noodles to cover with thin red sauce and waxy flakes grated from bricks of hard cheese.

"Perhaps you could be trained," she muttered. "We could use a helper around here."

"I would help, but I feel awfully sick right now," I replied, not mentioning the kitchen experience I'd gained at the CREIA. The churning of the freighter against the waves was unsettling. After the cook gave me a tablespoon of baking soda in warm water, I felt slightly better and ate dinner along with everyone else, alone in a corner seat, wishing I had long hair again to hide my face from the sailors' inquisitive stares. When the cook came out with dessert, a creamy rice pudding, I looked up long enough to notice one of the men was younger than the others. Dressed in a navy jumpsuit and black rubber boots, he might have been my age or slightly older. He gave me a secretive smile and a quick nod.

I didn't smile back, but returned the nod and looked down into my rice pudding. The boy finished his own dinner and brushed past my table on his way to deposit his tray at the overflowing sink. I didn't look up, but followed the path of his boots until they disappeared.

"It's maddening how they toss these dishes around," the cook complained. "As I said, you could be trained to help. You wash dishes?"

I just nodded and wished to disappear because my injured arm had become hot and itchy.

"Perhaps I'll inquire with the captain," she said, returning to the steamy kitchen.

I slipped out to look for a private place where I could replace the bandage. Upstairs, I circled the main deck, breathing in the wet air and holding my face into the droplets splashing up from the dark river. During the hours I'd spent sitting in the lounge, the ship had stopped to deliver a stack of wooden crates and a mountain of burlap bags filled with beans. Through the cafeteria window, I'd watched the sailors carry the goods onto the embankment, pick up a stack of empty, discarded crates, and come back onboard. I realized then that the journey to Raidho could take some time, perhaps a few days, and that, with luck and effort, I could find a tool onboard to remove the metal wrist band.

"Hello," someone said.

The young man from the lounge had come up behind me. He smiled with encouragement when he sensed my hesitance.

The captain had said there were bad men on board, but I was somehow sure they were locked in a cage in the hull, not standing before me in plain sight. As the wind whipped between us, the boy motioned me to follow him down a set of short stairs, then down another set. When we were in the bottom level of the boat, I followed him into a wood-paneled room that held a table and long bar.

"It's not wise to stand on deck like you were," he said. "The crew will toss a net over you."

"They will?"

"They've been known to play jokes."

His name was Averitt, and he was the captain's son. He told me that he'd lived his entire life on board, except for breaks to take exams, attend funerals and ceremonies, and occasionally shop for supplies in the city. He had wavy light-brown bangs that sometimes fell into his eyes, a straight and square chin, and a way of pulling his mouth to one side in a smirk. His worn navy-blue jumpsuit was too tight in the shoulders and missing a top button. The cuffs were rolled up halfway, revealing well-developed tendons in his forearms. Around his waist was a black leather belt loaded with metal objects.

"We don't have many convicts like you," he said, "meaning that you're a girl. Most are men and boys. We did have a belligerent goat once. He was on his way to a soap farm."

The word "convict" stung at my pride. "I'm not a convict," I said, hiding the bracelet into a fold in my skirt. "Just cited for loitering and not holding identification." I wanted to mention my status as a resident of *Cherish the Past*, but thought better of it.

"Why don't you have identification?" Averitt asked.

"It's a personal story, and I can't share it now."

A loud whistle blew from above.

"That's for me." Averitt slid off the stool. "I've got to get on deck, but let me show you to your room first."

"Room?" I followed him back into the narrow space under the stairs where Averitt turned into a hallway that smelled of mold and gasoline. A roar overhead indicated that we were directly below the engine. We walked through a cleaning supply pantry, a laundry room, and then into another alcove, where he opened a door to a tiny space, no bigger than a closet, holding an aluminum cot made up with a thin pillow and a cotton blanket.

"You can sleep here," he said. "Usually, prisoners are in the hull, locked up, but since you're a girl, Father wants you by yourself. This is where the janitor sleeps, but he can stay in the bunks with us while you're here."

"Thank you." I only hoped he'd never find out my crime.

"You're welcome, Miss ... Miss what?" He held out a hand.

"Kiehl," I said, foregoing my first name. His hand was like a warm woolen glove over mine, so alive and comforting that I held on a moment longer than necessary. When we broke the clasp, it was as though we agreed to bring it together again soon.

"Good night, Miss Kiehl," he said, turning on the heel of one boot. He pointed to a door at the end of the corridor. "That's the bathroom. Watch out for the loo—it's low pressure down here." His eyes lingered on my face before he went off.

I quickly locked myself in the room and sat on the cot to remove my shirt and bandage. Nearly two days had passed since I'd been able to look at my wounded arm. The old bandage was limp and loose, useless. Underneath, the perforated skin was blue-red, swollen into a sensitive mound. The tube of ointment from my knapsack was flattened, oozing, but there was enough to cover the area one more time. The remaining length of bandage went around twice when tied tightly.

Never would I have found a hard, narrow cot so inviting and comfortable as I did at that moment. With my boots and clothing off for the first time in so long, I curled under the blanket and wrapped my arms around myself, breathing the stale air as the humming motor propelled me into a deep and dreamless sleep.

CHAPTER 17

*H*ollis. Sometimes the memory of her was faded, like an old and brittle sheet of paper.

I remembered her long dresses, calicos with lace trim, and the rambling wave of her hair when it hung loose. My sister had dark lashes, enviably dark, and slanted brooding eyes that could sweep silence over a conversation. She would take me by the hand and drag me along to the barn, through the garden, deep into the forest path where we hunted for mushrooms, truffles, and pawpaws big as pillows. When I misbehaved, she'd lightly slap me on the wrist or cheek. When she outgrew her clothing or decided she didn't like a certain hat or pair of mittens, I acquired them. When she needed a pair of hands to lift sections of her hair when braiding it, I was the one. Hollis ordered me to walk straight, sit with my legs crossed like a lady, to cover my knees, to be polite when talking to the bus driver or field workers.

But at some point, her proud bloom withered. My sister became less than what she was, quieter, her eyes intensely troubled. An intricate resistance formed around her, and it was secret and shaggy like the forest moss. It became impossible to pull her out, as it thrived in crevices and corners invisible to all of us. Hollis disappeared first for one night, then several, returning sometimes in the late afternoon where she would eat, wash, and sleep until midnight, when she'd leave again.

At ten years old, I understood that the house was quieter, that Papa's hair was white at the temples, that an angry ambition had overtaken my brother. Most of all, I understood that my sister's puzzling behavior shouldn't be mentioned. Sometimes I'd hear my father speaking to her sternly, but he spoke of things I didn't comprehend. As she was home less and less, and eventually not at all, I became the caretaker of all things female in our house. The trinkets of jewelry and hairpins, a crocheted purse, a sewing box overflowing with thread and notions, old buttons, gloves, and scraps of paper lying about. There might have been more I never saw, tickets and photos that Papa had held onto.

Then, one winter morning, Darden Knowles, Papa's good friend and the owner of the lumber yard, showed up at our door one winter morning to tell us that Hollis's body had been found on a shore in a distant town. No one ever told me the name of it. She was in a muslin nightgown buttoned to her chin, face bloated beyond recognition, her dark hair tangled with long weeds and roots. We buried her the next day in a cemetery of small, unmarked stones.

She was seventeen years old.

From the small janitor closet on the cargo ship, I remembered my sister's death, turning over each detail, reconsidered every shred of memory. The review seemed necessary because—technically—I was her; after all, the tight metal band on my wrist said so. The mirror tile in the toilet chamber where I brushed my teeth said so, too: the girl gazing back looked like Hollis might have in her final days. My cheeks had sunk into spaces I didn't know I had. It was only in my eyes that I recognized myself. I whispered my name and pulled my real identification from my knapsack and allowed the memory from the square to flood through my flesh.

On the morning of my second day on the ship, I brushed my short hair and washed my skin in the little bathroom, covering my head with a cap and pulling up my collar to cover the skin on the back of my neck where the LUSH stamp had branded me. There were no clean clothes to wear, but the hours of rest and hearty dinner the night before had helped with my nausea. Going up to the lounge at dawn, I stopped for a few seconds to gaze out at the horizon. We had traveled a long distance during the night and had likely stopped several times. In my deep sleep, I hadn't been aware of the activity on deck, where the crew had been delivering and picking up goods at the little towns and villages sitting on the riverside.

"How much further to Raidho?" I asked Averitt. We were in the card room, that's what he called it, after a breakfast of buttered bread and eggs.

"A few hours."

"So soon?"

"The river is only so long, Miss Kiehl. Will you ever tell me your first name?"

Hiding the wristband in my skirt, I admitted that my name was Isla.

The ship rocked from a strong wave. "Why does your tether say another name?"

So he'd already seen the stamp on the band. I imagined the sunlight hitting it as we ate breakfast in the card room. A strong wave caused a slight sideways tilt and I accidentally slid toward him. I tried to steady myself and keep a distance, but couldn't keep my left knee from hitting his.

"Don't worry," he said. "I won't tell anyone your secret. This is a ship and we have our own rules." He held out an arm as if scooping up the entire river. "There is no country here, no orders. No boundaries or institutions." He lowered his arm and shifted to lean on one elbow. "Did you know this river is covering what was once a civilization? If you put on a suit and dive in, you could swim around in it. I've done it. At one time, this river was a town of houses and roads, even highways. It's all still there, underneath us right now."

"What happened to all the people?" I asked.

"You know what happened. They drowned."

It was true. I did know.

"At home, we have a long strip of untended land," I told Averitt. "There are houses from all points in time." I reached into my bag and found the postcard. "This came from a metal box on the front porch of one of them. My friend Sorrel said it was common for Citizens to send messages to one another. Short messages with short sentiments on them. It was a practice they enjoyed."

Averitt looked at the card and stroked the illustration in the corner. "I've heard of this system from my grandfather," he said. "The number stamped over this tiny picture stood for an area of land. The continent was divided into thousands of them with a private box at every residence. There's a similar kind of box at the port of Raidho, but it's always empty."

So close to Averitt, I took in every inch of his face. Full eyebrows, elegant arches over his blue-green eyes. And there were very small, faint freckles at the top of his cheeks. I liked the way he smelled of cotton and fish. "What have you found under the water?"

"Nothing much. It's impossible to retrieve anything valuable because we don't have enough oxygen to get all the way down. And all the artifacts are crushed and crumbled. I usually look for dead bodies—bones and skulls." He seemed embarrassed. "I don't know why, but that's what I want to see."

The ship picked up speed, a reminder that our time together was evaporating.

"Please tell me where you came from." Averitt took my hand into his.

In the comfort of our clasp, I told him the whole story, starting with my arrival at CREIA, the holographic spiders and drugged water, the hours I'd spent in the bus, Mr. Drexin's assault, the bomb, ending with my arrest in the fishing village. I finally broke our grasp to pull my real identification from my knapsack.

"This is you?" Averitt asked.

The girl in the photo—she seemed like a girl to me, like someone I used to be friends with—looked out at us as if asking for rescue. She had long red-brown hair, full cheeks, and dark hazel eyes that, I realized, were nearly identical to her sister's.

"Yes. I'm Isla Kiehl. Hollis was my sister, but she died a while ago. And—there's something else I should mention." I withdrew my hand from his.

"What is it, Isla?" He tried to take my hand again, but I shied away.

"When I was in Peorth," I began, "after the explosion, I mean, I encountered a girl I knew from the CREIA. You might have heard of her—Ashleen Seranack. She's the daughter of the rogue governor. We had a confrontation and, in defense of myself, I dropped a grenade given to me by a rebellious man, one of the Unsaved." I exhaled, feeling less burdened, and pulled myself straight to look him in the eyes again. "The grenade ... I believe it killed her. Maybe another as well."

Averitt absorbed my confession. "I've never heard of the girl you named," he finally said. "And I've heard no news of her death or any others over our radio, although I did hear of the violent incident in the square. And you were defending yourself, Isla. If not them, it could have been you." He reached for my hand again, and I allowed it. "And I am very glad it wasn't you, and that you found your way onto this ship. We have a good home here, and I wish you could stay a while longer, even for just one more route up and down the river."

We fell silent, looking over the gray waves into the sky, the palest blue I'd ever seen. The warm clasp of his hand in mine was calm and soothing. For the first time since boarding, I felt hope that my trauma could come to a reasonable end, that I would not be viewed as a murderess but simply as one who defended herself. But the hope was fleeting; I had killed Ashleen and her death would be vindicated. Nothing could be more certain. For that reason, I had to get home as quickly as possible. My deepest wish was to see Papa and Perrin again before I was taken away, yet Averitt's offer to stay moved me in a way I'd never known. What I would have given to have both, to resume life without the guilt and shame that clouded every view of my future.

"I wish the same," I admitted to Averitt. "But the bracelet I'm wearing monitors everything I do, every place I go."

He pulled back my sleeve and examined the metal wristband, running his fingers over the tender skin around the bond. "Damn this thing," he said.

"Yes, it's tight and uncomfortable."

In my room earlier, I told him, I'd tried using my knife to cut into and remove the restraint, but its metal was much stronger than my blade.

"I'm expected to get on the bus at Raidho when I exit your ship, but I can't do that because someone could recognize me. They could even be waiting for me. I'm going to walk home instead and pray that the bracelet won't trigger an alert to the police."

My plan alarmed him, but he didn't discourage me. "Wait here," he said, jumping up as though he had a plan. He soon returned with a set of sharp, pointed metal jaws as large as Papa's pruning shears.

"If this doesn't work, I don't know what will."

When my forearm was stabilized between two blocks of wood nailed to a platform on deck, he was able to pinch about a millimeter of the band with the points and pierce a tiny cut into the metal. After a few seconds of grunting, straining, stopping and restarting, he sliced into the final section of the band, freeing me. We smiled in relief at the sight of my bare wrist.

"Thank you," I said. "You put yourself at risk to help me."

Averitt folded the cuff in half and threw it into the water. It sailed in a low arc, splashed into the froth, and floated for a few seconds before a wave swallowed it.

"As far as I know, you jumped overboard," he said.

I imagined the metal band falling through a school of catfish and landing in the wreckage of history. My sister and I would share a secret suicide.

The freighter began to shake and a few members of the crew came up on deck to anchor the vessel at the next stop—Raidho. I could see the town off in the distance; from the shore, it was a landscape of squares and peaks and clusters of trees. In the short time I'd been on board, autumn had arrived to transform the foliage into hues of fiery orange and aged green.

Averitt turned to me, taking my hands. "After you leave, I'll listen carefully to the radio news," he promised. "And I can perhaps trace back in the chronicle of events, finding out details about those who died in the bombing you endured. If there are names, hers will likely be listed. How can I find you again?"

The ship was pulling into port, sounding a loud, smoky horn. The crewmen threw out ropes and began to shout commands, anchoring us to the pier. The physical draw to shore also pulled us closer together. The proximity made my head light, my heart pound.

"My town is called Naudiz," I told him. "But I live in the countryside. Our neighborhood is called *Cherish the Past*—it's part of an educational tour. But I don't know what the situation is at my home today." I turned my face away so he couldn't read the emotion in my eyes. "I suppose what I mean is that I don't know where I will be."

"I understand." He helped me with my knapsack, adjusting the straps so it was on my back in a comfortable place. The crew was calling for me to leave, but we had a few seconds for a final goodbye. "But remember our name, the ship's name, it's called *The Hudson*. The next time we dock at Raidho, I'll put a card in the box for you. This isn't the end, Isla. I am hopeful and I am sure."

Averitt opened a cabinet behind him and pulled out a bright yellow cloth. "Take this with you," he said. "If you can ever come back, tie it to one of the trees on the pier at Raidho, near the dock." He nodded to the platform. "I'll stop the ship to pick you up. Even if there's no cargo."

I took the cloth and looked down when he pressed his lips onto my cheek. We clutched each other for another second, and I wished desperately we had a private moment, but we were far from alone and had to break our embrace under the eyes of the crew. One of the men winked at us. Averitt ignored him, pointing out the metal box on a pole in the distance.

"Goodbye for now," he said, helping me down. "I'll think of you every day."

I took in a last glimpse of Averitt before he slipped away to return to his daily work, to his father and the crew they commanded. And even though I felt vulnerable by standing in a spot where I could be recognized, I kept my eyes on *The Hudson* until the ship's silhouette blurred into the horizon.

CHAPTER 18

*A*rriving into the port at Raidho, I traveled around the pier and sat on a shady bench to unwrap the wound on my arm. Under the bandage, white pus was forming around the angry red gash. Pressure of more than a few degrees was nearly too painful to endure. I covered the wound again with the bandage, foregoing the ointment. What good was it anyway? I needed a doctor.

And I needed a map. At a commissary store, I kept my cap pulled down and bought a small wheel of cheese, more water for the canteen, and a block of aspirin. There were no maps for sale. When I asked the clerk which way led to Naudiz, he gestured toward the west. I decided to follow the water in that direction and hope that, eventually, I'd be on the bank of the stream running through town.

I walked with persistence, crossing every barrier, including a highway overpass. At times, the rugged woods kept me many yards from the riverbed and I had to use my senses to stay near the shore. Other times, I was just inches from the lapping waves, balancing the soles of my boots into the jagged rocky bank. At all times, I worried that I'd be seen by the cars and buses that occasionally came into view. In my worn clothing, thick boots, and stocking cap, I was a curious sight. I took a break in an isolated section of an overgrown field, lying in a spot of sun for a short nap and waking to gnawing hunger. Deep in my knapsack was the tightly wrapped salami I'd stolen from the CREIA during that first week. My knife cut into the thick plastic easily and I ate every bit of the oily meat while resting on a boulder.

The sunlight waned.

I shivered even in my thick sweater, facing the fact there was no choice but to spend the night outside. In a wooded thicket, I found a mulberry bush that had grown into and around a fallen tree, its weeping branches draped into a dark green inset. The new bedroom was comfortable after I laid down a floor of dry grass. I thought a fire would keep animals away—already I'd seen some coyote tracks—but there were no firestarters in my knapsack. What I did have was the mirror I'd stolen from the commissary. When held at a precise angle, the sun's dying rays heated and ignited a tinder bundle of twigs and brush I'd gathered. I dropped the burning bundle into a pyramid of sticks a few feet from my sleeping quarters and sat down with my legs crossed as the sky dimmed into deep gray and, eventually, blue-black spotted with countless sparks of starlight.

Nestled in the grassy bed inside the mulberry hut, I listened to the woods, focusing on an owl with a consistent and comforting hoot that helped me ignore the mysterious shuffles and brushes that could be coming from a hungry bear or coyote. The fire was strong, crackling and smoking from the circle of rocks I'd used to surround it. With my eyes closed, I imagined myself back at home in my real bed. There would be clean sheets and a warm quilt, and the familiar sounds of our house: the creaking floorboard when Papa or Perrin walked by, the splashing of the basin when they washed, the whistling winds over the field outside my window.

And then I thought about Averitt, the feel of his hand in mine, and his words: *This isn't the end, Isla. I am hopeful and I am sure.*

The yellow cloth smelled of dust and lake water, but it was a cushion of comfort as I drifted into a light sleep and dreams of difficult footsteps taking me in wide circles around a grove of cinders and mountains of sharp black twigs. The dawning sunlight arrived a few hours later, peeking through the leaves and the dried black husks of old mulberries, urging me to get started again.

The cold night had extinguished into a sunny morning. Sitting on a log near the charcoal pit, I ate some cheese and peanuts, and watched the birds fly around and call out from the trees; they came together in clusters, chirping out their directions for winter travel. Even though I had long ago lost track of the days of the week, I could tell from the naked tree branches and the crisp leaves on the ground that cold weather was at our door. If I hadn't been a fugitive, I might have even enjoyed those few minutes sitting alone in a beautiful, peaceful place.

The water canteen offered a few more drinks before I tightened my boot laces and resumed the journey, following the stream a few yards from its rocky bank. The highway I'd spotted the day before had ended and the area I traveled through was densely wooded and isolated without any marked paths. Snakes whipped through the tall grass and I had to avoid them by twisting through winding bushes and weeds to stay near the water. Eventually, the stream grew wider and the trees taller. I walked through a forest of slender pines and hesitated when I heard something unusual ahead in the distance—a mechanical rumbling and grinding. A half a mile or so later, I discovered the source of the noise. Tucked into a forest clearing was a small village of cabins circling a long building made of whitewashed cement.

Buried so deep in the wilderness, I speculated that the camp I'd arrived to might be a home for members of Seranack's brigade. Or, perhaps the opposite was true and the residents were outliers with their own plan of life.

Crouched behind a big oak, I watched as two bearded men dressed in dungarees, boots, and white cotton shirts came out of the building and waved in a big truck rumbling up a slope on the other side of their camp, sputtering to a stop inches from them. Another man in a blue uniform emerged from the building and they all talked to one another in earnest tones for a few minutes before opening the truck's bed to load it with dozens of plain boxes retrieved from the building.

A young woman about my age, maybe slightly older, came out of one of the cabins and stood at one corner of the cinderblock building to watch as the truck was packed. She had auburn hair in long waves and wore a coat made of furs sewn together.

Still well-hidden in the brush, I willed myself to stay still and take in every detail. It was obvious the residents of the cabins were making something; maybe it was whatever they were loading into the truck. A smoky smell hung in the air, a charred and pungent odor. Although I didn't see any people other than the three men and the young woman, there was a pleasant bustle rising from the small cabins and buildings, a sense that a worthwhile industry was taking place, one delivering prosperity to the residents. I could hear voices but couldn't make out words. From time to time, there were sounds of whooshing and sucking, as if water were being transferred through a set of pipes. The wet noises were punctuated with snaps and slides and I imagined that doors were being opened and closed. With conjured nerve, I peeked out and got a better look at the men, taking in a breath of shock when I recognized the younger one.

"Gareth," I said, shooting up from my hiding spot and running down the trail toward him. My boots sunk into the soft mud, but I felt as though I were running across clouds.

"Gareth!"

"Isla? How did you—?"

We embraced for a second, the curious eyes of Gareth's truck-loading partner—introduced as Tom—upon us.

"Come with me into the lodge," Gareth said. "We have a fire going and Elizabeth is making soup. She usually helps us with the loading, but it's not a good idea for her right now."

"What sort of work happens in this place?" I asked once we were inside, resting on a hard stool near the flames.

"Our job is to process plant pulp into paper," he said. "The paper is rolled up and piled into the truck outside. Tom drives it to Raidho, where it is then loaded onto a cargo ship."

I didn't tell Gareth about my injury or that I'd just been to Raidho and come off the vessel he mentioned. He didn't seem to be the volatile boy I remembered, but a sincere young man who had filed away the thoughts and wishes of his younger self.

"But aren't you living in the city? You were leaving the night I saw you at the commissary."

"I was never too sure about it," Gareth said. "After more thought, I went to your farm to speak with you again, but your father and brother said you'd been taken away by Ms. Hardin. They were panicked at your absence, but couldn't leave because of their responsibilities to the tour buses. I told them I would go off to find you, but I searched and searched with no result. Your brother then told me of this mill, where cheather and other fibers are fused and flattened into paper, and I came here to find work. The man who runs this place is of the right mind, and we are collecting our strengths to someday go forward with change in the city." The firelight revealed the tense furrow in his eyebrows. "What happened to your hair, Isla? And why are your eyes so wild?"

My cheeks warmed with embarrassment. "If my eyes are wild, it's because I'm a fugitive." I stood up with resolve. "My presence here puts you at risk. I should leave right away."

Gareth stood with me and was about to speak when the girl I'd seen outside—Elizabeth—came to the hearth.

"Have some soup first," she said. "Please."

The scent of mushrooms and cream lured me into accepting the offer. She poured the portions from the head of a long table, the ends of her russet hair falling over full breasts. When she turned to the side, I noticed the wide belt of her dirndl skirt was hiding a slight swell in her abdomen, a proportion inconsistent with her slender limbs.

"Here you are." She handed me the hot cup of soup and smiled politely, but I sensed a hint of wariness in her tone.

Gareth laid a protective hand just below Elizabeth's belt. "Another week to go," he said to me, as if that was explanation enough. I tried to keep my reaction neutral, but my blood surged with the understanding that Gareth, the one for whom I'd so strongly pined, was now another girl's love. But the baby in her womb—how could it be his in such a short time since I'd last seen him?

"I never expected to become a mother so young," she said as we ate the hearty mix of mushrooms, onions, and peppery cream, a curious silence hanging over us. "My family is from the mountains, but I always yearned to get out, agreeing to marry a man from the town below ours. He died of a virus right after I fell pregnant." Elizabeth ran her hands over her abdomen. "A group of traveling missionaries came through to anoint him and I left with their flock, hoping to find an income. This camp was one of their stops. I never left because I loved the woods and the productive work."

"They returned to marry us a few days ago," Gareth said, looking into his nearly empty bowl of soup.

I wanted him to know I wasn't hurt. I wasn't angry or disappointed or jealous. But the right words to express those notions were private, remnants of the natural force that had brought Gareth and me together that day at the commissary, and couldn't be spoken in front of the girl that fate had led him to. And I would be silent about his behavior with me as it appeared he had reconsidered his rude ways.

"Thank you for the soup," I said, rising. "I better return to my path before too much daylight passes."

They both resisted the idea of letting me go, but after a few minutes of earnest pleading, assurances, and insistence on my part, they allowed me to go off on the condition that Gareth lead me up the hill and ensure I was pointed toward Naudiz before resuming my hike.

"We don't have much food to give you," Gareth said at the bend. "But you should take this can of liver."

"No, please, no," I said, but allowed him to drop it in my pocket.

"I must mention something else," he said. "I was a crude ass on the night we met under the stairs. For that, I am deeply sorry."

We both smiled.

"I can excuse you with ease," I told him. "And I'm happy about your love with Elizabeth and the baby, but—" I stopped, remembering the eyeless child in Perrin's workshop on that night that seemed years ago. "There are many deformities among children due to toxins in the water. Perrin has found cheather to be a preventative. Perhaps if she were to drink it in some tea or take a tincture—"

He interrupted me with a finger to his lips. "You must speak in low tones, Isla. Our spot out here is not as secure as the camp. And, yes, Elizabeth is taking such precautions. What I must tell you is that, when you arrive at your home tonight, do not rush inside. Things there are somewhat different than when you left."

His words trembled in the air, and I was nearly too afraid to ask what he meant.

"A while ago there was a small fire in the cheather field," Gareth continued. "Your father rushed out with a water hose, but he fell into the flames and was badly burned."

"My papa," I said, the vowels choking in my throat. "He was burned?"

Gareth took me into his arms, smoothing the brush of hair under my hat. Fearful he would see the LUSH stamp, I pulled away and backed up.

"I must go now," I said. "Thank you for searching for me."

"Won't you stay with us tonight?" Gareth pleaded. "Daylight is already fading."

But I backed away and turned toward the bend with a wave of farewell.

Despite the interlude, my body was exhausted. I relied on the cooling wind to ease my fever as I pushed through the tangled weeds, fallen twigs, and the sickly chills tingling in my back and neck. The pain in my arm intensified but I carried on into the late afternoon, finally stopping to rest on a flat boulder to sip the last few drops of water and futilely hunt through my backpack for a cracker to go with the canned liver. I tucked the empty canteen into my bag, stood up on weary legs, and merged into the dusk. The path near the stream had opened into a narrow dirt road and walking had become easier. From time to time, I saw tire marks in the cracked muddy earth, a clue that the road had been used recently.

Just as the sun was setting, the trees thinned and the trail curved to reveal one side of a ramshackle wood fence bordering a vast field of clover. Bathed in the grassy scent, I closed my eyes for a second's rest and opened them again to take in the hovering orb of the setting sun. Climbing over the fence would be dangerous and risky, so I walked along one edge, stepping nervously in fear that a farmer or fieldworker could see me. The rushing sound of a car from the opposite end of the pasture lightened my heart. A paved road was close, so I pushed forward.

Moments later, I opened my arms and laughed.

There they were, running in the dying daylight, their silvery skin and gritty hooves tumbling toward me. It was the married couple, the dappled horses I had fed so many times while waiting for the bus. I climbed over the fence and met them in the field's center. The animals snorted and whined, demanding snacks I didn't have. I took a few seconds to stroke the wife's velvet nose. She butted against my hand—a sure request for a carrot.

"Soon, soon." I waved them off with a whisper, creeping to a quiet strip near the log fence partitioning the pasture from the road I'd walked so many times when going to school with Esme. My mind was dizzy, but I was now only a mile from home. I worried about Gareth's warning, that things were different, and I dreaded seeing Papa with scars and injuries from the fire. I had suffered my own abuses, of course, and explaining them would be nearly as painful as living them, but I was proud to be returning home to tell them of the freedoms I'd found—the thriving city, the unregulated freighter ship, and the organized effort to bring Seranack down.

The dizziness passed and I gathered the strength to carry on, focusing my burning eyes into the darkness.

While walking the road, I took in the familiar surroundings and strode along insecurely. Even though my final destination was close, I was arriving as a lawbreaker and fugitive. The owner of the horses, who could have seen me in the pasture, might have heard that a girl from Naudiz had escaped from the CREIA. And how would I announce myself to Papa and Perrin? They might have been punished for my recent escape.

Esme's house looked no different, still squat and neat, its bluish siding and tin roof shining in the moonlight, the back room lit with the yellow glow of an oil lamp. I imagined Esme's mother alone in her sewing room, basting a hem or trimming the frayed edges of a pant cuff, sadly absorbed in her work. She might be thinking of her daughter, wondering if she'd ever see her again. For a moment I considered knocking on the door. Would she take me in?

But the light in the house flickered off as if in answer.

With reluctance, I willed my fatigued muscles and joints to carry on. The wind was cold but I began to sweat because of the fast pace and the fever raging inside my flesh. I turned onto the dirt landing leading to our house and could see the rooftop slanting into the indigo night sky. Gravel scattered under the soles of my boots as I began to run, pushing forward with every ounce of energy I had left until arriving at the end of our front path, breathless.

Home.

I fell forward onto my knees and shrugged away the burdensome knapsack.

Home, with its fading paint and blotched roof, the sagging

eaves and overgrown boxwood bushes. Home, with the old rocking chair on the porch, swaying in wait for the next to sit with a bowl of beans. Home, with the heavy oak door, the one through which my mother's body had been carried. Home, with the scent of cheather and apples and the row of barrels where we made candles and butter and soap. Home, with the rustling sounds of the barn and the chattering squirrels. It was so close. It was right in front of me. But I couldn't step into the house with the night so cold and dark, with Papa and Perrin undoubtedly asleep and not expecting an intrusion.

Fighting a wave of vertigo, I returned the knapsack to my sore shoulders and snuck around the back side of Perrin's workshop. The door was locked but I could see the mess of vials and beakers littering the table, and the big stove supporting the usual set of large metal pots. I could even see the cage where he'd been keeping Aura. It was empty.

Behind the workshop stretched the cheather field. In the windy darkness, spiked shadows rose from the dry earth with determined resilience, their wavering leaves beckoning in silvery tones. I considered the mist above the plants, the intoxicating cloud invisible in the darkness. The plants had grown to harvest height and were as tall as I was, but there was an irregularity in the perfectly laid plots—someone had walked through many times, flattening the foliage into a path from the far-left corner into the strip of evergreens. I could make a camp in the old lot for the night and announce my presence to Papa and Perrin at sunrise.

The pollen fogging from the ripe cheather blooms lightened the way through the uneven mounds and occasional rocks. The golden moon was my only companion, a full bright eye expanding against a backdrop of blue-black and winking white stars. About halfway through the row, I caught a glint of light coming from a few yards ahead, off to the side.

I remembered the intrusive visitor, the one who'd arrived right before Ms. Hardin had lured me into her blue sedan. In a panic that whoever was inside the old dwelling would see my shadow moving in the field, I stooped to hide among the plants. I quickly lost balance, tripping in a patch of rocks and roots and falling face-first into the dirt.

An owl cooed, its cry echoing into the deepest part of my soul. With my last shred of will, I pulled up and tried to walk again, but a paralyzing fatigue gripped me as I wobbled toward the pines. As I wavered on the edge of the lot and tried to focus on the electric light, I heard a clicking sound. The door opened with a rush, spreading a fan of white over the spindly stairs where a figure stood tall and straight. It was a young woman with long curls, dressed in a flowered gown.

"Who's there?" she asked.

My vision was ringed with darkness, a spinning and sickening blackness.

"Who are you?"

Her cool voice passed across the night air, challenging me to answer. We were surrounded by the tall pines rising into the dawning sunlight.

"I'm—" But my voice stuck and I was aware of a shooting pain through my skull, then a creeping numbness in my injured arm. Both came with the certainty that I was not well, that my fight was not yet over, that in fact another journey—a more perilous one—was about to begin.

"I'm Isla." The words echoed as my knees buckled. "Who are you?"

I fell to the ground before she could answer, palms sinking into the earth. Fully collapsed, I laid helpless and unable to move. I listened to her come down the stairs and step toward me, the toes of her pointed shoes inches from my head.

"Isla," she said, stooping down and peering into my face. Through my delirium, I sensed hesitation and concern in her tone. "I've heard about you. Let me help you up. I suppose you should go to your house. Can you stand? Concentrate on your feet and legs." The young woman wrapped her arms around my waist, helping me rise. We traveled a few yards into the field, stopping when we heard a rustle and crunch ahead.

"Who's there?" she demanded.

Two tall plants were parted with the nose of a rifle—but the person behind them was not an intruder. It was my own dear Papa.

"Isla," he cried, laying down the gun and holding out his arms. "How did—"

"Papa! Is it really you?" I ran into his arms, overjoyed in his secure strength.

But then a blank and quiet blackness took me fully into an angry grip.

CHAPTER 19

I woke later that morning to the woodsy nuts and velvet butter smell of muffins cooking in the oven. The luscious scent filtered through the mesh of my soul, nourishing the flesh and bones of the one known as Isla Kiehl, the one I had been and wished to return to. Through the haze, I felt hands on my skin—supple hands equipped with cooling medicine. There was a trio of voices harmonizing and colliding, making decisions about my tights and sweater and the bandage on my arm. A cold cloth cleaned away smoke, dirt, and grease.

"She needs warm fluids," said a voice. "If she would only wake up soon."

"She needs a doctor," said another voice. "What have they done to her?"

"I'll put on her dressing gown." This came from a woman. "Boil water for the tea."

My mouth and throat were sore and dry. I could only wince instead of speak.

"Can you open your eyes?"

With tremendous effort, I swam the dense fog and remembered where my eyes were. Once located, opening them required mental strength. I finally saw the owner of the voice—the girl who'd escorted me from the lot—standing at the end of my bed. With long brown hair around a heart-shaped face, she was very pretty and familiar in a way I couldn't place.

"She's awake," the girl called out. "Mr. Kiehl, Isla is awake!"

The young woman introduced herself as Janie Frost. She helped me sit up in my bed, supported my head with a pillow, and explained that she hadn't meant to surprise me the night before but had come out only because of the strange sounds she heard while folding laundry in her trailer. Thank goodness she had; otherwise, she said, I would have fainted in the field without anyone knowing.

"I was about to go to bed, but heard something outdoors."

Across the room, near my closet, was the tattered bag I'd carried for so long; the very sight of it seemed to trigger the pain in my arm. Pulling away the bedcover, I saw the wound had been covered with a cotton wrap, but the ache inside was as strong as ever.

"Thank you," I told her. "I feel as though I'm in a dream, being here in my bedroom."

Janie stood up to adjust her chestnut hair in my bureau mirror, tilting her head to avoid the chipped section. She turned and smoothed the wrinkles from her skirt. "Your papa and brother have been panicked at your long absence," she said, arranging my blankets, "but I told them not to fret so excessively. They told me you were at the CREIA and must have been held. I've been to the CREIA myself, you know." She sat in the wooden chair beside my bureau. "You've been unconscious for several hours. What do you remember about being there?"

Papa came in with a small teapot. "Dandelion root," he said. "Won't taste good, but should take down the swelling. Perrin is making a pumice for your wound. There's something very small deep inside your arm that must be drawn out."

Janie held back my hair while I took tiny sips from the cup.

Papa watched with worried eyes. "What have they done?" he asked. "Tell me what they've done to you."

My mind tripped around to recount the blurred and disorderly sequence of events. When I began to speak, my words were at first weak and hesitant, then more strongly spoken and certain. I told them of Ms. Hardin's trickery, my escape, the bus ride, the time in the city, my arrest, the trip on the cargo freighter, and the long walk back to the farm. I didn't mention the confrontation with Mr. Drexin or the grenade I'd thrown at Ashleen.

"Why did you cut your hair so roughly?" Papa asked. I noticed the burned scab on his forearm, a streak of dark red.

"Because I am now a fugitive. That's why I tried to hide in the lot instead of coming inside. Has anyone come looking for me?"

"We've heard nothing about your escape and no one has asked about you," Papa said. "But not long ago, an officer arrived to tell us there would be no more tour buses to any of the homes in our program. No reason was provided, but they took down all the official signs and told me to think only of ourselves from now on."

I was about to ask about the fire that had burned his arms and hands when Perrin appeared in the doorway, a cat under each arm. "We have two felines on the farm now because Isaac returned from his wanderings while you were gone," he explained. "He and Aura decided to mate, and kittens are on the way." The two cats were plump, wide-eyed, and twisting from his grasp to walk the blanketed landscape of my bedcovers. I ignored the pains of my body and petted their heads, enjoying the grassy animal smell and demanding meows.

Janie took my empty teacup, standing to allow Perrin to claim the bedside chair. They seemed to be friends, I thought, comfortable with eye contact and brushes between their bodies.

"I barely recognized you last night," my brother said, holding one hand to my forehead. "What happened to your long hair? You look like you fell in the threshing machine."

With my good arm, I patted the uneven haircut and arranged the longer strands around my neckline. The LUSH stamp was behind my bedclothes, but I felt the need to ensure its secrecy by holding my head rigidly.

"I had to cut it with a knife," I told Perrin. "To become unrecognizable."

He adjusted his glasses and accepted a tray of supplies from Janie. "Let me examine your arm and apply the poultice." With the bandage off, he applied the warm mush of ginger, garlic, and cheather to the wound, wrapping my limb loosely in a fresh band of cotton. "Sit still and allow it to soak. In a while, I'll try to purge the object inside. What is it, do you know?"

"A needle," I told him. "Broken under the skin."

"What happened?" Papa demanded, but Janie spoke before I could answer.

"I've been to the CREIA myself," she said again, circling Perrin to clean up the bowl and wet rags he'd used to make the poultice. "And the girls are subject to many physical exams."

"Yes," I agreed, willing to stall the explanation. Although I appreciated her diversion, I was increasingly curious about her knowledge of the CREIA and how she'd come to live in our old lot.

"Suddenly I'm very hungry," I told Papa. "Could you please bring me a muffin with butter? And some grapes." I knew our dark-red grapes would be ripe on the vines, plump and delicious.

"I made the muffins just for you, my Zasha," he said, standing. "Perrin will get you the grapes. The vines are loaded down because you haven't been here to pick them as usual."

"I'll get some radishes, too," Perrin said. "They've been growing tall and no one likes them but you."

Once I was left alone with Janie, I continued the conversation we'd started before Papa and Perrin had come in.

"My father and brother seem to like you very much," I said, shifting my position to keep the poultice from seeping out of the bandage. The medicinal concoction was doing its work; the angry sting meant the infection was under attack. I listened to the cats purring and felt their healing power. "How have you become friends?"

"I met them both a few days after you left." Janie leaned

forward and spoke quietly. "I can explain my presence, but please keep my words a secret," she said. "My father insists on hiding me here. He's a member of the Lower Polity, very powerful, and I was born to him off the record. For most of my life, I lived with my aunt and uncle in Ironcove, but when I came of age—I'm twenty-one now—my aunt unexpectedly asked me to leave. It was my father who knew of this place, the abandoned houses and trailers left without occupants. He promised to restore one to suit me, but when I arrived it was in terrible condition without even electric power or running water. Soon after you disappeared, my generator caused a fire that spread into the cheather field."

"That's how Papa was burned?"

"Yes." She took a breath and lowered her eyes, which I noticed were strikingly light blue. I knew those eyes from somewhere, I thought, and a coldness settled into my ribs. "That was how I first met them."

Aura mewed and settled her warm body against my leg. I stroked her head, feeling the bliss of wellness. "And why were you at the CREIA?"

Janie stood and moved to my window, pulling the thin curtain over the glass. "When I was eighteen, my mother took me there for a ceremony in the hope that I would stand out in some way and make my father proud of us. But he became angry instead, accusing her of putting him at risk. I was there only for a few days, then sent back to Ironcove."

Papa and Perrin interrupted us with a tray of apple muffins, butter, grapes, radishes, and sour cherries. Janie excused herself to go home, promising to return later, and left us alone. Although I was unable to eat much, the muffin and grapes infused me with an optimism that all would be well, perhaps, and that no one would come for me.

Perrin removed the bandage and pronounced it time to perform the small surgery required to remove the needle.

"Brace yourself for a bit of pain." He swabbed the wound with peroxide and gripped the spot with such force I had to bite my lip to hold in a scream. But the tip of the offensive needle emerged within seconds. He used a pair of sterile pliers to extract the segment and lay it on a cloth. The slender tube, smaller in diameter than the spoke of a dandelion seed, lay in a smear of blood on a white handkerchief.

"You walked a long way," Perrin said, standing. "I'll let you rest. Later, if you're strong enough, I'll call Janie back again and she can help you take a bath."

"Does she sleep alone in the lot every night?" I asked.

"Well, of course." He gathered his surgical supplies and went to the doorway, turning back to appraise me from the doorway. "Let the cats stay with you for a while. Everything is going to be fine, Isla. You're home."

A few days later, with my arm nearly healed, I was restless from the long bed rest. Perrin and Janie proposed a picnic, so we went with Papa to the walnut tree, far from the road, laid out a tablecloth and set out a loaf of bread and a ring of bologna. We prepared our plates and ate quietly, half-listening for what we were all worried about: an arriving car in search of me.

It was Papa who brought up a solution. "I believe it's best if Isla stays in the barn from this point onward," he said. "Eventually I'll have to find a way to have her declared dead so there will be no more concern of her capture." He exchanged a glance with Perrin.

Dead? I was already dead to who and what I'd been before. I explained to Papa that Staris had promised to tell the CREIA that he'd killed me, but Papa said the town bus driver wasn't to be trusted.

"He's an erratic character," Papa continued, "who skirts around the law when it suits him, but plays it nice with Polity to keep his driver position. No matter what he said, it's better if no one knows you are here. Over time, the people who care about your escape or encountered you along the way will forget and move on. In the meantime, you'll be safe and secure in the barn with plenty of company among the goats and ponies." He chuck-led. "In fact, those rascals could use an eye on them at all hours."

I understood Papa's way of thinking, but he didn't know I'd killed a girl. I thought of Averitt, who had pulled off the tracking band and tossed it into the water. The memory of him and the closeness we'd shared cast a stone of sadness into my heart. I wondered what he was doing at that very moment. Would he think of me again, or would he—as Papa had said—forget and move on?

Back in my bedroom later that afternoon, I untied my satchel and spilled the contents onto the floor. There was the knife I'd used along the way to cut my food and strike tangled branches from my path. Wrapping it in a clean cloth, I stored it at the bottom of the bundle of belongings I would take to the barn. Next, I found a pencil often shared with Esme and thought of my friend with wistful despair.

The last item on the floor was the rebel newspage handed to me by Alexander the day before his death. I unrolled the long sheet, which smelled of smoke and ink, skimming the headlines. Most referred to people and places I didn't know of, but I did catch one about Ashleen, who was referred to as "Seranack's eldest daughter." The article admonished her for attending the CREIA to participate in the "frightful genetics project that makes a travesty of humankind." The writer of the article hadn't known the aloof girls had visited only to promote Ashleen's cosmetics, or perhaps because they were bored.

And now she was dead.

CHAPTER 20

*E*very time Janie came across the field to visit us, she was quickly whisked away by my brother. He said they were just stirring up and bottling the cheather tincture for delivery to a new cancer pharmacy, but through the small square windows, I could see them laugh and brush against each other, giddy with lust, kissing without discretion. Perrin would stroke her long chestnut curls and whisper in her ear. Janie would smile. From my home in the barn loft, I'd pretend to know nothing.

Conferences of blackbirds spiraled the sky, announcing the first snow would soon fall. With the old postcard in my skirt pocket, I walked alone one day to the old lot to visit the small yellow house where I'd found it so many years before. I circled the rough path bordering the relics of lives lived and lost, understanding that we too would someday be nothing but dusty fossils of things we owned and used. I was beginning to see that Papa's diligence toward tradition was not so tiring after all, that he was right in putting value in such things. Walking home, I decided to write the story of my lived days on paper, so that perhaps someone of the future could read and know the events of my time in the world.

And I would live these days, I vowed, as the best of myself and those before me.

We were in fear of every car that passed, that it might signal my arrest. I continued keeping the knowledge of Ashleen's death to myself, covering my head and face with a scarf as I walked over mounds of fallen leaves to the house for meals and to bathe. I made egg sandwiches and crocks of broth for lunch, candied nuts and thin crackers baked with salt and cheese, filling the kitchen with the warm smell of butter.

"Your food is delicious," Perrin said.

"Yes, delicious," said Janie. She didn't meet my gaze, still avoiding the story she'd begun on the day I'd returned. They left the dishes to me with a claim that more important work was on hold in the workshop.

My barn bedroom was the uppermost loft, two flights above the ponies and well-hidden behind walls of stacked hay bales. I arranged my toiletries and flashlight along a narrow crossbeam and hung a fan from the rafter to bring a breeze through the window. I sewed a mattress from muslin bags, stuffing it so tightly with chicken feathers that the seams strained when I laid down. Yet it was a comfortable bed. With the animals snorting and shuffling below, I slept in a deep cloak of security knowing that any intruder would be loudly announced with an orchestra of whinnies and stomps. When night came, I'd bury under a thick quilt with the cats and look up to the night sky to trace designs in the stars and make wishes on the first ones to appear. I asked them for reassurance that my soul would recover from its trauma and prayed that no one from the CREIA would ever appear at the door.

In the deepest level of my thoughts and fears, I wished with all my being for protection against the authorities that were likely looking for me.

Or were they?

The road outside the farm was often so quiet I could hear the gravel shifting in the breeze. Cars occasionally passed, some speeding, others slow, but none stopped. I began to have faith that Staris's lie about my death had effectively convinced Rielle and the others that I'd never made it home. And even if the officers in the fishing village figured out I wasn't my sister, they would have tracked the tether to the bottom of the lake and made a supposition that I'd committed suicide, meeting my demise in a tangle of watery weeds.

As time passed, I began to accept that my new life was encased in the fictitious death symbolized by the broken bracelet in the river. But Mr. Drexin's rubbery lips and his forceful needle into my flesh quivered in the canals of my memory, a drape of denial pulled over a window. To open the drape, I felt I had to tell others what I knew.

I had ample paper and pencils, but when I took them up to craft my tale, the words refused to appear on the page.

∾

Three weeks into my confinement, a car arrived in the driveway. The black vehicle parked near the hitching post as I watched through a corner of the loft window. Two men, both in twill work clothes, short hair and beards, crossed our front lawn and traveled up the porch steps. The older of the two knocked on the front door, three short knocks that interrupted the icy peace of the cold morning. No one answered—I suspected that Papa was out taking measurements and that Perrin was feeding the mules—so the man kicked at the door with his boot, shouting, "Open the door."

I was angry at his coarse behavior, but couldn't make myself known and withdrew from the window to huddle behind a bale of hay. After sitting there for such a long time that my hunger was unbearable, I came out to find the car gone, the house sitting as though nothing had occurred.

"Who were they?" I asked Papa, finding him in the kitchen where he was cutting potatoes into squares. "Did you see them?"

"Saw them and spoke with them." He rubbed his forehead. "There is news you should know. Mother Cordish went to her God several weeks ago. The two messengers you saw came this morning with an order from her eldest son, the one who takes her chair." Papa poured the potatoes into his dented metal stockpot. "We are to prepare the lot for new residents, many of them, who will arrive to clean up the old houses and trailers for their own use. Our project is no longer for us alone. Others will come to live among us, and there will be no respect or regard for our family legacy."

"Oh, Papa," I said, leaning against the counter. "That's terrible." But, inside, I was set at ease by the news. The men hadn't come for me, but for an unrelated reason that could even be to my advantage. With a larger population around us, I could perhaps emerge from seclusion occasionally without notice. Maybe some of the new residents would be interesting, kindly folks who would make our lives less lonely. And we'd worry less about rats and cockroaches with the lot dwellings renovated and improved.

"I can sense your thoughts," Papa said. "While this may not be the worst situation, the many unknowns must be immediately addressed. This afternoon, I will gather our almanacs into the wagon and ask Perrin to take them to Darden Knowles' paper mill. Perhaps he can go next week, on a morning when it's quiet and still. The history inside them is the people's greatest treasure, one that cannot be degraded by the Cordishes or anyone else. The books can be kept there under the floorboards."

When Perrin came back in for lunch, Janie at his side, he readily agreed to the trip.

"Janie will come with me, of course," he said.

"The messengers didn't mention your presence in the trailer," Papa said to Janie. "Have you been informed of these impending new neighbors?" He was always polite and reserved with her, I'd noticed.

"No, no one told me anything," she said, looking down at her plate. Without another word, she began to eat her grains.

~

Like an old friend returning, my hair grew to my shoulders and covered the mark on my neck. I gained weight and felt more secure in the boundaries of the farm, beginning each morning with a trip to the house to make black tea for us before going to the chicken coop to collect eggs from the squawking hens. I hid my ID card in a birdhouse swinging from the cherry tree, kept my hair in a scarf, and pulled the eyeshadow from the trash pail to darken my eyes. When I wasn't doing chores or eating meals, I sat with the cats in the loft and knitted a set of squares for an afghan. With a scrap of stiff leather, I cut out and sewed a waist holster for my knife and wore it around my thigh day and night. Aura soon birthed a litter of three gray tabbies and I watched them grow from pink wriggling forms into plump kittens chasing each other in the rafters.

I thought of Esme and the fun we'd had together as children, the many walks to and from school, the way we'd giggled and flushed when sewing our gowns, the way she'd condemned me for liking Gareth Teague, the slant of her dark eyes revealing that she was jealous I had his attention.

"I'm cursed with the memories," I told Aura, who would only purr and knead her feet into my thigh as I tried to write my thoughts without success.

Sometimes when Papa was napping or had gone to town, I'd sneak to the orchard to a strong branch that held my body well, nestle into my coat for warmth, and watch the workers till the cheather field in preparation for next year's planting. Under the gloomy sky, their drab figures bobbed in the distance, outlined against the light film of pollen clearing into the cold.

One day I was dusting the pantry in the kitchen and noticed there were only a few jars of green beans and peach preserves, and no tomatoes at all.

"You weren't around to do the canning this year," Papa said from his desk when I asked him why. "Your brother and I didn't give it a thought." He motioned for me to sit in the chair across from him, patting the seat the way he did when there was an important discussion to occur. I remained standing.

"When I'm forever gone—and that day will come," he said, "both of you must take over the farm."

"Of course," I said. "I can't go anywhere but here. But Papa ..."

He inched back his chair and considered me with a shifting gaze. "I'm concerned at the way your brother carries on with Janie," he said.

At that moment the two of them were in the workshop, clinking bottles and laughing behind their closed curtains. Janie was with us every day, all day, leaving just before dinner if she didn't choose to stay.

"I've told Perrin to keep his distance," Papa continued. "To no effect. I'm not sure where she comes from and who's watching her, and she changes the subject when asked about it. I can no longer count on him. That's why I must begin to educate you about operations you've previously been uninvolved with. You were once in charge of canning green beans, and now you must take on some new responsibilities. I want to teach you record-keeping." He waved to the desk ledger penciled with hundreds of tiny entries. "To predict the rise and fall of the sun and the moon, the temperature of the earth, to measure the rain, snow, and wind."

"You mean, write an almanac?"

"Yes, the almanac. Although we cannot keep the old ones here any longer, we must continue the work."

"But who uses the almanac, Papa? Only you."

"The tradition is what matters. Learn, listen, and you'll soon understand."

Sitting at his paper-strewn desk, I tried to pay attention to his first lesson on moon phases. It had been a long time since I'd been so close to my father—when had his hands taken on so many freckles and warts? The bushy sideburns running from his temple to jaw were gray as steel.

He pointed to a drawing of crescent shapes and a penciled sliver. "See here." He cleared his throat and squinted, holding the paper far away from his face. "This is the moon at ten percent."

I nodded. "Papa, give me your shirt later today and I'll sew it a new button."

"Pay attention." He sat back with a scrutinizing gaze. "I thought you had matured and strengthened your mind while you were gone, but maybe not."

"I'm sorry. You're right, I'm sorry, Papa." As I spoke the words, a commitment firmed itself and I made a mental promise to review his instructions every night before bed. "Show me, Papa. I'll pay attention now."

I learned not only the lunar phases that afternoon, but also the names and qualities of the full moons. The day following was a lesson on humidity, then one on dryness. We walked the farm to gather samples of soil and condensation, woke in the black morning to precisely time the rising sun, sat together outside the barn at night to observe the constellations through the clouds. I gauged the thickness of the ponies' bulking coats and counted the woodpecker population in each tree to assess the hardiness of the impending winter. We ignored Janie and Perrin's reckless laughter in favor of treks to the woods to count mushrooms and record the absorbency of the ground. We watched the sparrows and finches cluster in the eaves. I learned to make pencil markings in Papa's ledger sheets, to use the ruler to measure out new ledgers, to file the sheets into a broad wooden drawer.

"Do you think I should hide forever?" I asked him one day, ripping a long sheet from its adhesive strip.

Papa was at the window watching Perrin, who was raking pine needles over the bare plots.

He didn't answer my question but made an unrelated pronouncement that surprised me. "Your brother is planning to move Janie to the mill," he said, arranging some papers into a stack. "They'll be leaving in a few days. She will stay, but he will return to continue his science. Now, where are my eyeglasses?" he asked with a pat on his back pocket to confirm its emptiness. "Out on the porch?"

He left me alone in the study, questions circling. Why would Janie go to the mill? She could live with us should the newcomers invade the privacy of her trailer. But, even more pressing was why Perrin would let her go. The two were obviously in love.

Love.

The very word made my spirits sag. Trapped in the prison of the barn, I saw no route to love, to the pleasure of companionship and promise of motherhood. I'd always longed to be a mother, but the hands of destiny had perhaps turned me onto a road with all routes closed.

The first winter storm arrived that afternoon. Puffs of snow flitted from the clouds to bury the cleared field and the browning lawn in front of our house. Lighting a fire in the barn was too risky with so much dry straw around, but I had a small stove to fill with hot coals that glowed angrily from their little nest. It was enough to keep me and the animals comfortable, and our stack of coal was plentiful thanks to Perrin's trips into town.

One quiet afternoon, thinking of a dusty guitar we owned, I climbed into the attic to retrieve it and hunt through some of my mother's things. There was a pair of scissors shaped like a bird, a jar of tiny glass beads, and a tin of talc powder with Russian words on the label. I also found a coat made from burgundy wool. Lined with creamy satin and edged with scalloped trim, it had been carefully preserved in a wood trunk, nestled in pine chips. When I walked out to Perrin's workshop, the hem dragged in the grass, catching the frost. The sleeves fell over my fingertips.

"Janie will take it," Perrin said. "She has no wool coat at all, only cotton, and you have your old one."

"I suppose." Handing it over to him, I wished that my frame filled the garment properly. "Was our mother tall?"

"Taller than you." He supported the coat on a hook and brushed it with his hands. "Can you make liver for lunch? It'd be good if you'd fry it in some fat and onions."

Janie arrived and tried on the coat, which fit her perfectly, the hem skimming just above her ankles, the cuffs landing at her wrists.

"Thank you," she said, allowing Perrin to take her into an embrace. "It's a beautiful coat. And so special."

We spent the rest of that afternoon telling her about our mother, explaining—among other things—how she'd been sent from her country to ours, her marriage to Papa arranged by the elder women of their church. The stories were shadowed fragments pulled from the attic of memory. But, once spoken, they rained upon the haunted thoughts holding me hostage, those fresh and fearful memories of the fourth-floor room and Mr. Drexin. Later that night, with an easy will and Aura purring at my side, I lifted my pencil to paper and was finally able to write.

CHAPTER 21

I woke at sunset, my writing on the floor, feeling uneasy. Aura had left her usual spot at the end of my cot to perch on the windowsill, sniffing into an open crack in the shutters. The fire in the stove had burned down, and my teeth chattered as I pulled on my boots and clothes and slid down the steps to replenish the coal, tripping along the way. The crunch of the coal landing in the stove must have deafened me to the sound of Janie running through the snow. It was the way she frantically jiggled the lock from outside that I heard first. The cats fled in different directions, scrambling into the lofts. I dropped the poker onto the floor and backed into the nearest pony stall, leaving the stove wide open, flames licking the air around it.

"Open up, open up," Janie cried, pounding the door. "Are you there? Let me in, please!"

Then I realized the pounding was coming not just from Janie, but also from a further away place—someone was pounding on the front door of our house, too. After I ran forward and released the lock, Janie slipped in and motioned for my silence with a finger over her lips. She was in my mother's red coat, a linen nightgown beneath, and a pair of battered canvas boots I recognized as the CREIA standard issue. She pulled me into an empty pony stall behind a stack of hay bales.

"Stay completely quiet," she whispered. "There's a car outside."

A crater in my soul opened, taking my blood as its sand.

"A car?"

"Shhhh, be quiet," she said, wrapping her arms around me. "Don't move and be silent."

The coal fire flourished outside the stall, casting a warm flicker into the dim space where we sat trembling. Even though I wanted to ask Janie exactly where she'd seen the car, my mind was paralyzed with fear and words were impossible. And I hadn't reset the lock on the barn door. Minutes passed and we gradually loosened our grip on one another. But just as I was about to suggest that the danger had passed, the ponies at the front stalls set off with nervous stomps and whinnies. The car was driving toward the doors, casting its white headlights through the fire's glow.

"She's here," Janie whispered.

She?

We listened as the car door slammed and a pair of feet crunched into the snow. After a firm knock, the door slid open and we heard footsteps on the floorboards.

"Janie?" a woman called. "Please speak so I know where you are."

"That's Ms. Hardin's voice," I whispered, my chest turning to ice. How did Janie know Ms. Hardin? I remembered the way my former teacher had so sweetly helped us prepare for the circle ceremony at the CREIA, the way she'd kindly brushed and braided my hair, the way she smelled like flowering chives.

Janie pressed into me. "Shhhh."

A morning sunbeam tricked down from the loft window, spreading light onto the haystacks fortressing us. The footsteps stopped, pivoted, and came toward us.

"I see you hiding back there," Ms. Hardin said in a sharp tone.

"Who is with you?" Over the rushing wind came a series of mechanical clicks.

"Janie? Answer me. Who is with you?"

"Don't shoot," I said, standing up on shaky legs and holding my arms over my head. "We're right here, Ms. Hardin. What do you want?"

"No," Janie sobbed and huddled into the hay bale. "No."

But I stepped forward.

In the dusty light falling through the beams, Ms. Hardin was smaller than I remembered, her stark white hair chiseled at the jaw, cheekbones sharp and angled under a stony and condemning gaze. She wore the CREIA uniform under a black twill coat. Her pale lips were pressed into a tight line. At the sight of me, she lowered the small white gun to one side, eyeing me with surprise.

"Well, what's this? I didn't come for you, Isla. But it's interesting to find you here."

I considered my defenses. The coals in the stove, still crackling. The knife around my thigh. A hysterical scream to bring Papa running. Ms. Hardin stepped closer, eyes simmering, the gun now pointed toward me.

"Staris said you were dead," she continued. One of the ponies shuffled in his stall and whinnied. "I should have known better than to believe him."

"You lied to us, to all the girls," I accused. "We thought—"

Ms. Hardin thrust the pistol forward. "Don't be a fool." The gun trembled in her tight grip. "Come around the haystacks and fall to your knees."

I knew I should beg for my life, but my throat closed against the plea. I knew it had been my will to live that had brought me to this very moment, the moment when—ironically—it could all end.

I fell to the ground and held tense.

"Don't you dare shoot her, Mother," Janie said, stepping from her hiding spot in the hay. "Let her go. She won't tell anyone about us. Just let her be, let them all alone."

Mother?

So that was Janie's secret. With my eyes locked on Ms. Hardin's boots, now joined by Janie's, I flipped through the clues that had always been there, so loosely tied that I'd never formed the knot of realization. The way Janie had seemed familiar at first —it was because her features were like Ms. Hardin's. I dared raise my eyes to behold the two women in front of me.

"That's what you would like, isn't it?" Ms. Hardin snapped. "To go off with that farm boy so I'd never see you again. Forget it. Your father and I have a young man for you back in the city. He's a Polity with a good station."

"I don't care about your plans," Janie pressed on. "I'm in love with Perrin and we've made our own plans."

"Perrin," Ms. Hardin sneered, waving the gun. "Is that what you want? Life on a farm?"

"Yes, I do. Better than being a sad old wench like you."

"Get in the car," she snapped, then turned to me. "Isla, stand and put your hands over your head. Don't try anything. I will shoot if I have to." To verify, Ms. Hardin pointed the gun at my head as I stood on shaky legs and raised my hands.

"You better not—"

Janie's words were interrupted by footsteps crunching in the snow outside.

"What's that?" Ms. Hardin turned around.

"Isla?" Papa rattled the door.

"Papa, no!"

The door slid open.

He had just a moment to take it in: Janie in the red coat, me running toward him, Ms. Hardin with the gun. I saw him back up a step and then the shot came, hitting him in the side of his neck. My papa stumbled sideways, hit the stove, then landed in a pile of straw.

Motionless.

Dead?

My ears rang. There was a smell of gunpowder, and the ponies screeched and thrashed in their stalls. Ms. Hardin turned to me with a shuddering gasp. The pistol fell to the floor, landing softly in the straw.

"Isla." Her face was as pale as her platinum hair. "I'm—I'm sorry."

PART IV
TRUTH

*M*s. Hardin found her pistol in the straw and used it to order me away from Papa's motionless body. He couldn't be dead, I thought in panic. But, if not, why wasn't he rising to slap the gun from Ms. Hardin's hands?

The three of us stood together, stunned.

"Maybe he's still alive." My words were hollow with grief, the vowels choked. "We have cats who can—"

"Quiet." Ms. Hardin's face was tight with tension. "This wasn't supposed to happen. Now I'll need to start a fire." She slapped Janie hard, leaving a streak on her pale cheek. "It's your fault. You weren't where you were supposed to be and now you've brought us into this miserable accident." She ordered me to find a harness and tied Janie's hands with the belt of her CREIA uniform. After I was finished, she ordered me to turn and tied my hands the same way.

"Please don't start a fire," I begged. "Just leave Papa here as he is. We must tell my brother right away."

Janie sobbed.

Ms. Hardin had no interest in my words or her daughter's sobs. She used the gun to force us around Papa and into the car.

Janie sat beside me, curling her body toward the window. Tiny bits of frost tinkled on the glass.

Ms. Hardin slammed the door on us. From the cold car with its dark dashboard, we watched her disappear inside the barn. Minutes passed.

"I want you to know how much I love Perrin," Janie said, quiet, looking off into the clouds. "I really do. How I wish he would come out now and save us from this."

I could think only of Papa—his lifeless body, the shock on his face—and frantically circled my mind for what to do. I strained against the tie on my hands with every bit of strength possible, but the belt was too strong to break.

"You must do as she tells you," Janie said, her voice flat. "Don't try to escape."

We both jumped at the blast—a burst of fire and heat and splintering wood on the other side of the barn doors. I closed my eyes and imagined the cats running off, the ponies somehow unharnessing themselves, the billy goats breaking through with their short, sharp horns, all the animals fleeing through the pasture into the woods to find shelter.

If Papa was dead, they must live.

If Papa was dead, Ms. Hardin should burn with him.

But she returned to the car a few seconds later, bringing in the smell of oil and ashes. With the gun in her lap, she pressed the ignition switch and shifted the gears, turning the car toward the road.

"Just stay still and don't cry, girls," she said in her teacher's voice. "Janie, after you calm down, I'll take off your ties."

"Yes, Mother."

The car started without issue. She moved the gears quickly, setting us to sail from the drive and onto the road.

Perrin, I screamed inside my soul. *Perrin, come out now!*

Turning for a last look, I found a way to hold hope: Ms. Hardin's fire had been poorly ignited. Through luck or the power of my imagination, the angry flames had extinguished in the cold oxygen of the morning air, imprinting the white sky with a thin trail of dusty smoke.

Janie sobbed and sniffed, leaning forward to take the pressure off her noosed hands. "We need handkerchiefs," she said. "Please untie us, Mother."

"You disobeyed. Reflect upon your actions."

The landscape of trees and brush skimmed the car windows, a motion blur of brown and green that held me hypnotic as the hours wound us into a dusky twilight. The roads we traveled were long and straight, then short, curved, and full of bumps and holes. Eventually, we passed through a dirt lane running through a wood that cleared into a majestic opening surrounded by evergreens. A water fountain gushed in the center of a median strip fortressing an entrance marked with a stern sign: *Private Property*. Ms. Hardin passed and slowed onto a long gravel lane, stopping at a white stone artifice occupied by a uniformed man.

"Oh no," Janie whispered to me as her mother recited an ID code to the guard. "I think we're at a frightful place."

Behind the white stone gates was a small city of cement buildings, each one many stories high, that dwarfed the trees and blocked the starlight. Janie remained in the car, still tied, but I was ordered out by Ms. Hardin, who nudged me through a gate and into an arched stone hallway. I was taken on by a thin young man with a tight grip.

"This girl goes into the vaults until a punishment is mandated," Ms. Hardin instructed the man.

The order, spoken so sharply, caused my hopes to shrink.

"I will untie your hands," the guard said to me. "But you must wear a blindfold."

The blindfold was made of stiff plastic material, secured in the back with three rivets applied so tightly that even sliding a finger underneath was impossible. It covered my forehead, eyes, and the upper bridge of my nose. He pushed me forward and I felt us moving down a damp, narrow stairwell.

I was locked into a barred cell.

"There's a toilet in the back corner," the guard said. "Feel around so you don't fall in. I'll return with your food after daybreak."

Feeling the walls with my fingertips allowed me to imagine what kind of space it was, and within days I had a picture of the stone cage in my mind. The bars were arranged in sets of three. Each trio of thick steel rods running vertically from the floor to the ceiling was intercepted with a small vertical space sectioned by a waist-high horizontal metal shield ending at the brick floor. It was through this top portion of the space that the guard brought the food. Usually, it was a powdery block of a substance that tasted like moldy chicken fat. I ate as slowly as possible, breaking the mound into thirds, holding each third on my tongue until it completely dissolved. He also brought a beverage, a luke-warm herbal tea that had a flowery scent. This I poured into the toilet hole because it was surely drugged. When my thirst became too insistent, I took small sips spaced far apart to minimize any sleep-inducing effect.

The blindfold eventually became loose and wet. Not from tears—I refused to cry or become consumed with worry that Papa and all the animals had died in Ms. Hardin's poorly made fire—but from the moisture emitting from the three cement walls and the dank air. I slept on the floor, also cement, but the sleep was delicate and easily interrupted. My ears learned to hear the faintest drop, prick, click, and whispers of open air and sucking drains. The guard came and went erratically, and I began to sense that I was a secondary duty to him, one he could put aside when other matters took urgency. The ceiling above me was too thick to hear footsteps, but I was sure there was activity occurring directly above my cell.

"Am I alone?" I asked him one day. "Where's Janie?"

He never replied.

"How long will I be in here?"

No response, just the clatter of the food tray against the metal shield.

Ms. Hardin had said "until a punishment is mandated," and I longed for its delivery. Time became my torture, time and anything that could consume it—even punishment—was preferable to its stagnation, no moment more remarkable or memorable than the next.

To keep my character straight, I made up stories and lived them as reality in my mind. Most were about the future, where a girl like me—not necessarily me, but someone like me—met a boy, fell in love, and had children. She lived in a land of animals and flowers and did as she wished every day with a cat following her everywhere. I tried not to think of poor Aura and the fate she may have met in the barn. When the made-up stories felt old and tired, I reviewed the best scenes of my life. With the memory of Aura's warm and purring body so vivid, I turned over every wish, memory, idea, desire, and impulse embedded in my psyche.

Perhaps the hyperactive synapses of my brain even expanded and contracted my skull. In a second I didn't anticipate, the blindfold on my face was loose enough to pull off, rivets intact.

At first, the unmasked space before me was nothing but a cloud of somersaulting molecules. As the molecules absorbed light, the cell walls appeared—planes of gray slashed with strips of black. For a short span, I saw what wasn't there as much as what was there. The old memories I'd been replaying materialized into a mirage of my mother as a young woman in her red coat. She looked down on me with concern, willing me to stand. I reached for her outstretched hand, but the vision dissolved. Turning, I was surprised to find that my cell had a window, a rectangle of glass against the cement wall. On my toes and looking out, I could see a courtyard of tall green shrubs and wooden benches. Several young women sat together on one bench, but my eyes were weak and began to water from the brightness, so I looked away.

"Up to your feet, girl," the guard commanded.

It was night, and the guard usually didn't come at night. Startled, I almost reached for the blindfold to pull it off as had become my custom when waking, but remembered in time.

Rising, I managed a "Yes, sir?"

"I've been ordered to take you out," he said, unlocking the door. "Step forward with your hands at your side."

He tied my wrists and used a tool to release the rivets holding the blindfold in place.

"Thank you, sir," I said, pretending it was the first time I'd seen anything since my capture.

He maintained his stony reticence, pushing me up the steep stairwell with an insistent thrust. I was weak in the legs and used all my strength to reach the landing where the guard cut away my clothing—I had been wearing my clothes from home—and put me under a shower of cold water falling from an invisible source above my head. The water ran into my eyes, but I kept them open to take in the surroundings. The bathroom was long, a tunnel of tiled wall supporting a long tub and a ladder of faucets and pipes.

"Use soap," the guard said, tossing the shavings onto the floor. I picked them up, standing again in a spell of dizzy *déjà vu*, and covered my skin in a thin lather, washed it away, and stood still as he dried and covered me with a clean sheet. In a different circumstance, I would have tried to hide my nakedness from a man, but since the guard had been my singular human contact during the prison term, I felt irrationally unconcerned. The sensation of clean skin, hair, and the ability to see was an intoxicating freedom.

"Please untie my hands," I begged.

"Not yet," he said, leading me down a dark hallway and through a set of double glass doors. On the other side was a white counter occupied by a woman in a gray coatdress. She looked at me with heavy-lidded eyes, uninterested that a girl with uncombed wet hair, draped only in a sheet, had been brought to stand before her.

"Name?"

"Me?"

"Yes, you. Oh, never mind. You're the one from the vault." She removed a sheet from a pile sitting in a tray, wrote on it, then ran it through a clicking machine.

"Room seventy-three," she told the guard. "I'll take her."

At the woman's words, the guard bent down to release my hands from the tight restraint. He left without a farewell and I followed the coat-dressed woman's hunched body to a room with "73" on the door. Behind it was a vacuous space that seemed to have no walls except the one I'd just crossed. The room was a sleeping quarters comprised of small cots, slim mattresses, and metal frames stacked on top of each other like train boxcars. The highest level was several yards above my head. Many cots were occupied by sleeping, snoring bodies. There was also a mirror and sink and a few wooden chairs clustered around a table. Just below the high ceiling was a panel of barred glass shaded pink with the beginning of dawn.

"Is this the punishment I've been assigned?" I asked.

"Hah! Hardly. We haven't received any word from Rielle or the CREIA, even though we've asked several times what to do with you. So we're assuming you go in with the rest of the girls," the woman said. "Take any empty bed. There are no assignments and you'll find gowns in the closet." She pointed to a rack behind a folding curtain and was gone a second later, shoe soles squishing down the cement hallway.

"Janie?" I said to the dim, snoring space. "Janie? Are you in here?"

"Be quiet," someone hissed.

"Sorry."

I dressed in a worn gown, light-green with small white buttons, and fought the urge to get into one of the little beds and fall into a much-needed sleep—real sleep in a bed instead of a prison floor. I heard rustling and realized the dozing bodies were waking up to look down on me from the various points in the room.

"Who are you?" This came from a small girl, very young, with black hair.

"Has a bus come in?" another asked. "How many have arrived with you?"

"It's just me, no others." I backed up toward the door to process the sight of them with my still-sensitive vision. There were many empty beds, all of them neatly made, but just about the same number were filled, all with girls my age or younger. They began crawling down the ladders attached to the sides of the expansive frame holding the cots in place.

Surrogates.

"Janie?" I said again.

"I don't know a Janie," one girl said, brushing by to claim a pair of boots from a rack of battered pairs. "Perhaps a Janine, and there's likely a Jane somewhere." She was sallow-skinned with dark crescents under her eyes. When she spoke, her collarbone rose out in sharp definition. "Who are you? I'm Ciera."

"Her name is Isla," came a firm, loud voice. "I know her from school."

I turned to face the speaker, not sure if I should believe my eyes.

The girl who'd made the claim was Leslie Snyr, my former classmate. Still the same with brown freckles and wiry hair, she regarded me with such trepidation that I was instantly certain that the worst tragedy yet to strike was not my time in the vault, but when the woman had run my sheet through the clicking machine.

Like the other hundreds of girls at the Center, I would become a womb incubator for the Composite project.

"You'll go in every three or four months," Leslie explained during recess that day. "The schedule depends on how many capsules are available. You'll be taken into the surgical theater—"

"Theater?"

"They call it a theater. I don't know why. Once you're in there, they play music, lullabies usually. The doctors pretend to be very nice and kind, but really they only care about getting the fertilization to succeed. It doesn't always, and when it does, the offspring most often die within a few days. It's depressing." She stretched her feet in front of her and raised her cheeks to the sunshine. "When each round is over, you get to come here for a while to recover until a new capsule is available."

The afternoon was cold and we were sitting on one of the wooden benches I'd seen from the window of my cell in the vault, giant shrubs and pines looming over us. Some were carved into animal shapes—a duck, a swan, and a moose.

"I refuse to be locked in a capsule," I told Leslie. "I escaped from the CREIA, and I plan to find a way out of here, too."

"You'll have no control over it or anything that happens here," Leslie continued. "Once you're in the theater listening to the lullabies, a doctor injects anesthesia and puts tubes in your body that keep you alive. The sleep is so deep that you know nothing. You never even know you're inside the plastic bubble until they wake you up when it's over. It rotates so you won't get bedsores."

I imagined all the girls asleep in their capsule, babies gestating in their wombs. "Why do they keep trying to make composites when so few survive?" I asked.

"I've wondered about that, but I have no answer. At times I think they don't care as much about making composite children as they do about keeping all of us girls in this prison." Leslie looked across the courtyard, which was surrounded by a browning lawn that disappeared into a holographic wire fence. "You were lucky when they gave you a place at the CREIA. I'd go back if I could."

"I only want to go home. Ms. Hardin is at the CREIA now and she—" I stopped before revealing that my father and our farm might be gone. Leslie had been through enough without having to hear about my tragedy. "Do any of us ever get to leave here, Leslie?"

"Only if you become very ill. There was one, a girl named Olive, who began bleeding badly after a failed attempt. They couldn't capsulate her anymore, so she was taken away one night. We don't know where she is now."

I avoided asking my old friend how many times she'd completed the incubation process or what her rate of success was, but I wondered if any of the girls became attached to the children they grew inside their wombs. In the hours I'd been at the Center, I'd encountered many of the former cadets, such as Marta Klein, but Breea was not among them. The thought of her rotating in a capsule worried me.

"How long have you been between capsulations?"

"I'm not sure. It takes a long while to recover from the anesthesia. Look around and you'll see girls just coming out of it. At first, there's no sense of time or place and everything hurts, as though you are bruised inside and out. Some girls cry a lot and want to see the child they made, but that is never allowed. Others are angry their fertilization didn't work and they were pulled out early. Eventually, you'll come to prefer capsulation to recovery. You don't have to think about anything when in the capsule. Here," Leslie gestured to the animal topiaries, distorted by the blowing wind, "you can only ponder how you will end."

We spent the rest of the afternoon shivering in our robes and talking about our hometown and people we both knew from school and the market, even smiling at some of the memories. Then I told her about the photographs they'd taken of me at the CREIA, Mr. Drexin, and how Staris had taken my token in exchange for a ride home.

"Do you still have your token?" I asked.

"No. Everything I took on the bus with me was never returned. I remember the bus driver you mention, not just from the CREIA, but from Naudiz, too. He used to wink at me when I got on. To think you were in with the luggage during that whole trip—I'm astonished! And you look so different now than when we were in school. Have you gotten taller?"

"Maybe just a little. You look different, too. Your eyes might be lighter in the center."

Leslie raised a hand to her cheek and pursed her lips, glum. "No, it's just that my skin is so rosy—the capsule is very hot—and they look lighter against it."

The afternoon sun was setting amidst lavender clouds and a flock of blackbirds dipped over the holographic fence, sparking a rainbow of jagged rays. They *caw-cawed* in pain and flew higher to prevent skimming the invisible border.

"Is it really better to be in the capsule than awake?" I asked.

Leslie stood up and tightened the robe around her small waist. "Oh, yes. It's a deep and peaceful rest, and the dreams—" she took my hand and we walked back toward the cement cylinder that housed room 73, "the dreams are long and lovely. Not like regular dreams, but magical dreams that are much better and more interesting than anything you can imagine."

CHAPTER 23

Over the next few days, I tried to formulate a plan to escape the surrogate center. I needed a partner to help me, but none of the girls were nearly as smart and brave as Sorrel had been; if any of them had once been smart and brave, those qualities had been stamped out through cycles of capsulation and recovery. Leslie and the other girls dragged around Room 73 and the courtyard like old women, waiting for their next dream-capsule adventure to begin. Those recently awoken arrived at our room at various times of the day and night, always escorted by the coat-dress woman. She would help them to a bed, take off their boots, and provide a clean washcloth for their flushed and sweating faces.

I'd been living among the beleaguered sorority for a few days when the coat-dress woman turned to me on a rainy morning and said my turn had come.

"A capsule has opened up, and you're next. Go to the bathroom and empty your bladder. I'll wait right here."

"But you haven't yet heard from Rielle about my punishment. What if she sends it when I'm inside?" It was the only reason that could keep me out.

The woman pressed her lips together, annoyed at my defense.

"Why worry about such a thing? It will likely not happen. And what if death is your punishment? Wouldn't you rather put that on delay?" She grasped the collar of my robe, pushing me to the bathroom. "Come on now, or I will have the guard return you to the vault."

The thought of lying blindfolded on the vault floor again was unbearable, so I obeyed. After I went to the bathroom, we exited the dully hissing doors into a chamber with white walls and glossy black hallways. I followed her past a nursery; the broad glass window offered a view of the rows of baby bassinets inside, but I saw only two or three infants. The woman stopped in front of the window and let me look in.

"Such tiny little creatures," she remarked, keeping a grip on my wrist. "My own boys were twice as big."

One of the composites waved at the air with red fists, rousing a nurse who lifted and cradled it to her breasts. She brought the bundle over to the window and pulled back the baby's blanket to reveal a round head and face that looked just like a normal baby's, only much smaller, no larger than an apple.

"Please let me go back to the room," I asked in hope that in this moment of tenderness the woman could agree to give me more time, but her face hardened and she pulled me away from the window.

"Stupid girl," she said, pushing me toward a door across from the nursery. "Your turn has arrived. Open the door and get inside."

"I—I don't think—"

But my argument was halted when the door opened on its own, revealing a young woman on the other side; she was pretty, with thin angled eyebrows and a slender nose.

"Don't be fearful," she said, holding out her hand. "I'll take care to make sure you are safe and have a good sleep."

But when I refused to accept the outstretched hand, they forced me into a chair.

"Please calm down," the pretty nurse said, sliding a clear tube under my skin.

My veins quickly filled with a cool fluid that took my senses to a state of euphoria. Words of resistance stuck in my throat and hung there.

"Now lean back."

The chair reclined and a lullaby began to play, pulling me into its clever tinkering tune. My legs were laid out, eyes closed and taped. I heard whispering, felt fingers pressing my chest, my pelvis, my thighs.

There was a cluck of discontent from the coat-dress woman. "She was a tough one."

And then I knew nothing about her, about the room, the capsule, or what my body was about to do. I knew only the sense of weightless floating, the soles of my feet meeting grounded earth, the silhouette of a small house on an orange horizon.

I began to walk inside the dream, moving toward the horizon with the wind at my back until I was standing at the front steps of the porch. The door opened on its own with a cheerful click. I passed through an arch and moved into a short, dark hallway lined with panels, stepping through one decorated with iridescent flowers and sparkling dots. On a wall before me, a flickering hologram swiftly formed into a moving photograph and I watched my mother, her hair light honey-blond, dark circles under her blue eyes, sitting on the porch snapping green beans. I was mesmerized by the confident way she moved her hands through the bowl. The screen shifted—I watched her marry a young version of my father in a small chapel, their hands held together over a large book, their profiles black curves against a multicolored window.

Then I saw my brother standing in the back field, a flash of lightning serrating the heavy clouds above him. Perrin untied a mesh bag of brown seeds and poured them into his palm, looking down with determination. The seeds fell into a plowed row where they were watered by steady rain. I watched the plants break through the ground and gain height. The rain became a light-green fog littered with what seemed like millions of pages of paper flying like birds on the wind current. When the fog cleared, there was nothing but a blank length of white-blue sky and a hazy moon.

Shaking.

Speaking.

"Up you go, sit up now."

A slap on my cheek.

"Who?" Strong light stung my eyes.

"I hate to admit so, but you were right. Now get up on your feet and we'll put you into a dress."

"Who are you?" My head ached in an effort to remember.

The woman was untying my gown, slipping my arms into a scratchy garment, fastening a row of plastic buttons. "You'll remember soon enough. It will take a spell of time, but you can sleep it off in the car if they allow you to."

"I was right? What was I right about?"

"It's not good news, I'm afraid. Your punishment has been delivered."

The woman pushed me down a hallway, with white walls and shiny black floors. An elevator plunged us down. The door opened with a swish that stirred my consciousness into proper alignment. We stepped into the stale office managed by the coat-dress woman, who I now recognized as the one standing beside me.

"Well, here she is," the woman said to someone. "You might need to tie her hands because she likes to try sneaky tricks."

A figure wearing a hooded cloak reached out for my hand. "Isla," they said, lowering the hood, "let's go." Their hand was warm, the grip urgent.

I tried to focus on her face.

Intelligent eyes, square jaw, brown hair that had grown past her shoulders. A tiny mechanism shone in one ear.

"Sorrel?"

CHAPTER 24

Sorrel's car was the same dark-blue model as Ms. Hardin's.

"It actually *is* Ms. Hardin's car," Sorrel said, shifting the gear lever into a backward motion, then forward. "Or was. Rielle took it away once we figured out where you were. Sorry it took so long." She was in a tan dress, brown boots ending just below her knees. The car turned onto a flat road and we sailed under a tunnel of bare branches, emerging onto a long stretch of grassy plain. We were on our way to the CREIA, she said, where things had changed significantly since my escape.

"After you left, the cheather you'd planted grew and bloomed," she told me. "The plants were as high as my chin—I'm astonished you had the courage to lay out the seeds knowing how large the plants can get. The flowers were enormous and the pollen from them collected over us and polluted the air. We had no choice but to breathe it in when walking between buildings. The drugged water stopped working and everyone began violating the daily schedule. No one knew when or where to get meals. Then one group broke out against the rules altogether. They went into the labs and disturbed the equipment, pulling out cords and destroying experiments. I wasn't in with them, but I enjoyed the new freedom."

"I suspected it would grow tall," I said. "But not so potent." I remembered how my small bottle of tincture had counteracted the drugged water. The seeds that Perrin had pressed into my palm had come from an extra-strong strain.

"You should have seen Rielle after she realized what was happening and called us all to the cafeteria. It was there that she announced our freedom. We ripped off our uniforms and threw them into a big heap in the middle of the floor. We danced in our underwear and the Grays took over the fourth floor, singing their work songs while hanging out of the windows. I got my hearing aids back just by asking for them. After we got tired of dancing and singing, we sat in a big circle—you know how Rielle loves making you sit in a circle—and she told us our water would no longer contain the passivity microbes. Instead, we will use cheather to bring us to high alertness. At that time, she didn't know it was called cheather. It was Esme who told her what it was."

"*Esme* told her?"

Sorrel turned a corner and picked up speed, heading toward a bright red building constructed from spindles and shingles.

"Isla, the cheather saved us—it exposed the lies, the slavery, the truth about who was controlling us. The girls and women at CREIA have united together, all of us equals. But—"

"So you don't work in the laundry anymore?" The impact of what she described was just beginning to sink in. What would it mean if the CREIA was no longer operational? Would I be able to find Janie and go home?

She looked over and smiled, the hearing aid sitting perfectly in her ear. "Just wait," she said. "You'll see what you caused. But you shouldn't meet with Rielle looking like you do, so blushed and panicked, so let's go into this market for a meal and new clothes."

"Sorrel, no. Papa might be dead, and the animals, too. Take me to the farm right away. I think I can figure out how to get there. We'll follow the river like I did before."

But Sorrel parked the car and turned off the motor, turning to me with insistence.

"You must come with me, Isla," she insisted.

I owed her my life, but couldn't agree. "I can't bear the thought of what could be happening at the farm," I told her. "And I don't know where Janie is. My brother will—"

Sorrel gripped my hand. "Who's Janie? Come back with me, even if only for a few days."

"But what if I can't ever get out again?"

"You must look beyond yourself. Imagine that you started to weave a beautiful rug, but got called away. The rug was left on the loom and your friends filled in a few inches of strands, but lost the pattern. But they need you to finish it, and you refuse to return."

My will weakened at Sorrel's passionate analogy. I reminded myself that the fire at the farm had long been tended to by Perrin, and although my anxiety about its damage and Papa's possible death was so strong I hardly cared about what was happening at the CREIA, I agreed to place trust in her promise that I wouldn't become trapped again.

And I was hungry, very hungry.

Inside the market, we ate roasted chicken legs with spiced sauce and found a LUSH clothing booth. Sorrel paid the vendors with credits from the CREIA account—I had no money or any belongings. Due to Ms. Hardin's early morning abduction of me on the day she'd shot Papa, I'd been taken away without anything but my nightdress, long since cut off and disposed of at the surrogate center.

We both bought new skirts, blouses, jackets and boots, folding my dirty gown into the trunk of the blue sedan.

"How strange to have a car to ourselves." I slid into the front seat and ran my hands over the dash. The hearty meal and fresh feeling of new clothing had buoyed my spirits, but there was a dampness in my soul. "And how did you learn to drive?"

"A bus driver gave me lessons," Sorrel said, steering onto the bright road.

"You mean Staris?"

"Yes, that's his name. You know of him?"

I explained that he was the driver from my hometown who had played illegal music for me on Saturdays.

"It was a long time ago," I said, watching the trees and pastures rush by in a blurry strip of brown and rust. My mind wandered back in time, reviewing the past, unfolding the events that had delivered me to this day where, unlike any other day of my life, I was wearing clothes I'd selected without any rules. Although the future was uncertain, I had for the first time a hope that it would be me—not Papa, not history, not the Upper Polity, not the CREIA—that would shape my destiny.

Sorrel asked me to describe what had happened at the surrogate center. "Did they—" She stopped herself. "Or, are you ... going to be a surrogate?"

The question hung between the car seats as we headed toward a horizon broken by long flat buildings and electric poles. We passed a wide dark-blue sign with white letters:

Center for Research of Ecological and Intellectual Advancement
(CREIA)

I explained to Sorrel that since I'd been pulled out of the capsule early, it was doubtful that fertilization had occurred. "I was also injected against such a possibility during the days when Mr. Drexin tried to assault me."

"What relief you must feel," she said.

We stopped a short distance from a tall fence rimmed with the wavering light pink halos I recognized as holographic energy indicators. My heartbeat surged with the memory of the horrifying green spider I'd passed my hand through in order to escape.

Sorrel used a pronged instrument on the car's dashboard to open the gate.

My breath grew short, my palms damp, the muscles of my abdomen and legs clenched in resistance.

"Sorrel," I said with panic. "No, I can't do this. I can't come back—"

But the car continued to move us down the broad paved lane. Up ahead, the familiar shapes darkened the afternoon sky. It was the CREIA campus I recognized, the place I'd risked my life to leave.

"Calm down." She pressed the gas, moving us closer to the courtyard. "And look up ahead."

I dared to look, and took a breath of awe when the realization descended upon me.

Cheather.

The courtyard and the lawns were covered in it.

The plants waved lazily in the light wind, lifting the intoxicating green dust above the heads of the girls and women strolling the walkways. The scene was as I remembered, but different. Doors were open and unlocked, held in place with boulders; windows were unshuttered, decorated with curtains and jars of bright flowers; the air smelled of coffee and sugar; a flickering television set illuminated the windows of the laboratory. I heard laughter and applause, heard footsteps thundering toward us as we parked the car and stepped onto the pollen-dusted bricks.

"They've arrived!" someone shouted.

I brushed the wrinkles from my new suit—a linen skirt with ribbon trim, a suede vest over a silk shirt patterned with dots, sturdy brown boots—and took in the festive energy rising from the crowd of smiling, clapping women and girls now surrounding us. From it stepped the person I knew so well, the one I'd deeply missed in so many complicated ways. When our eyes met, every grudge and unspoken bit of anger fell away. I fell into her embrace.

"Esme!" I whispered into her dark brown hair.

"Isla!" she said into mine.

We released each other, smiled, and stepped back with our

hands clasped in the air above us. There was a loud cheer as I scanned the faces for those I knew: Robin, the Grays, Cistine, Gem, Alise. The girls now stood as equals among the teachers.

Nowhere among them was Ms. Hardin or Janie, but a familiar face caught my attention. Hannah stood at the edge of the crowd, her long hair down and face shiny, dressed in a beltless teacher's uniform. The skirt was ripped at the hem, the collar cut into sharp points. With it she wore the same pair of shoes I'd last seen on her when we were locked on the fourth floor together. The heels were worn, the soles held to her feet with green jewels. Our eyes met and I instinctively went toward her, but Esme took my elbow.

"Walk with me to the library," she said, circling us around the applauding crowd with a firm hand on my back. "Rielle is waiting."

"Yes," Sorrel said, joining us. "There isn't much time."

Hannah had made her way to me and I dismissed their commands long enough to accept her embrace and congratulations. "I have so many things to tell you," she said.

"Come with us if you want," Esme spoke to Hannah sharply. "But let's go now. The moments are passing quickly. We have a plan for tonight and the sun is already beginning to fall."

A plan?

Whatever their plan, I wasn't sure I could help. The recent hours under anesthesia, nourished only with a feeding tube, had consumed my strength. When I had the chance to close my eyes for a few seconds, as I did while we sat in a circle waiting for Rielle to arrive, the memory of Papa lying motionless on the barn floor presented itself in vivid detail. The calls and cries of the escaping cats and ponies echoed in the caverns of my mind, intermixing with the voices around me. The girls spoke in low tones, plotting the night ahead.

"A coalition of men from the Lower Polity is on the way here, arriving in two different cars late tonight," Robin said. "They have no knowledge of how the cheather has liberated us. We must wear our uniforms and pretend everything is unchanged, that we live just as when we drank the passivity water. They'll have their refreshments in the dining hall and proceed up to the fourth floor for their bastardly intentions with Hannah and the others who were once locked there."

Everyone in the circle looked at me and Hannah. I reached behind my neck instinctively and pulled away my hair to show the others my branding.

As Sorrel excused herself to heat the water kettle, I told the girls about the night I'd been locked up and stabbed by Mr. Drexin, pulling back the sleeve of my new shirt to show them the scar, which had healed into an irregular white crescent. On my arm, it looked like a closed eye with scattered lashes.

Esme didn't seem to understand. "He stabbed into your arm? Why would he injure you in that way and not just use a gun?"

I looked to Hannah for help in answering. She was wordless, so I pulled an explanation from my foggy brain.

"His intention wasn't murder, but punishment for my refusal of his intimacy," I told her. "Mr. Drexin and all the men go to the fourth floor for luxuries and physical stimulations. The drawers are stuffed with chocolates and nuts of all shapes and sizes, dusted with salt. They drink wine and fermented brews, sleep in wide, plush beds, and watch television without restrictions."

"Yes," Hannah joined in, turning to reveal the LUSH mark on the back of her shoulder. "The girls who live on the floor are frivolous playthings for the men, like flowers in a vase to enjoy and toss in the garbage when time causes them to decompose. And no one girl lives in any room—they rotate around them to ensure variety and interest."

"That's abhorrent." Esme thoughtfully arranged her skirt into a fan around her thighs, eyes down.

Sorrell poured out cups of tea infused with cheather pods, and the bitter green taste and earthy smell made me wish for home. I sipped slowly, watching the sunlight dwindle on the other side of the library's color-washed window panes. My thoughts lightened and the blood in my veins sped vigorously.

Esme finished her tea within seconds, setting the cup on the wood floor with a hollow clank. "We have only a few hours to prepare," she said.

"But where is Rielle?" Robin asked. "I thought she'd be here with us right now."

"Writing her telecast, I believe. She'll be here soon. She made an announcement earlier today to reinstate the old procedures. Hannah and Isla, you'll wait in the fourth-floor chambers. Who else was up there?"

Hannah gave the names and Robin wrote them down.

We stood as a group and were holding hands to confirm a commitment to our missions when the door opened, unleashing a panel of orange light from the hallway beyond. Rielle stood in the center, not wearing her usual uniform, but in a belted dress made of patterned silk. Her dark brown eyes shifted in anticipatory light when she saw me.

"Isla," she said, coming forward to take my hands in hers, "it is time for us to forgive one another."

I wasn't sure how to respond; certainly, there was no reason to apologize for my escape, but it didn't matter. She quickly took over the group, giving instructions and cautions, sending Robin and Hannah off to conduct room-by-room inspections.

"Everything must be in place," she said. "All residents of the campus should appear asleep with the windows closed, doors locked, and lights out. Esme, you must sit in the garage because the bus is on the way. When it arrives, keep it and Staris hidden until dawn. I'll be telecasting early in the morning. Immediately afterward, the bus can travel to the surrogate center to retrieve and bring back as many residents as possible."

"I'll go along to help Staris take them out," I offered, relieved that Rielle's plan would free the surrogates. "And wait with Esme, too."

"No, Cistine will help Esme. You and Hannah will return to

your rooms on the fourth floor where the other LUSH girls are already stationed. Seranack and his posse will be going up for their soirées." She pulled us closer by the hands, excluding the others. "You two have the most important job of all. When the male visitor shuts and bolts the lock, pull it back without his notice so I can enter."

"But what if I can't get to it?" Hannah asked, worried.

"You *will* get to it." Rielle squeezed our hands with force and pulled us even closer. "Don't question your ability to do so. Be absolutely discreet, and be quick. There is a shortage of time. Go now and get prepared." She released Hannah, waving her off, but held me back for a question.

"What gave you the idea to plant the seeds here? Such defiance could have led to punishment by death, you understand? Polluting the air is a felonious offense. The CREIA was and will continue as an institution of ecological advancement. You should have brought the seeds to me on your arrival for the scientists to study."

I looked down to avoid Rielle's penetrating gaze. The pockets of her brown skirt slumped with the weight of objects inside, and I remembered the collection of door controls she carried everywhere. But what was in the other pocket?

"Please forgive me," I said. "At the time, I didn't fully understand how successfully the seeds would grow, that they would cause a dramatic difference to the air. I planted the seeds only because my brother asked me to spread a new strain."

"All right, then. Go off now to the fourth floor. Put on the gown and wait quietly."

I took the elevator to the fourth-floor chambers. Since I'd left, it had become dirty and poorly maintained, with bits of litter and dirt on the floor and fingerprints on the controls. It was obvious that some of the girls—freed from restrictions—had been living in the luxurious quarters. Several of the lights were out, and the hallway door hesitated to open until I coaxed it with my hands. The room I'd occupied on the night of my escape was sloppily prepared, with the bed covers thrown on the mattress carelessly and the closet floor covered with rumbled uniforms of all kinds, some of them ripped and reassembled into patchwork compositions—sleeves and bodices connected in unorthodox ways. Undressing, I put on a pink lingerie set that seemed somewhat clean, dumping the dirty clothes from the closet into the chute that had once been my escape hatch. After a thought, I tossed my new clothes down the chute in the hope that I could have them back after the plan was enacted.

At the piano bench, I played the keys softly and allowed my thoughts to spin. The need to see the farm and confront the fire damage was urgent, but since freeing the surrogates was possible, I was willing to wait. If Rielle's plan went off as we wanted, the Polity would be locked in the chambers tonight, giving her the chance to release the surrogates and negotiate new liberties for all Citizens. Certain that Papa would want me to help in such an endeavor, I decided to stay.

Seconds later, the doorknob turned and a man walked inside.

My heart jumped.

The male visitor was much older than Mr. Drexin, taller and more slender in the torso and legs, with a balding scalp and bushy whiskers lining a square jaw. His colorless lips pulled into a tight line as he engaged the bolt lock on the door and stepped toward me at the piano.

"Good evening." The dark pupils of his eyes bored into mine, not unlike the holographic spider's. "My apologies for the late arrival."

"Hello." I looked down at my hands, picturing how they would soon unlock the door.

We sat together on the sofa, where I tried to pull the thin gown over my upper legs.

"You are much shorter than the girl I usually visit," the man said. Up close, I could see pocked marks in his cheeks and the growth of white whiskers above his upper lip. The irises of his light green-blue eyes sharply contrasted against his dark brown skin. His rumpled suit, dark-blue with white stitching, smelled of charcoal and gas. The acrid odor brought up the memory of the bomb in the city square.

I must have grimaced or put on a negative expression, which he immediately noticed.

"The girl I prefer to see doesn't hold her face in such an unattractive manner," he said, crossing one long bony leg over the other. "Show me your smile," he said. "I'd also like a cup of hot tea —no whiskey. I don't drink like the others do."

"What is your name, sir?" I asked, unsmiling, preparing the tea at the counter of the small kitchen. To the warmed water, I added a portion of dried black tea and a dose of tranquilizing powder that was stocked with the medical supplies. Stirring the powder into the tea, I delivered it to him on the sofa, stooping awkwardly to keep the gown from slipping from my shoulders.

He unbuttoned his jacket—revealing a gun strap with a pistol tucked in the pocket—and accepted the teacup, sniffing at the steam.

"I'm Seranack," he said. "You were unaware of my identity? Why am I not with my usual girl? She normally drinks a cup of tea alongside me."

"I'm sorry, sir."

He seemed offended at my empty hands, so I returned to the kitchen to make my own tea, watching as he drank the beverage at an agonizingly slow rate. I heard a door open in the hallway and the soft thudding of footsteps and speculated that the first of the Polity had been locked up. Nervous there might be more telltale sounds to alert him, I sat down with Seranack on the couch and asked him to tell me a story.

"You must see many compelling events as the head of the quadrant," I remarked. What would he say if I were to mention his daughter Ashleen? Would he become a sad and grieving father? Or was he cold and uncaring as Janie's father had been?

"I am not the head of just this quadrant, but oversee all four quadrants. My other girl knows that much. The director here— what is that homely woman's name again?—should better educate the concubines for my sessions."

He cleared his throat with force and I noticed that his eyes were not as open as they'd been on his arrival. I sipped my tea with enthusiasm to encourage him into another long drink.

"Her name is Rielle. And your power is at a fascinating level, Mr. Seranack. Please tell me about your life. I miss my own Papa so much. Do you miss your family too?"

A low whistling breeze came through a crack at the bottom of the locked apartment door and a spree of footsteps thundered in the hallway behind it.

Seranack looked over, softened, finishing the tea in a single swallow. "I think often of my daughter Ashleen." He turned and leaned a knobby shoulder into the tweed sofa cushion, stroking my kneecap with his thumb. "She has a brilliant sense of economics. Just last week she received an award for her business success."

"Last week?" I asked, trying to hide my shock. He spoke of Ashleen as though she were still alive. My mind circled for an explanation, but there was no time to ponder why he'd spoken of her in the present tense.

"Yes." Seranack sighed, hanging his head to the side, "Yes, she is a brilliant girl."

He soon fell into a snoring sleep. I gently removed the empty cup from his clasp, set it silently on the tray, and went as quietly as possible to the door to deactivate the bolt lock. I hovered at the entryway, turning to keep an eye on his slumped form. When he emitted an especially loud snore, I dared to turn the knob and peer into the empty hallway.

At the far end, the entrance door to the stairwell was propped open with a heavy rock. I longed to slip away and run toward its

beckoning light. Four flights of stairs were an easy route to freedom; it was an uncertain type of freedom, but one preferable to
my current situation. The crystal chandelier teased me with a
path of triangular prisms, but I didn't step out.

A shadow slivered the light and Rielle appeared. The drooping
pockets of her brown skirt swished as she came closer, stopping
beneath the chandelier to hold my eyes in question.

"He's asleep," I said silently, enunciating with my lips as I had
when Sorrel was without her hearing aid.

Rielle reached into her left pocket to remove a black pistol.
She waved me aside, stepping into the room with slow delibera-
tion. I kept the door open with a stopper, following behind and
holding a breath as she raised the weapon toward his forehead and
readied herself. Seranack's eyes twitched under his lids.

"Put on his restraints," she whispered to me. "Do the hands
first."

The supplies had been secreted in a drawer under the television. The cable ties were identical to the ones I'd worn myself
when Ms. Hardin had taken me into the surrogate center. I
looped each end and tip-toed toward the sofa, aiming at the
easiest target: a limp hand hanging over a cushion. The tie went
on without trouble. After fastening it well, I located his other
hand tucked under his head and hesitated. Rielle saw the impossible situation—there was no way to secure his hand without
jostling his head.

"Remove his gun," she whispered. "Give it to me."

His gun?

Later, I would replay what followed in my mind over and over
again.

Rielle and I could have left Seranack with a single hand tied to
the sofa, locked the door from the outside, and proceeded with
the next stage of the plan. But, like most bandits good or otherwise, we had committed ourselves to the best possible outcome.
In the moment, the sleeping, snoring moment in which everything so far had gone very well, it seemed logical to empty his

holster and leave him without a weapon. His gun was within reach —the back-strap conveniently protruding from his left hip, held in place with a snap that popped open with light pressure from my fingertips. Coaxed from the holster with a firm pull, the pistol was in my hand within a second.

Seranack was still snoring.

I took a backward step, eyes focused on the center of his chest with full intention to shoot should he wake up. So focused on the buttons of his shirt, I didn't notice when his eyes opened.

Seranack lunged forward and snatched the gun away from me, pointing it at Rielle.

"Run!" she commanded.

I found a hiding spot behind the kitchen counter, cringing at the sound of the shot and the blast of powder and smoke.

"Old dogs like you are hard to kill," I heard him mutter. "You think that—"

"Hell's waiting," Rielle said with a weak gasp.

A second shot blasted through the room. I knew something awful had happened but didn't dare rise from my hiding place. Yet as the moments passed, I knew I must confront the scene.

Rielle had been hit and was bleeding from her chest, but she'd fared better than Seranack. He was still latched to the sofa, bloody from her bullet and still as a stone.

"I need help," she said, crumbling to the floor. "Help me, Isla."

In my memory, I watch us leave the room from a point above. Not a defined point on the ceiling, but a portal temporarily opened by the event itself. I see Seranack's body; my ripped gown, tangled hair, and dirty knees; Rielle's anguished face—nearly as white as the towel I took to her bleeding wound. I see myself pulling her up, allowing her to lean onto me.

Yet Rielle could go only as far as the foyer before her persistent strength extinguished, falling from my support to the carpeted floor. The chandelier absorbed this final action, its dangling crystals tinkling a cacophonic melody over her last words.

"The speech," she said. "Take my speech."

A paper was in her pocket, folded around the door controls.

"Your speech is in my hands now," I assured, holding her eyes to keep her alert. "Do you want me to—"

But Rielle was gone.

CHAPTER 25

I stood at the podium in the library auditorium with Esme, Sorrel, Hannah, and Robin at my side. The camera before us flashed a light as the telecast began. With the blood-spotted paper in my shaky hands and a photograph of Rielle projected behind us, I prefaced with an explanation.

"Dear Citizens. We are here to tell you that Seranack is dead," I said to the camera's mechanical eye. "And so is Rielle, the director of the CREIA. Her final speech will soon be printed and distributed throughout the quadrants."

The girls around me shuffled and shifted their weight on the creaky planked floor.

"At this very second," I continued, gaining confidence, "the Polity who challenge the order of our time are locked in a fortress of their own making, and we have the key. In the days ahead, we will negotiate their punishment on conditions set forth by you."

Esme moved forward to stand beside me at the podium.

"Our chance has arrived," we said together. "Tell us, Citizens— what do you want to change?"

CHAPTER 26

*M*ore than anything, we soon learned, the Citizens wanted answers.

But the answers were embedded in the broken strands of the past, sealed with strings and wax, packed in dusty pockets and the eroded memory of an eager civilization that began to move forward so quickly there was no reason to look behind.

The day after the telecast, Staris went to the surrogate center and collected the residents onto his bus. Sorrel and I stood at the gate and cheered their freedom, relieved to see Breea, Marta, and Leslie among them, but the girls themselves were quiet and uncertain. It was only when they were stationed in their rooms, tucked into comfortable beds with plump pillows and windows closed against the frost, that the possibilities of freedom became apparent to all of us, including me.

"Could you teach me to drive?" I asked Sorrel.

I quickly caught on, steering one of the blue cars through a crooked path of cinder blocks, around the courtyard, onto the main road and back again. After a few more lessons, I was ready to drive home to the farm. By then, the Polity we'd locked up on the fourth floor agreed to resign their positions and surrender their weapons in exchange for release. But they would remain under the eyes of the Citizens. Each man and every member would wear monitors, tracked by holographic geography for the rest of their lives. Any indication of them meeting together would instantly alert the head of the newly formed Citizen brigade that had formed in the city, headquartered in the gold skyscraper once occupied by Seranack.

"The CREIA can begin a new research mission," I said to Sorrel. "We'll study the cheather plant. My brother has already discovered how it helps sick people, but it can do even more. Come with me to the farm. I can't wait another day."

"Of course I will," she said.

Esme stayed behind—everyone agreed she was the best person to replace Rielle.

"Once we're there, I'll find a way to send your mother to visit," I told her.

"I'll drive your mother here myself," Sorrel offered.

"And perhaps she can live here with me." Esme slid the door controls into the pocket of her dress and folded a blanket into the trunk of the blue car we were packing for the trip. My side of the trunk held only a stack of books I thought Perrin would like, a change of clothes, and a thick wool coat. "I miss my clothes and shoes, all the things from my bedroom. It's been so long since I was there."

The three of us turned to each other in a small huddle, the wind blowing at our backs.

"We're different now," Esme said, raising the hood of her white jacket. Her face had filled out, the hollows under her dark eyes erased, a blush on her cheeks. All of us were eating better— portioning out meats and cheese at every meal, stirring peas and beans into the fat drippings, scooping mashed potatoes. The composite children sat with us in the cafeteria, quiet and inquisi- tive, with plates of noodles and cheese. Leslie had discovered their mean, aggressive nature calmed down when a dose of powdered cheather was stirred into their juice cups. They became sweet as puppies, polite and shy, giggling at jokes and the funny songs the Grays sang to them.

Sometimes I thought backward, reliving in my mind the days before I'd first escaped the CREIA. Had I known the tremendous power of the organization that had—through Ms. Hardin—lured Esme and me onto the campus, I'd probably never have dared to escape and hide on the bus. Even so, that girl who knew so little about what she faced and what lay ahead lived inside me still, was at the root of all I said and did each day. There wasn't a way to dismiss the more innocent version of me, yet I could not look at my surroundings without regarding the tarnish of my struggle and a twisting funnel of digested fear.

The blue car's engine ignited with my voice command. Esme watched us leave, waving farewell from the highest point of the arc-shaped exit path. It felt strange to drive the car away as though I was a participating member of the institution that had tried to kill me. The car gained power and sped through the opened gate.

Change. I glanced at Sorrel, who seemed to share my thoughts.

Yes, we were different.

~

"I have a stop to make on the way to the farm," I told Sorrel once we had passed through the city. "There's a metal box attached to a post at the cargo port in Raidho."

"Oh, good. I need to stretch my legs, don't you? Is the box far from here?"

"I'm not sure."

We drove another hour, following the road that wound around the river, passing through the fishing village where I'd been arrested, and then a long stretch of empty fields and granite mines.

"We could plant cheather here," Sorrel said. "Look at all the space."

I'd been taken over with nervous energy. What if Papa was not at the farm when we arrived? My throat constricted and I nearly decided to avoid the stop in Raidho. But just at that moment, the port came into view. I turned the car onto the winding lane, which took us down a steep hill that ended at the wooden dock.

I opened the door to the smell of saltwater and pointed to the box. "There it is!"

Sorrel smiled, uncertain. "What do you want to do here?" she asked. "It's just a box."

"It's a box for postcards. Can you reach back into the seat and hand me the pad of paper? It's probably all for nothing, but I want to try."

She waited in the car as I went to a salt-soaked wooden bench near the yellow box and spread a sheet of paper out, smoothing it with the vertical edge of a cloisonné pen that had once belonged to Rielle. For a few seconds, I listened to the lonely cry of seagulls and considered forgetting all about the idea. How could I put a set of words together in a way that would express my feelings but protect them, too? It was as though a rare flower sat at the center of my heart, one that could be nourished only by a certain poem and pouring of sacred water.

Dear Averitt, I began. The pen seemed to move on its own, carrying the simple message of my mind onto the paper. I folded it in half, then quarters, wishing there was a photo on the front. In my bag, I found the old newspage from the city square and ripped out an illustration of a mountain range and folded it around the note, tucking the corners neatly.

The metal box opened easily. Inside the dark mouth of space, my fingers brushed against something solid. There was already a postcard inside.

My heart skipped. Fortunately, I remembered to slip my message into the box before I rushed back to the car.

Dear Isla, he'd written.

I wanted to speak to you in person, but you must know this—after

some questioning among the ship crew who have wandered around
Peorth, I have learned specifics about the bombing in the square
and the event that has caused you so much shame and grief. The
person you named and her company are still alive (although not
without harm—a facial scar and a small limp)! I've learned this
news recently, along with the fact that she fails to remember much
at all. This is common with traumatic injuries, I hear. Write back
soon.

Yours truly, Averitt Lynch

I tucked the card in with my old clothes. Seranack was dead but his brilliant daughter was still alive. And I was not a murderess after all. I turned to Sorrel as we drove away and told her the whole story, admitting the relief I felt.

She reached over and swept a loose lock of hair away from my face. "I'm glad you're released from such guilt. And soon you'll be home. I've been thinking—is there a way to grow the cheather inside instead of outdoors? That way, we wouldn't have to wait until the warm weather arrives. I've heard of systems like that using electric lights and tubes of water."

But my attention was consumed by the sight before us—the familiar lane leading home, flickering in the panorama of the car windows.

"Look," I pointed to the bus stop, "that's the exact bench where Esme and I waited every school day. If you look past it, you might see two horses, a female and male." I tried to glimpse the married couple myself, causing the car to weave on the road, correcting the steering just as we passed Esme's family farm. There was a final stretch of cobblestone, and then the sharp arc that took us to the bottom of the hill.

"That's it." I coaxed the car onto the path leading to the house. "Sorrel, I'm home!"

We stopped in the spot at the hill's crest. The farmhouse looked normal: bushes pruned, the porch cleanly swept, the door closed with the old flowered curtain hanging behind the fogged glass. My body moved without thought, leaving the car door open as I rushed around to take in the sight. The barn was still standing, but a section of the roof had been reshingled. Shielding my eyes against the sun, I saw a stretch of charred wood—an irregular patch of sooty residue shaped like a half-moon—running like a bruise from the loft window to the double doors. The unmistakable sounds of whinnies and snorts and the flutter of hay on the other side drifting up the muddy hill assured me that some of the animals had survived.

The door to the farmhouse opened with a creak.

"Papa?" I called hopefully. "Papa?"

But the figure stepping from the shadowed porch was not Papa.

"Isla?" she asked. "Isla? Who is with you?"

Janie was wearing my sister's old pale blue cotton frock, the faded dirndl skirt frayed at the hem.

"Janie? How did you get here? And where is—" My question wandered off, already understanding what her pained expression meant.

Janie looked down at the porch planks. "Your father—he's not here." A breeze from behind me reopened the door she'd just closed.

"But why?" I asked, terse, backing up toward the car. "Where's Perrin?"

Janie didn't know the dress she wore had once been a bed sheet; the cornflower blue spotted with white blooms, each bloom with three petals bursting at the top like exclamation points. Behind her, the house was dark, airless, and she stood squarely at the threshold, hiding something.

"Who is *she*?" Sorrel whispered, coming up behind me.

"Her name is Janie Frost." I might have added that I wasn't afraid of her or what she was hiding, even if it was my father's body or her mother and a gun. Maybe she was hiding one of the Polity or a sympathizer, someone like her mother, or even

Ashleen, who no longer held a position over others. Many had been removed from their homes and put out to fend alone. Perhaps my brother was inside lying on a death bed. That last thought put my feet into motion. "Let's go inside."

"Your father—he died that morning and Perrin took him to the mill," Janie blurted, her eyes on Sorrel. "I wish it hadn't happened through my mother's actions, but your brother has forgiven us both. We didn't think you'd be back so soon, maybe not ever."

Sorrel took my hand. The wind seemed to circle us, pulling up browned leaves and pebbles, flipping a small branch away from my feet. Behind the house was the seesawing cry of a blackbird. He was looking for his flock, lost in the hour between day and night. The sun disappeared by degrees, I knew, but there wasn't a measure for the invisible folding of sun's rays, fingers curling away from us.

"He died for a reason," I said to their respectful silence. "But I wasn't done knowing him yet."

And it was the settling sadness—the cold certainty that my days and nights with Papa had snapped shut like a record book with all entries filled—that made me collapse to the ground in grief.

CHAPTER 27

When I was a small child, the thought of leaving home was unfathomable. We belonged to the farm in the way that the trees did. We were planted there, driven up from the soil to hold our arms out and say, "This is our land, our air, our dirt." We carried a flame forward not only for ourselves, but for the animals we raised and the food and grain we harvested. The farm was our spot on the planet, a place to live and die.

Despite the almanacs lining the shelves, our concentrated attention to the seasons of year and passing seconds of the hours, we never understood the mortality of the farm itself, that we could be standing at the end of its story.

In Peorth, the Citizen brigade dismantled *Cherish the Past* and, with it, our ownership of the property. We would live as equals among others, Perrin announced, and the lot once hidden by Effort Kiehl's pine trees was soon opened to Citizens eager to build new lives. With Aura and Isaac in the car, I locked up the farm on a warm morning in March and traveled to the paper mill. Once there, I set up a weaving and writing studio in a roomy cabin built by my brother and Gareth Teague. Sorrel promised to visit, but she was busy working at the CREIA where they were turning the laboratories into water gardens and teaching the composite children how to raise plants of all kinds.

Some nights I'd sit at my loom for hours, mindlessly working the heddle through the warp where I was making a flag for our camp. I wove the final dark-blue and red threads into the cloth the day before my brother's wedding.

"Things keep on changing around the quadrant," Perrin said, sitting on the hard bed we'd set up for him in the spare cabin. The board of managers had enacted a wise rule from the past, one saying an engaged couple shouldn't see each other right before their wedding day.

"Such as?" I stood on my toes to retie my scarf in the bureau mirror. I'd spent the entire night with my hair wrapped in fabric strips and unwound them to release the long curls. I ran my fingers through the stiffened strands, glancing at my brother's reflection while he took off his shoes and reclined on a pillow. With sideburns long around the ears, he now looked more like Papa.

"There is a kind of passion in people today. Too much, maybe. I want to stay out here, cut down an acre and put up a new house, attach a workshop to the back. Wouldn't have to worry about anyone getting in my way." He stretched his long legs onto the bed. "Where's Janie?"

"You can't see her, you know that. The rule, remember?" I turned toward him.

"Rules should be broken."

"Rules have reasons behind them."

He smiled. "I brought a gift for the party—the bus driver sold it to me. You won't believe what it is."

"Tell me."

"You'll see. Or hear, I should say. But you must wait until after the ceremony. I'm not sure it works right."

I left my brother to take a nap and went out to look for flowers. It was still early in spring, and I found a few crocuses and wild roses in the garden and used my knife to cut them at the base.

They could soak overnight for the bridal bouquet. Before going off, I checked the peonies I'd uprooted from the farm and replanted. It would be a year or two before they would bloom again.

I carried the cut flowers into the kitchen, found a big can, and filled it with filtered water from the nearest rain barrel. Above, the trees were bursting with buds, showering the earth with white and pink petals. It had just rained and the air held the strange scent of cheather pulp steaming from the metal vats that hissed on the processing building's roof. I'd gotten used to its pungent odor, tolerating the smell as I might grow accustomed to an uncomfortable bulge in a bed pillow or a wart on my thumb. In the same way, I'd become accustomed to the LUSH stamp hidden by my hair. I didn't worry about it being seen, and I was even proud to share the story of how I'd endured and escaped the CREIA's traps.

"Good morning, Isla." This came from Lorene, one of the camp residents, as I walked back to the studio. She was married to Jack Redding. I'd first met them in Perrin's workshop long ago, when they'd come looking for a syrup to help their son. Hutch had been born with a serious deformity—his eyes were covered with skin, casting him to blindness.

"A lovely day, isn't it?" I asked, meeting her at the doorway. Behind her, Hutch was sitting at a table with a small guitar. The skin covering his eyes had been surgically opened by a kind doctor in Ironcove. The surgery had been incredibly delicate, Lorene told me, and also very risky because no one was certain that Hutch had eyes at all. But when the skin was slit, there they were, beautifully big and bright.

The flowers needed sun for their wait, so I excused myself to set them on a wide railing in the screened arbor in the weaving room. Janie's gown—made from woven cheather fiber, nicknamed "chax," was hanging from a rafter, swinging gently. One of the cats —Isaac—was nearby, stretched in a sunbeam. Our spring had been very cold with many episodes of icy rain. Janie and I had been unable to do much except make our meals, read, and talk the hours away. Perrin built persistent fires in the stone hearth in the main room as I told everyone about my time on the prison floor and the last hours at the CREIA, and gazed into the flames as the bad memories—once spoken—burned into ashes.

I woke at dawn and sat up from a dream that hadn't been about people and places, but about an emotion happier than sorrow, yet not completely sad. Papa, my mother, my sister—not one would be present for Perrin's wedding day. Even Esme would be absent. She was at the CREIA, helping her mother move into one of the remodeled bunkers and managing the construction of a new wing.

Outside, I walked over to the spare cabin, passing Ms. Hardin and her morning stretch group. She was holding a warrior position, arms overhead, averting her eyes away from me. I didn't speak to her often, but had learned that she was taking care of Gareth's baby while he was in the city helping the others. His wife, Elizabeth, had hemorrhaged during childbirth, sacrificing her own life to bring a healthy boy named Eli into the world. Some of the camp residents, including my brother, were insisting that I treat Ms. Hardin with forgiveness. I had to force myself to remember she was as much a victim as any of us.

I knocked on the door and Perrin let me in.

"We need a camera," I said, stepping over the shoe polish kit he'd spread out on the floor. "If you didn't bring one, I think you can make one from a box. We have paper, and you can use an emulsion to develop the photograph under the sun."

"Don't worry. I have a camera with real film."

Perrin tied his polished shoes and stood up, already dressed in his wedding attire: a clean white shirt and trousers held in place with thin suspenders. He'd be wearing a dark-red tie of Papa's.

In three hours, the main room would be filled with people and candles and laughter. Life was coming up from the earth, cycling into rebirth as it had been doing for all of time. Inside every one of us, I thought, walking back to help Janie drape the windows with boxwood branches, there's a ghostly print of what came before. And even though we try to change the ghost, we can't control the power behind it, the place it came from and the place that brought us here. We're seeing only tiny sections at a time, not aware of the larger design made of all of us and everything. The design was why Perrin had looked at a cheather plant and wondered what it could do other than provide fibers. Why Papa had measured and predicted the path of planets and measured the melting snow.

I stopped on the path to look for the pails of boxwoods we'd cut the night before, aware of a stirring in the woods behind. I stood straight, daring to hope.

There was the crunching of twigs, footsteps on the bend. And then Averitt was there.

"You came," I said, lightheaded. I hadn't seen him since the day I'd left his ship, so scared and injured and weighted with crime.

"I did." He wore a suit, clean and pressed. He was tan and taller than I remembered, as confident on earth as he'd been on water. "And I've never been to a wedding before, so you must guide me through the ways. Should I throw rice on the bride and groom as they leave? I've heard this is a lucky custom."

"Unless it's cooked," I said.

We laughed and came together, gathering up the boxwood branches as though not a moment had elapsed since we'd last parted. We slipped into the main room just as the pipe flutist and drummer began to play the prelude march.

Perrin was at the altar, rocking back and forth in his polished shoes, hands clasped. Janie, beautiful in her long, flowing chax dress, her hair curled in tendrils around her heart-shaped face, came down the aisle. Their exchange was quiet and sincere, led by Ms. Hardin, who was dressed in a long robe. A few guests sniffed and dabbed at tears. A babbling baby in the back of the room had to be taken out, and there were a few loud sneezes. When the ceremony was over, Perrin and Janie kissed and sailed down the aisle, steps nervous but smiles sincere.

Everyone was hungry, so the party began with platters of salmon and roasted potatoes. Perrin's gift to the party was a music player purchased from Staris. We listened to the ancient music and drank a fermented carrot beverage made especially for the event. It had a sweet tingle that made Jack Redding's jokes a little funnier. There were toasts with dark-red wine and, in a moment of suspense, Janie threw her bridal bouquet.

The bundle of blossoms landed in Averitt's hands and the guests around us laughed.

"More proper this goes to you," he said.

"I thought you didn't know the customs of a wedding," I replied, taking the bouquet.

"But I will learn."

Everyone laughed, light with joy, and began dancing under the beams.

There were any number of reasons to be happy that day, I thought. For the first time in what seemed an eternity, there was no reason to fear the future. True, the future was always an unknown, but the warp of the weave was strong and I held the crossing threads in my own hands. I had found a route without detour or danger, a brimming path blooming as full and lush as the roses in my arms.

Walking it, I was no longer alone.

EPILOGUE

When my mind is silent, a door deep in my memory sometimes slides open to review a night long ago when I was just sixteen. My questions about the world had begun to whisper, and I went out on a dim evening for a walk. Out of habit, my feet followed the cobble path to the main road and up the hill to the bus stop. I wore my orange skirt and white sweater, the uniform of autumn, and was feeling like myself all the way (except for a slightly stuffy nose), weighing the indecision about where I was going, not just on that night but for all the days and nights ahead.

Sixteen years of life, it was then, each one tucked under and over to the edge. I was a paper fan without an inch left for the next fold. Where was the next sheet?

I now know this new sheet was the object of my search that night, of that quiet walk I took alone in the danger of darkness. The wind froze off the insects or owls, bare trees clawed the blue horizon, reaching to the sharp stars, and the night put its eye on my slowly moving figure, a rusty slow-stepping girl who, once at the bus stop bench, hesitated a few too many seconds before deciding to turn around and go home. What happened next can't be logically explained.

In the sky overhead, the two dappled horses who grazed in the pasture behind the bus stop bench—the married couple who begged for carrots—were dancing in the air, so far up I could barely see them. I first thought their owner had duplicated them into holograms, but as they descended, the flap of their wings and snorting noses left no doubt they were the flesh and bone pair I petted every school morning.

The light around us brightened as I watched them land, husband followed by wife. Their wings, still stretched over the wobbling wind, were so white and expansive they reflected the moonlight, a milky aura that seemed to be protecting them. When they saw me, the aura took on a translucency before disappearing. The horses folded their wings, shrugging the knobby joints into a space between their shoulders and spines, burying the feathered tips into their spotted coats. I'd violated their privacy and should walk away, I thought, but then they spoke to me with their eyes, asking what I wanted.

I wanted to ride into the air with them, I answered, on the husband because he was wider through the backside and could support my weight. The wife could lead us under the clouds in a circle around the field.

They came closer, inviting me to climb on, but I pulled back. Sensing my indecision, the beasts turned and slogged away through the field, slipping through their back gate and into the barn.

To this day, I've never again seen them spread their wings. But if they ever show me the secret again, there's no question I will take the ride and look down at the world in joy. Even if it never happens, the memory of that night is always there and it has become my own power. Every moment I lived in fear, even the blindfolded, tied-up fear of a prison floor, I always knew the horses had wings, that they were free. And because I knew that, I was free too.

I was always free.

ACKNOWLEDGMENTS

LUSH took many years to write. My journey from idea to publication was not unlike Isla's as there were many obstacles and challenges along the way. I have a few people to thank: my husband Patrick, who read the book only when I really needed him to and let me keep it a secret until then; the editors of *Five on the Fifth*, who published my short story "Secret Fields"; Pat, Nikki, and Anna from Royal Oak Timed Writing, who inspired me with their dedication as we typed away at the Office Coffee Shop; all the beta readers from Fiverr who offered criticism and feedback; Nathan Phillips, who provided an insightful editorial eye. And, of course, Michelle Lovi, who saw something and took this little bird into her catalogue at Odyssey Books.

ABOUT THE AUTHOR

Anne-Marie Yerks is a creative writer from metro Detroit, MI. A graduate of George Mason's MFA program, her work has appeared in literary journals such as *Juked*, *The Penn Review*, and in several anthologies. She has freelanced for many magazines, publishing non-fiction articles about wellness, fashion, real estate, crafts, home improvement, and education. A longtime writing teacher, she loves traveling to literary destinations and occasionally presents at AWP and the Winter Wheat Festival of Writing. Anne-Marie is also a certified seamstress (but prefers the word "sewist"), a fiber artist, and a beginning gardener.